The harsh sun was bigger and redder than the one he was used to. The planet was a world of purple shadow. They were on a hill covered by a sort of clover. Below them a forest started, blackish trees with tentacle-like fronds that seemed to wave on their own. "The atmosphere is thin," Asher said, his voice penetrating the trickler.

"Aye," the Digger said. "Remember this: on the Warrior Planet, you must always have a trickler and enough oxygen to get you where you are going.

"This is your first test. At this moment twenty warriors are two thousand meters to your south, heading toward you. They intend to kill you. Your task is to defeat them. You have all the time you need, until your trickler runs out. Good luck, Asher Tye."

Asher whirled. He caught the briefest glimpse of the alien's form as the airlock cycled the Digger inside. He was alone.

WARRIOR PLANET

# DON WISMER

WARRIOR PLANET

BAEN BOOKS

WARRIOR PLANET

Copyright © 1987 by Don Wismer

A Baen Books Original

Baen Publishing Enterprises
260 Fifth Avenue
New York, N.Y. 10001

First printing, May 1987

ISBN: 0-671-65642-2

Cover art by A.C. Farley

Printed in the United States of America

Distributed by
SIMON & SCHUSTER
1230 Avenue of the Americas
New York, N.Y. 10020

# Prologue

There was the faintest whisper of sound behind him. He whirled on the ball of his foot.

The animal was in the air, in mid-leap from a house-sized boulder that he had just passed. It was steer-sized, six-legged, with a mouth hinged like a shark's, green and spotted with blotches like sun patches on sward. Detail merged into horror; he saw a confused swirl of claws and teeth.

In panic, he threw up his hands, arms rigid, palms at a ninety-degree angle toward the beast. Green flame wrapped around his wrists and focused. Fire shot out at the beast.

Even as he did it, he knew that it was a mistake.

The October One looked at him from the height of her ornamented chair. Two powerful Adepts held him, one by each arm, standing in front of her, just behind the yellow line. His head hung; he could not look her in the eyes.

"You killed an animal," she said in her gravelly, flat voice. He made no answer, could think of none.

"You used your Skill in a way visible to all, in fire and smoke and flame. You . . ."

1

There was desperation in him. He thought he was about to die.

"There was no time!" he cried, his body trembling, looking at the floor.

"Nonsense!" she thundered. Her black hair seemed to swirl with a life of its own. Her face, ageless, expressionless, held two glowing yellow eyes, which he dared not look upon.

Her downward slash of a mouth opened. Her voice came again. "We were watching; it was The Test. You could have taken one step aside and placed yourself in Shadow. You could have . . ." She paused. There were several other ways, none that would have attracted the attention of anyone nearby. There were even ways he could have killed without notice, without sound.

But killing was not the issue here.

He waited for the judgment that he knew was coming. He was eighteen years old, and there was nothing in him but fear.

He glanced desperately at the man on his right. Cor-Reed, his teacher for seven years, stared unmovingly ahead, gnarled face set in its habitual frown, streaked hair thin and half gone on a glistening scalp, lips turned forever down in impatience with the universe, almost sneering. No help would be found here. When he had failed with the animal, he had failed Cor-Reed most of all.

The hand on his arm tightened, until he could feel the pain.

"Enough!" the woman grated. Her voice was so low that it was almost a whisper. Asher gasped, and the pressure eased. "Judgment and punishment are mine. You, Cor-Reed, might defend this boy. You might tell me of his training, of the flaw that you and other Guild teachers have worked on for the seven years, of the hope you had in the promise of his other attributes, his aptitude toward the Skill."

She breathed. The boy had not heard any intake of breath from her since he had come to her chamber almost eight minutes ago, and he was attuned to such things. For the first time now, she breathed.

"Enough." She passed her hand over her eyes, closing them for a moment. The boy could feel the weariness in her. But then she hissed, and he could feel the strength. "The Law of October is plain. 'Six years, and no more than seven, shall an Apprentice labor, whereupon the Apprentice will be tested, one Test and one alone.' This one has been tested.

"Look at me, Asher Tye." There was finality, grim and hard, in her inhuman voice. The boy's head drew up, and his eyes looked into hers. He did not want to, resisted with all his strength, but she had the Power in its full measure. He was but a failed student of it.

Hazel eyes met yellow. She used no further force, merely looked into him.

"You have failed the Test," she said. "The Test beyond which there is no appeal. In accordance with our Law, I decree that you will be Erased, and expelled from the Guild, and sent back to your home world. Without Skill. Without Power. Without the Guild."

Erased . . . The taking of his mind. The message of the words, the force of the yellow eyes, hit him like a nail-studded club. Violent emotion, fear, terror, a sob coming out of the lower depths of his body without his volition . . . His head shook as the frustration came into him, beating against the other emotions that were brimming to the surface and drowning him.

The woman saw it, and he knew that she saw it, and so he understood exactly when she whispered: "The flaw."

She needed to say no more.

Then, in a movement of creamy fluidity, she stood. The black, gold-edged robes of the October Guild fell around her gaunt, unseen body. Her black hair writhed silently. Within it, there was the occasional tiny, bright flicker of static electricity.

"Cor-Reed, Dan-Gheel," she spoke to the two men

who held Asher Tye. "The Judgment is finished. You will take him to the Probe."

The men inclined their heads a fraction, the closest to a bow that the Guild ever allowed. The hands tightened around the boy's arms, and he felt himself turning and walking out of the chamber.

Walking toward the Mind Probe.

Terror overflowed altogether then, and he struggled, kicking the shin of Dan-Gheel, trying to tear away from Cor-Reed.

But they placed a Calmness on him which he could not resist. Yet the Calmness was external, controlling his body alone. He raged inside.

The Mind Probe would erase all the Skill out of his mind—cleanse seven years out of him, and leave him as he had been when he had come here.

An eleven-year-old child—in an eighteen-year-old body.

# Part I:

## FLIGHT

# Chapter 1

He had asked the wrist computer what day and time and year it was, and whatever the computer had replied, only one thing seemed to echo in his brain, back and forth like a steel ball. September had ended only moments before; the computer had switched to October in mid-sentence.

Across the bubble, with all the colors of the rainbow, the stars streamed past in lines like a thousand claws, scratching across the luxglass of the observation port, red and yellow, yellow like eyes, and green and purple . . . Purple, like light, exactly the same shade as . . . as . . . claws and purple light and yellow eyes . . .

Out of the corner of his eye, he saw a nose-shaped alien scuttle out of the room, and . . .

He remembered.

He sat suddenly upright in the lounge chair in which he had been lying. A few of the other passengers looked at him in surprise.

He remembered! The October One. Cor-Reed. The beast from the rock.

And the Skill!

He stood up abruptly. He was on the observation deck of a starship, watching, with some of the other

7

passengers, the stars as they fled by in lines, while the ship bore through interspace. Several other passengers turned to look at him, to divine the reason for his sudden movement.

Almost trembling, he made a slight motion with his left hand, and pointed to the viewport with his right. The heads looked that way and forgot about him.

It was the Cloak of Unnotice, part of the Skill. In all the minds that had been looking his way, the image of the brown-haired boy was diffused and tinged with a deep unimportance. The eyes had seen, and if they looked his way again, they would see again. But the minds would not notice, as long as he kept the Cloak in active force around him.

He'd been on the ship two standard days. He remembered coming aboard with the wonder of an eleven-year-old, gaping at the immense ship in orbit around the October World as his shuttle drew close. He had spent most of the two days right here on the observation deck, watching as the ship pulled out of orbit, watching as the red October World dwindled behind them until it popped out of view as they entered interspace and the lining of the stars began.

He had felt no special emotion, other than a child's wonder. He had felt no separation, no regret, no sadness at leaving a world that had been his home for seven years, at leaving an opportunity that would have made him great in his own mind.

All he had felt was the awe of a child looking at the universe.

Now his mind reeled with sadness and regret, but also with surprise and joy and hope. Memory! Skill! It was as if someone had given him a mouthful of medicine that had tripled his knowledge all at once.

He sank slowly onto the edge of the lounge chair, trying to grasp what had happened.

He remembered entering the Probe chamber. There Cor-Reed had pushed him away, not hard, with a kind of studied contempt. Asher had wept hysterically and clawed after him, too late to follow him through the closing door. Then he had been alone in the chamber. The lights had turned violet, and become so bright that . . .

That was when the forgetfulness had begun. After a while two men had come in to him, men that he did not recognize at the time, but now knew were Dan-Gheel and Cor-Reed. The latter had looked at him with hatred, and Asher had wondered why. He had felt fine. He had wondered where he was, but that was all.

The men had taken him to a room, where they dressed him and handed him a suitcase. He was on his way home, they explained. He had felt happy about that. His parents must be waiting.

But what about the training? Somehow he had known that he was in this place for training of some kind. No, they had said, he had not been able to start the training. He had failed some kind of aptitude test.

That had puzzled him. He hadn't remembered any test. Never mind, they had assured him. He did have a great aptitude in robotic logic. They were sure that the Robot Guild would be the place for him.

So they had bundled him aboard the starship. As the shuttle had neared it, he had seen its name in metallic mosaic on its angular hull. *The Pride of Caldott*. Caldott was a planet near the Core, an important place of commerce and finance.

His own planet, he had recalled, was Barnard's Refuge, in the outer swirl of one of the galactic arms. That meant that this world he was leaving was even farther out from the galactic core; it must be truly one of the fringe worlds, on the very rim of the galaxy.

He remembered now that he had sat in a sort of hazy stupor for the two days, going to his cubicle only for sleep, and to the common dining room for meals. He had spoken to very few people, and to no aliens at all. At one point, a matronly woman in the company of a Digger, an ugly little alien that buzzed instead of laughed, had struck up a conversation about inconsequentials, until Asher, even in his eleven-year-old naivete, had wished they'd go away. He hadn't liked the Digger, whose snout reminded him of a mouthful of worms.

Another time a teenage girl, bored with the travel, had tried to make his acquaintance, and had become first puzzled and then fearful at his boyish babbling. An attractive girl, he thought with regretful irritation.

Looking around now, he saw neither the woman and alien nor the teenage girl, not that he wanted the company of any of them. Instead, he . . .

A man was looking at him. Asher looked back with fear welling up inside.

The man was dark-haired, shorter than average, with liquid black eyes. He was staring directly at Asher, directly through the Cloak of Unnotice.

Asher looked away, trying to seem casual. He had seen the man before, he knew, without taking any special notice. The man had often eaten at the same time Asher had on the ship, and he always seemed to be on the observation deck whenever Asher was.

What if the man were an Adept? Would he notice the Cloak?

Of course he would. And if he were in fact an Adept, he would have Skill beyond anything Asher could command.

The man was starting toward him. Asher could see him out of the corner of his eyes. What did it mean?

His mind whirled frantically, but he could think of only one way to account for this man's presence. He must be some sort of Monitor for the Guild, a fail-safe mechanism in case the Probe did not take.

For that was what must have happened, Asher realized suddenly. Maybe the Probe did not always work. Maybe it broke down sometimes, or maybe some people had a sort of natural resistance to it.

The man was threading his way through a tight knot of passengers, human and alien, who were blocking the long aisle in which Asher sat. There was an exit nearby, much nearer to Asher than to the stranger. Asher's leg muscles tensed; he would run.

But even as he thought it, he knew that it would do no good. All the man would have to do would be invoke some arcane aspect of the Skill. There was one, for example, that senior Adepts would use on occasion to save an Apprentice from proceeding forward with some ill-considered application of Power—a single Word, hypnotically engraved in all Guild minds during Apprenticeship. It would stop him in his tracks, and that was not the only trick that could be used on him.

Fear. Nervousness. The flaw was there, as it always was, bedeviling him with self-consciousness. Perhaps this man had no sinister intentions. Perhaps he . . .

The man cleared the gaggle of passengers and began to move more quickly. There was nothing friendly in his face or his movements.

Suppose some people were resistant to the Probe? Then what could the Guild do to safeguard the October secrets? It couldn't just let failed Apprentices circulate around the galaxy, using and abusing various aspects of the Skill . . .

In a moment of amazing clarity that Asher would remember all his life, he knew that the Guild had only one way out. When a failed Apprentice somehow escaped the Probe, the Guild would have to kill.

Surprise. He would have to do something that would take the man so completely by surprise that he would not have time to invoke the Skill. Something so overwhelming that it would befuddle him—blind him, perhaps. Blind him . . .

He would never expect, in a crowd of passengers . . .

In a single fluid motion, Asher rose to his feet and threw up his arms, palms at a ninety-degree angle. The man's eyes widened, and he opened his mouth to say the Word.

Green flame wrapped around Asher's wrists, focused, shot toward the man. The man threw a Shield up, as

Asher had known he would, and the Word was muffled
into silence. Green flame cascaded off the Shield and
onto the vinyl chairs, which erupted into black, oily
smoke. Someone screamed, and a chorus of cries and
honks and shrieks rose up, drowning out any chance of
the Word being heard.

Asher bolted for the exit, the smoke obscuring for a
moment the man with the dark eyes. Blinded . . .

As Asher dove through the doorway, he glanced behind him and paled. The man was in the air in an
impossible leap, twenty feet over the billowing smoke,
heading toward him. It wasn't low gravity that allowed
the leap; the ship was on standard one g. No, it was the
Skill, one of several types of levitation.

In that single glance, Asher saw that the man's mouth
was open and his Shield down. But the screaming bed-
lam from the passengers blasted around them, and
drowned out anything the man might have tried to yell.

Then he was through the doorway, and out of the
man's sight.

# Interlude

Nearly one hundred and twenty years ago the October Ones had raged out of the Sculptor's star-blotch and reached the outer arm of the main galaxy. Their first landfall had been the world later called October, and from there each had set out and taken a piece of the galaxy, a pie sliced ten thousand times. And they had begun to rule, but only a little at first, only a tiny piece of each slice because the galaxy was so large and populated by so many beings: a hundred *billion* inhabited planets with life forms swarming in their abundance and adaption to the inconceivable in environment and lack thereof. The effect of October was like a drop in the ocean, a sand grain on the beach, a single cell in the human body.

But they would not expand their own numbers, would not create new October Ones. Alien, they were a race that was ultimately paranoid, and they not only feared one another (which was why there were so few) but could feel no rest until they knew that they controlled, directly or indirectly, the actions of the billions in their sectors and ultimately in the entire galaxy. They would never rest easy until they had complete control, and for that they sought and fought. And they sometimes re-

13

membered the self-effacement of the Teacher whom they had deceived, and wondered at it, and thought it weak and stupid.

Perhaps, once they achieved complete collective control, they would eliminate one another.

But for the moment, the only way their influence could spread was by teaching Skill to members of other races whom they could easily control. To their collective annoyance, they found that few among the trillions had any aptitude at all for the Power.

Certainly the October One herself had found it so, in the human segment of the galaxy. She had been the One to remain on that first planetfall; she had considered her environment and found it wanting. Its inconsequential human government disappeared when she devoted a millionth of her attention to it.

Perhaps the Ones should have penetrated directly to the central galactic government; but there had been no way of telling in advance whether any rival Power existed among the myriad swarms of sentient beings that they found. They well knew that if a Power did exist to challenge them, it would be able to conceal itself.

And so, at first, the Ones hovered in the backwaters of the galaxy, waiting and probing. But in 120 years of siphoning information to the One in the human sector, they had felt not the slightest whiff of alien movement in the Power, not the tiniest ripple in its etheric embrace that they did not cause themselves or account for among the lesser beings who touched, feebly, one or another of the lesser Skills.

They then formed a "Guild," a legal entity in which, in theory, was gathered the body of a particular learned profession. Guilds were among the few institutions of any influence among the chaotic jumbles of races and economic interests and potential conflicts that the galaxy represented, the Galactic Police being another. The influence of October began to spread more and more rapidly.

As for herself, within a year after settling on her

World the One had been named Guildmaster and had begun human recruitment—and found it hellishly difficult.

The human race seemed to have but the rarest and most unpredictable grasp of Power of any race that the other Ones described to her. But she set up a testing network on each planet she consumed, and found those few who had Skill potential; and as she gained followers one by one, planets in her sector fell under her influence. She absorbed each government and, if there existed any people of intuitive discernment, she destroyed them. That she was thereby eliminating the most creative and talented of the human race did not interest the October One.

Eighty-nine years after she had taken the October World, the October One sent a newly-passed Adept named Cor-Reed to the planet Edom. It was his first mission. He was to take over a planet.

Bribing his way up the highly stratified social ladder, he reached the chamberlain of the third son of one of the most powerful dukes.

"I represent the new faction in the Guild of Personal Protectors, about which you have heard," the sour young man intoned. "You have only to consult the Galactic Database to read of our ascension." He stood at ease, his face reminiscent of a carnivorous rodent's.

The chamberlain consulted the database and found this note appended to the description of the Guild of Personal Protectors, also called the Bodyguard Guild: "While known and respected for its careful adherence to an elaborate code of ethics, internal dissension has arisen in recent years. The older Guild leadership is currently under challenge by a new group which seems destined to assume control; for at every test of professional skills so far arranged, the younger challengers have humiliated their superiors. It is assumed that the next Guild election will see a change of command."

The chamberlain pondered. The world on which he lived was ruled by forty-six noble families, among whom wealth and power were concentrated. Attacks on them were common, but the nobles controlled the in-planet police too.

Everything is a question of being seen, the chamberlain thought. Of no distinguishing characteristics, he well knew that he owed his present post to personal public relations and a great deal of luck. But he was chamberlain only to his duke's third son, and there were layers above him to which he aspired. Visibility . . .

"Would you," he said in his best convivial voice, "consent to a test? I have to tell you that our Bodyguards have proven adequate to this point, and this is a violent society."

"Were I or my designees to serve as M'Lord's bodyguards," the gaunt man said, "nothing and no one would ever come near him."

The chamberlain smiled wearily. The duke's first son, second daughter, and third wife had all been assassinated. In turn, the duke had ordered the deaths of scores of actual, potential, and imagined opponents.

"I will see what I can do," the chamberlain said.

Cor-Reed smiled. This greasy sycophant was annoying him, and Cor-Reed wondered when and where he could take revenge. For the moment he would use him, for even in this stratified society in which family members were often hostile and isolated from one another, the duke would hear from his third son now and again. . . .

At length, an auditorium-in-the-round was set aside and the duke and his family, surrounded by bodyguards and their families, assembled to see what promised to be a private and enjoyable show.

After long and florid obeisances to those in the audience, an impressive feat of memory because he had not only to name each one, but list their titles, the chamberlain came to the point:

"And as we have, in effect, a challenge, the Fifteenth Duke of the Scarlet Flame, His Honorable etc., etc., has commanded that the local members of the Guild of

Personal Protectors choose a representative to face, in full and fair combat, this newcomer from off-planet, who represents a controversial faction within the Bodyguard Guild itself."

From one side of the stage came a woman, stepping just within the circle of a spotlight. Everyone in the crowd knew her. She was Tessa Fyrestall who, with her husband and children, shared the round-the-clock protection duties of the duke himself. She had personally foiled sixteen separate attempts on his life. Her husband, older daughter and son had accounted for another twelve among them.

She was a tall woman, handsome in a grim sort of way, with close-cropped hair that seemed to be of alternating blond and brown strands. She moved like a dancer.

But she was not dressed like one. She wore soft leather boots, from each of which the haft of a dagger protruded. In her belt were a blaster and a needler, and the cermonial sword of her Guild hung with polished scabbard and functional haft. Loops of apparently ornamental leather were studded with the gripping ends of a short, dagger-like shuriken, or throwing knife.

The people assembled knew that she practiced the deadly skills at her command for three hours a day. She was an expert among experts. In the crowd, her husband Ast and three of their children watched. The youngest was Miri, six years old.

From the other side of the platform, Cor-Reed appeared, and the crowd gave one long, collective gasp. For his only weapon was a metal billy club like police of old used to carry.

"Begin," said the duke, a heavy man in flowing embroidered robes seated on a raised chair. The chamberlain, mouth still open, looked wildly around and then leaped for safety. For already Tessa's needler was out and she was firing at Cor-Reed. But she was unaccountably slow, and his club, flung at her, knocked the weapon from her hand. Its beam flashed momentarily, and Cor-Reed, seizing the opportunity, caused it to catch the chamberlain before it winked out, hitting him low on the spine. The chamberlain was dead before he felt the attack.

Later this would tell against Cor-Reed; the duke would reason that the beam could just as well have hit him. But at the moment no one paid much attention, not even the duchess. For Cor-Reed's club had taken an incredible bounce on the floor and knocked Tessa's blaster out of her holster even as her hand was grabbing for it. In the audience, Ast Fyrestall was on his feet.

Her sword was out now as she leaped at the rat-faced man, but the club was there on the floor and she couldn't seem to avoid stumbling over it. With cat-like grace she recovered in a single step, kicking the club away from her. It flew through the air—and Cor-Reed reached out one hand and, again incredibly, had it.

*Sting.* One of the little shurikens was, all at once, sticking out of Cor-Reed's club as he held it before him. *Sting! Sting!* Another and another. And then she was upon him, and no one in the audience, save Ast, believed that Cor-Reed had a chance.

To Cor-Reed, who had nudged each weapon with his mind as he had needed to, this was the hardest part. He could blast the woman's brain to jelly with a quick mental blow, but he knew that it would reveal too much of his Skill. Ast, in the audience, was being hauled to his seat by other members of the Guild. It would be highly unethical to interfere, they yelled at him over the din. Tessa would be disgraced if he did.

The sword descended on the club, and the steel, folded and tempered thousands of times in its manufacture, should have cut through the apparently softer metal like butter. But Cor-Reed seemed to twist the club at just the right moment, with the descending sword just between two of the imbedded shurikens. To Tessa, it felt as if she had hit concrete. Something seemed to seize the sword by its blade, and at the same time she lost all strength in her fingers. The sword flew out of her hand toward the rear of the stage, and Cor-Reed, for his minor amusement, caused it to fall point-first into the back of the fallen chamberlain.

He swung the club against the side of Tessa's head and, at the same time, delivered that shattering mental jab.

She fell. He clubbed her two more times before she landed, just for form. Everyone could see her eyes, open and fixed, as they stared at nothing and everything, looking into infinite distance without fear or pain.

The crowd was transfixed. A sort of moan came from it, of ecstasy and pain, the corrupt society mixing with the members of the Bodyguard Guild. Cor-Reed, panting, stood looking out at them, keeping a close watch on Ast.

"Since the honored chamberlain can no longer speak for me," the Adept said then, between gasping intakes of breath, "I do hereby submit that you replace your old and inept bodyguards with . . . ah!" A sharp, involuntary gasp of pain burst from him as a tiny shuriken imbedded itself in his calf.

Just in time, he threw up a personal mental Shield, something he should have done before, but he was as yet young and with little experience; it caught an incoming shuriken and bounced it aside, to fall harmlessly on the platform.

Everyone, not the least Cor-Reed, looked to see where all this was coming from. Cor-Reed had thought that the rigid, self-sufficient ethics of the Bodyguard Guild would have saved him from attack, except possibly from Ast, who, in his grief, might forget himself. But he had been watching Ast.

A little figure stood on the stairs, a figure not even half grown, but every eye could see the resemblance to the corpse on the stage.

"You cheated! You killed my mother!" the little girl screamed. She flung another shuriken, scrambling up the steps, and dove for the fallen blaster. Cor-Reed suppressed the impulse to blast her brain too; but how could he have concealed the obvious use of psychic Skill from this distance?

"Miri! No!" the little girl's father was yelling frantically, uselessly. The girl had hold of the blaster now, and was raising it, pressing the firing stud . . .

The club had been aimed at her head, and Cor-Reed, wanting it to touch her so that he could kill her, was dismayed to see her twist aside. But he whirled its end against her arm, and as the bone shattered, the blaster tore a hole in the auditorium ceiling. The girl staggered, and then other bodyguards had her, and were hauling her away.

"I'll find you!" She was screaming and crying at the same time. "I'll find . . ."

Cor-Reed's "faction" failed to win the ducal contract. After the demonstration the duke rose, his old bodyguards clustered around him, and declared with an air of cultured bombast, his florid face grinning at the crowd:

"A little girl defeats him." The group roared.

"The chamberlain regrets him." Such wit, the crowd acclaimed.

"And I don't like him!" This time, the crowd was carried away in delirious enthusiasm.

Cor-Reed, enraged, had nearly blasted the brains of everyone in the room, but caught himself at the last moment; it would have been too dangerously public. Instead, he withdrew with ill grace and set about converting a rival duke, whom he convinced by assassinating the first one.

After a time, Cor-Reed's Bodyguards had all of the ducal contracts, and violence lessened on Edom—one of the few planets where the rule of October resulted in even temporary good.

Ast Fyrestall had agreed with his raging daughter that something had been wrong. That last shuriken had seemed to bounce off of nothingness itself, and others among the bodyguards in the audience had remarked on it. But Fyrestall's efforts at raising an inquiry ended when, just two days after his wife's death, he was seized by a massive heart attack. It was as if something had grabbed hold of the muscle and held on tight, the doctors had said. The family was dispersed; Miri was sent to an obscure uncle off-planet, and Edom lost track of her.

# Chapter 2

Asher raced down the corridor in hysterical panic, his legs churning, darting around surprised passengers, skidding around corners, almost blind in his fear. The Cloak was gone, forgotten as the uproar in his head crowded it out.

At length his breath began to come in gasps, and his terror dug deeper into him. He blundered along, oblivious to the stares of alien and human alike. Get away, get away, his mind shouted. Get away . . .

Nearly tripping over an Andalian snail, he staggered forward, off balance, and collided with an elderly gentleman, off whom Asher careened and then grabbed at in an instinctive effort to keep the man from falling. For a moment they clung there, the man clutching at him, pain in his eyes, Asher trying to steady him. The snail cast them a look of contempt, and oozed away.

"Sorry, sorry," Asher babbled inanely, panic transferred for a moment into a fear that he had injured the old man, or was maybe causing a heart attack.

The man caught his balance, and the moment he did so, backhanded Asher across the face, sending him staggering. The blow was weak, but it brought tears into Asher's eyes.

"Reckless young fool!" the old man hissed, adjusting his clothing with a feeble dignity. "You ought to be locked up. All of you. I . . ."

Asher moved unsteadily backwards, remembering why he was running, fear rising again within him.

"Sorry," he said again. Inside him, the thought came that he was showing the flaw. The flaw that had caused him to fail the Test.

The man stepped forward suddenly, hand raised to strike. The boy backpedaled out of reach, and then turned and scuttered to the nearest corner a few steps away.

When he had gone down several hallways at random, moving more deliberately, no longer calling attention to himself by wild-eyed flight, he stopped and leaned against the curved wall. With an effort he controlled his panting breath. He wanted the casual passerby to notice nothing, not even the depth of each breath as he dragged it, karate-like, into the pit of his stomach, slowly and steadily, with the discipline of an opera star. Something more that he had learned on the October World.

He pretended that he was consulting his wrist computer, a common enough sight. He did not use the Cloak. The Adept would sniff it out, like a hound after a scent.

Reason it out, he told himself. Reason it out, master the flaw, pretend that you did not fail the Test. Bring your mind and body into your service, into your mastery, where they belong.

At length, as his mind began to quiet, he began to think with some rationality. He quieted his racing thoughts, his fear, with a wrenching effort of will.

Will. That was the key to everything, he thought. A powerful will could do almost anything with a body, a mind, a total human being. It could force athletic prowess through rigorous training, mental acumen through study and practice, and even skill in handling people.

A human being could, and would, if he had any

intelligence at all, observe the most effective people around him, and by an effort of will, emulate them—practice their body language, use of words, dress, politeness, habits—until some of it became second nature, that part of it that eventually fitted oneself.

Only in the inevitable deterioration of age could a strong will fail, and even then the weakening could be slowed by deliberate attention to diet, exercise, discipline. And a will could itself be exercised and developed, until it could conquer indecision, fear, pain, in a way, even death itself.

His flaw had a lot to do with will. But he would conquer it now, here, this minute. He had to.

Or he would very likely die.

Where was the Adept this minute? On his trail? Perhaps just about to round the nearest corner?

He needed information, badly.

Within the molecular structure of his wrist computer was stored a good portion of all human knowledge, with the rest accessible by radio with the nearest database.

"Computer," he mumbled. No one had yet figured out how to feed thought itself into a computer. A voice was needed, even if it were a mumble.

"What," he asked the machine, "is the latest news bulletin from within the ship?"

"At thirteen standard days to Loblolly, your Social Director has a challenge," the computer intoned. The voice itself seemed to come from everywhere, but no one else could have heard it. It came from an implant behind each ear just under the skin. Everyone had them; the computer spoke only to his own receivers now, conducting sound through the mastoid bone directly into the middle ear.

"Take your choice," the computer said. "An exciting evening of music with the Pied Pipers on Deck G or, for chlorine breathers, the crystal show on Deck . . .

"Stop," Asher said, irritated. "All I'm interested in is news about the observation deck!"

Without hesitation, the computer said: "We're sorry, but an electrical short has caused the closing of the Oh-Two observation deck for about twenty minutes. We invite you instead to view the stars from the Flamingo, the restaurant of the gods, with delicacies to delight all the senses . . ."

"Stop," Asher almost shouted. "That's it?" he demanded. "Nothing about Security after someone?"

"Nothing," the computer said in its efficient, friendly way. All wrist computers were friendly, without being sickening about it—although there was some variation in the friendliness factor, as manufacturers struggled for different parts of the market. Asher's computer was only moderately friendly. The October World did not go in for friendliness.

He was not a part of the news. The Adept was not, either. Perhaps they were both being sought by the ship's police, but even as he thought it, he knew that it was unlikely. He had been, after all, screened by the Cloak of Unnotice, and it was very likely that the Adept had been, too. Perhaps many eyes had seen that incredible leap, but minds had not registered the act.

"Electrical short," indeed. How the ship's maintenance robots must have been puzzled by the melted chairs.

So it was likely that Security was aware that something suspicious had happened, but didn't know what to make of it. And it was unlikely that the *Pride of Caldott* had its own Adept on board. Members of the Guild hired themselves out, of course; it was that kind of commerce that kept the Guild alive. But an Adept's services were expensive, and the Guild's main clients were planetary governments and large corporations on the trail of security leaks, as Asher had been told. Not enough ever happened on a passenger starship to bring its holding company to the point of employing traveling Adepts.

But an Adept *was* on the *Caldott*, looking for him, discreetly asking about an eighteen-year-old boy with brown hair and brown eyes and a sort of wild look.

The old man. His agitation would be instantly apparent to an Adept. "The hoodlum went in that direction," the man would say. "I hope you catch the young . . ."

Suddenly Asher shouldered off the wall and began to walk. An Adept could quiz any of the passersby, alien or human, with a minimum of words and a maximum of effect. Around the corner he might come any minute now, Asher thought. Any minute.

He tried to keep his eyes from darting nervously about. He was aware that in his flight, he had been heading instinctively toward his cabin by the shortest route, and he began moving in the same direction as rapidly as he could without calling undue attention to himself. The Adept would, of course, know where his little cabin was, at least if his purpose for being on board were to keep an eye on Asher Tye. And the man on his heels had not caught up with him yet, so the coast ahead was presumably clear. Probably Asher owed his life so far to the fact that the corridors were not well traveled at two in the afternoon, and that the route to his cabin involved many turns, cutting down on the likelihood that the Adept would meet passengers who were traveling Asher's route in reverse.

As he hurried along, Asher's mind dwelt on several unhappy thoughts. How, he wondered, could he avoid a full Adept for thirteen days, until planetfall on Loblolly? And then, how could he get off the ship without the Adept's notice?

There was virtually nowhere to hide. There weren't any broom closets or maintenance areas on a modern starship that were in any way accessible to him. Maintenance was performed by robots, whose quarters were airless and almost without heat. Empty cabins were sealed tightly against intruders, and none of Asher's primitive Skill could penetrate their security without setting off alarms somewhere in the ship. He could not stay indefinitely in restaurants or entertainment nooks without attracting notice or using up his money, or both. Nor could he penetrate the areas of the ship reserved for chlorine- or methane- or water-breathers; with his oxygen-breather's equipment, he'd stand out like a cat in a birdbath. And here, if he used the Cloak, he would be broadcasting his whereabouts to the Adept, rather than hiding from him.

Suppose he managed to avoid contact until planetfall. There were only two debarking gates for oxygen-breathers, alien and human. They were side-by-side and fed by a single corridor, to the shuttles that would take passengers from the orbiting starship to the planet below. Debarkation through the other sections—water, methane, or chlorine—was reserved for the appropriate life forms, without exception. And Loblolly, now that he recalled it, was a methane world. A sweeter trap could not be imagined.

Nor could he somehow steal a lifeboat. The starship had plenty of them, of course—enough to ensure the survival of all passengers and crew should some disaster befall the main ship itself.

But the boats were sealed away behind tightly closed security panels, and only electronic commands from the bridge, or the failure of gravitational, electrical, or life support systems, could release the boats to passenger access. Not only would an attempt to penetrate a lifeboat set off alarms in security areas all over the ship, but even if he made it inside and separated from the ship, there were only two possible destinations on the fuel the lifeboat would have.

One was the October World, where death or more thorough Erasure certainly awaited. The other was Loblolly, where the police would pick him up in orbit, and where the dark-haired Adept would inevitably find him and wipe him out. The *Caldott*, with its superior speed, would get to Loblolly well before its own lifeboat, and the Adept, perhaps with dozens to back him up, would be waiting.

But he had to try. He could not just roll over and say, "Here I am, take me!" He had to fight back, somehow, even though he might have no chance at all.

As he neared the cubicle, he told himself that he had maybe five minutes to grab his things and get out. The entire interior of the ship was dangerous to him, but no place was more dangerous than the tiny cabin. While he could not have penetrated a cabin's security, a full Adept could with ease.

Should he throw himself at the mercy of the ship's security police, Asher wondered suddenly, stopping for a moment to let a six-hundred-pound Tessorian slither past. For a moment he felt a wild surge of hope at having found an answer, but then he knew that it was no good. He himself could have befuddled a run-of-the-mill security force with his Apprentice skills; an Adept could walk right through them as if invisible, which to them he would be.

The walls were now curved; his cabin was near the outer hull. It was just out of view now, maybe twenty yards away, down the corridor's beige floor that was like hard rubber, with a door set into the pale yellow plas-steel wall.

He came up on it then, and looked nervously up and down the hallway. Back the way he came, a foot-tall Ghiuliduc was rolling away from him, but the alien was no threat. The other way, there was no one.

Quickly he placed his palm on the plate next to the door, said the voice-printed access word, saw the door slide away. He took a single step inside, and . . .

He looked full into the face of the Adept.

In blind reaction, he leaped backward, or tried to. The door had unaccountably shut already, nearly taking his backside with it. He bumped into it, and threw a foot forward to catch himself. He slammed a hand onto the inside door plate, practically screaming the code.

Nothing happened.

Asher threw up his arms instinctively, palms rigid, looking at the man, his mind blank with utter terror.

The man stood tensely across the room from him, liquid dark eyes intent, looking fixedly at the door, hands ready at his sides. Asher screamed in his mind for the Green Flame. It did not come. The man was not moving . . .

Asher's ears picked up a low buzz to his left, and involuntarily he darted a glance that way.

In the cubicle's single chair, there sat a woman. The same woman who had talked his ear off on the observation deck, when his mind was still that of a boy. There was a smile on the puffy, matronly face. And next to her was her alien companion, sitting on the end table, ugly snout buzzing with . . .

Laughter? Frantically, he looked back at the Adept. The man was still there, not moving, not blinking. The Green Flame would not ignite. Asher tried again.

"No," said the woman. Her voice was low, but carried an assurance with it. "It won't come."

"But . . ." Asher croaked. He tore his eyes away from the unmoving dark ones in front of him, toward the heavyset woman and her odd companion.

"He's in a time of his own," the woman said, humor in her voice, gesturing with one lazy arm toward the Adept. "He thinks only a microsecond has passed since he came here. You sure stirred up the Power when you came alive again. Lucky we were closer to your cabin than he was."

"A Time Stop!" Asher breathed. He realized that his arms were still extended ridiculously, in their futile attempt to summon the Green Flame. He lowered them suddenly, and looked back at the dark-eyed man.

"Aye, a Time Stop," the woman said softly, eyeing Asher. The Digger stopped buzzing, and the room's silence was almost a noise in itself.

"But he's a full Adept—he must be," Asher said lamely. He looked again at the pair to his left, and leaned weakly against the door. They were making no threatening moves. But caution was in him. He would have jumped into the corridor and run, if he could have. But they had done something to his door, and evidently to his Skill.

"So is Digger," the woman said. "And so am I. The fool rushed in here to lay a trap. He didn't think a trap would already be here. Although, I admit, the trap was not for him, but for you."

The import of the last few words made no impression on Asher for a moment, as the thought struck him that he had been a fool. The Adept had not been dogging him, seeking him out through human and alien who might have passed him by. Instead, the man had run directly to his cabin, to lie in wait and blast Asher down when he came, as he inevitably would.

Maybe if I didn't have the flaw, I might have foreseen that, Asher thought. I . . .

And then the final few words did hit him, and he gaped at the Digger and its fat companion.

The tableau held for a long moment.

Then he drew himself erect. If a single Adept could not stand against two, then an Apprentice who had failed the Test to become an Initiate would have no hope at all.

At length, the silence grew oppressive.

"Get it over with!" Asher said at last, his voice a painful ghost of itself.

"Get what over with?" the woman inquired with a sweetness that was terrible to Asher's ears. The alien began to buzz again.

"You have to play with me?" Asher said shrilly. "That's not the way I thought the Guild did its killing."

"No doubt it's not," the woman said, making her form as languid as its bulkiness would allow. "But then, we are not Guild." She threw back her head and laughed with a suddenness that made Asher jump. Asher wondered if she were unbalanced.

Asher rubbed a hand over his eyes. His mind kept reeling from one thing to another. He couldn't keep things straight.

"But you said you're Adepts," he said weakly.

"Yes. But not of the Guild," the woman said. "I was once, but not anymore. And the Digger never was."

"Come off it!" Asher shouted. He was still convinced that he would not leave the cabin alive. "All Adepts are October Guild. By definition!" The Time Stop was a very difficult technique. In training Asher had practiced its close kin, the Death Trance, slowing his own body down to death-like quiet and then reawakening it. But it was one thing to order one's own mind into such a state; it was quite another to impose it on someone else, and that someone an unwilling Adept. Skill of a high order was at work here. Asher wondered if it was the Digger, the woman, or both of them together. They had to be October!

"Digger, our young friend is so sure," the woman said, laughing that same, overly loud laugh. "Must we disabuse him?" The Digger buzzed.

Asher sank to the floor then; he just didn't think that his knees would hold him up anymore. The flaw, of course, was there, playing riot in his mind.

Across from him, the Adept glared balefully, lost in timelessness.

The woman's voice came:

"You are not October Guild, not any more. And you are an Adept."

"I'm not," Asher said. His voice was stammering; he tried to control it. "I'm not even an Initiate. I failed the Test."

"So what?" the woman inquired. "You have many of the Skills, at least in their raw state. They didn't give you the name, is all."

When Asher did not respond, she said: "You're not the only one, for Egel's sake, and neither am I. I suppose you could call us Rogues; is that good enough for you?"

# Interlude

Nearly a dozen years before, the gigantic online files of the Galactic Concourse—one of the many services of that feeble federation—had carried a story that had escaped the notice of most galactic citizens. That was not surprising; nearly every news story escaped nearly everyone's notice. The reason, of course, was that there was too much news for anyone to absorb more than a minute fraction at best.

This particular news story concerned a new splinter group within the Guild of Personal Protectors. The Bodyguards had been absorbed by October for twenty years now; Adepts held the top positions and maintained them by demonstrating, through mental trickery, better martial skills than anyone around them. The bodyguard-in-the-street often wondered at the obvious lack of physical development among the top officials, for they seemed to train rarely; yet they seemed invincible in open combat.

The splinter group was headed by a young woman of extraordinary accomplishment and persuasive power. In her local sector she had won every combat tournament in every martial skill tested. The few images that had been captured against her will showed a woman of fluid grace, tall and strong, with hair that alternated blond and brown and a face grim with past memory and present determination. But she had learned not only fighting skills; apparently she had studied the social development of the galaxy, and did not like what she saw.

When she felt that she could begin, she circulated a document among selected Bodyguards titled "The Protector's Task." In it she described interplanetary corruption, syndicates operating in the open, carrying drugs and contraband while planetary governments looked the other way. She described people living in squalor; she described torture, and takeover, and injustices of every kind. And she laid out the task of the Bodyguard in simple, unadorned language:

*We are trained to protect; yet when those we protect kill or oppress, some among us look the other way. I say that such is cowardice. I say that such Guards have sold their moral sense for a job. I say that we, who have the skills, also have the responsibility of advising those we serve, and refusing to participate in anything they do that spreads hate and evil to other beings. If they will not hire us on that basis, then I say that this Guild should refuse to serve such ones.*

Her name, she said, was Tova; and followers began to come to her. She tried to stay in the background, to place this or that of her followers as figurehead, but it soon became impossible to do. Some of her followers were puzzled by her uncharacteristic reticence; but she knew that should the October Guild connect her with the little girl Miri of long ago, her group would be destroyed within days.

One day Tova's group took concerted action. On one planet, a military general was ready to implement a carefully-laid plan to take control of the civilian government. One last peg was ready to be hammered into place. Not having heard of the October Guild, he hired a group of Bodyguards to murder thirteen top civilian leaders.

The number turned out to be unlucky for him. The Guards in question were of Tova's faction, and they surrounded the general in his office and broadcast his image over the planet, with a running commentary of their own. The plotters were arrested, and the Guards were heroes.

But on that planet alone. The leaders of the Guild of Personal Protectors, horrified that Guild members had broken a contract, sought disciplinary action against the group: they would expell them and then punish them with elimination, quietly carried out by the top leaders themselves.

That was the plan. But the little group suddenly disappeared, taking a hefty financial award from the planet they had protected. It was then that the leaders discovered that Tova was a name that they could not trace beyond half a dozen years. She had apparently come out of nowhere.

The story was of passing interest to a few. Cor-Reed saw a summary of it, but not the image of Tova. He dismissed the incident as the work of young hotheads.

Tova tried to have her group recognized as a separate Guild with the name "Transfer Guild." But Bodyguard/October agents at the Galactic Concourse deflected the application.

A drug-running starship was on its way back from Caldott, where it had dumped a shipment and gathered tangible payment in iridium and other rare metals, when three of its crew suddenly took control. Victims reported that the attackers had overcome them with bare hands and feet. The attackers sent the drug-runners, half alive after ideological indoctrination, to the nearest planet on a lifeboat, and the hijackers disappeared into interspace. "Thus," they declared in an online story, "will the Transfer Guild deal with drugs."

It did not take many more such incidents for the news media to begin calling the Transfer Guild "Thieves";

soon it was popularly known as "The Guild of Thieves."
Real thieves were insulted, but some were intrigued.

Other incidents ensued, but Tova wanted, above all,
to mount a direct attack upon the October Guild. She
used the online files too. Only the October Guild possessed the abilities that she had seen at the death of her
mother—and, she now guessed, her father.

She knew, at last, who her enemy was. What she
needed now were Transfer Guild members with powers
to match those of October, or at least capable of shielding themselves from October attack.

While she searched for such resources, she taught
and molded and fought, and formed specialists in instant reflex and combat with any weapon, or with none.

Careful watchers of the databases might have caught
the correlation. Two things had to be put together: the
underlying purpose of October, and the threat to it that
pure idealists could offer if they had appropriate mental
weaponry. The October One herself had glanced for a
fraction of a second at the Transfer Guild in its early
stages, before the name "Guild of Thieves" became
current. But she dismissed them as self-rationalizing
pirates.

And as the tachyonic stream of news information
poured out of the galaxy, engulfing the satellite systems
and reaching the other members of the galactic super-
cluster, there was one who did put the factors together.
What intrigued this watcher especially was that no Thief
ever broke training and came out of cover. It implied a
teacher of unusual effectiveness, using techniques it
might be well to learn.

# Chapter 3

"Close his eyes," Asher breathed.

The two looked at him. On the woman's face was amused boredom. On the alien's . . .

Asher couldn't tell.

The woman stirred, and said: "Why not? Digger."

The little alien turned his head. Then, looking like a walking nose, he scuttled toward the dark-haired man. The alien's half-sheathed claws clattered on the plassteel deck like a bony drum-roll.

Asher leaned against the door and watched. He knew that eyes left open under a Time Stop would tend to dry. When the spell was later ended, the irritation would alert the individual that something odd had happened. The best way was for the action to happen, literally, during the blink of an eye.

As his cilia writhed horribly, the Digger's mouth moved. His head tilted and he looked up at the rigid man. Then he spoke, the first sound other than a buzz that Asher had heard from him. The voice was low, bubbly, ghastly somehow, distorted by the cilia into incomprehensibility. The alien reached up with one blunt arm, claws retracted, underlying prehensile fingers making a sign in the air.

36

As if dragged down with weights, the man's eyelids slowly closed. Asher was dumbfounded; he would have had to do it by hand.

"We should have let him go blind," the woman said. Asher shot her a look of surprise and anger. The woman, seeing it, waved it away.

"Never mind, kid. Let's go."

The Digger stopped his signing and moved toward the door, head turning completely around like the turret of a tank.

"Where?" Asher demanded. The woman had risen, and was already almost on top of him.

"Out," she said tersely. "You want to be here when he wakes up?"

There was something crude about her that Asher did not like. The manic laughter of a few moments ago was gone; she was now as grim as an undertaker.

"A moment," he said. Quickly he grabbed his satchel and began to stuff it with a few garments and personal things.

The woman grabbed his arm: "What the devil are you doing?"

"Why," Asher said, stammering, "getting my clothes."

The woman grabbed the satchel with one hand and shoved with the other. Asher stumbled backward and sat heavily on the bed.

"Digger, did you imprint all this?" the woman rasped irritably, pulling Asher's possessions back out of the satchel.

Asher found his voice. "Give me that stuff back!" he shouted, and thrust himself off the bed. The woman straight-armed him in the chest, and he went reeling backward again. The little alien burbled and seemed to take hold of Asher's objects by an invisible hand—or rather, many invisible hands, or tentacles, or whatever.

Telekinesis—moving objects with the mind—was commonplace on the October World. Asher tensed to spring off the bed again, but the woman's hand was still on his chest, her face close to his, her breath pouring over him.

"What did they train you for, to become a professional idiot?" she demanded harshly. Her hard eyes glittered. "If anything is out of place in here, that Adept over there will know it and know that a Time Stop was at work. And then he will know that we, or someone like us, are aboard, and then we'll be in for it!"

The Digger was arranging the things as they had been. He had long before imprinted on his mind the entire scene—the cabin and its contents—like a photograph. He nudged the items with delicate little pushes of the mind into places not even a millimeter apart from where they had been. Asher, thinking now, watched him and wondered at his Skill.

He didn't want to look at the woman. Instead, he let the tension slip away from his rigid muscles.

"Okay," he said dully. Of course they were right. Why couldn't he ever make the proper decision?

The woman seemed satisfied. They waited until the Digger had arranged everything with exactitude. Then Asher rose and the Digger smoothed out the bed, even poking a little dimple into the slipcover that had been there before.

"Let's go," the woman said.

Asher shot a final, nervous glance at the Adept, who was still standing there, the aura of menace around him made somehow ludicrous by his closed eyes.

Asher stepped to the door and was stopped by the woman's outstretched arm. The Digger had said something, his knobby eyes fixed on the door.

"Someone outside," the woman said. "We'll wait 'til the corridor is empty."

So the Digger could feel through walls.

Among the Guild, they referred to anyone with that particular talent as one who "had Sight." Although it was not an unusual Skill, Asher had spent hours trying to learn it, or even understand it, without any hint of success.

The Digger, he supposed, could "see" around corners, feel the underlying mental vibrations of thinking, conscious beings nearby. Useful, indeed, were one to desire concealment. As useful, perhaps, as the Shadow . . .

"The Shadow!" Asher said suddenly. "Why not place ourselves in Shadow? That way it won't matter who's going by."

The woman hit him across the mouth in a movement that was so casual that Asher had had no idea it was coming. It was the second time that day that someone had hit him.

Instinctively, his arms jerked up for the Flame as anger surged in him. Then he recalled that that weapon was useless against her.

"Halfwit," she said loudly, her voice holding malice and contempt. She didn't even bother to look at him. "There could be five hundred Adepts on this ship. Use the Shadow, or even the Cloak, and they'd all be on top of us as if we were painted with orange and purple spots yelling 'Here! Here!' " Irritation was on her face, and petulance, as if she hated to provide him with an explanation at all.

Asher, though, had to admit the truth in what she said. But she had hit him . . .

The door suddenly opened—Asher hadn't seen either the woman or the alien touch it, so there was some more psychokinesis at work—and the three moved out into the hallway, which was deserted. The door closed softly behind them.

The woman looked at it with eyes that seemed as hard as granite.

"In fifteen minutes he awakens," she said as if to no one. "We should have killed him."

The Digger mumbled and hissed angrily.

"All right, all right," she said irritably. "I suppose you're right, about the security police anyway. Still . . ." Her eyes glittered at the door. Asher shuddered.

They moved silently down a series of intersecting corridors, around corners, and then up three levels and down one, in a tortuous pattern that Asher finally realized was dictated by the presence or absence of life forms in the corridors just out of sight ahead of them.

Eventually they came to a cabin indistinguishable from the one Asher had held. In all the time they had traveled, in the middle of the ship's day, they had seen no one else, neither human nor alien.

The Digger's Sight was very good.

"My name," the woman said, "is Kerla. No middle name or last name. Just Kerla."

Asher was sitting on the fold-out bed. The woman was on a chair, facing him, her fat body lying back in loose relaxation. The Digger was between them; Kerla was using him as a footstool, with no evident discomfort to him.

"You're not stupid all the time," the woman's harsh voice continued. "You've thought about ways of escaping the *Caldott*. Aren't any, are there?"

Asher said nothing. He didn't like this woman. But she was right. There was no way off the ship without crossing the path of the October Guild, whether the dark-haired Adept was alone or not.

No way alone, without help . . .

"We're going to leave you here for a while," the woman went on. "It would look funny if the two of us should suddenly fail to show up at the hangouts we've used. Other passengers know us, if only by sight.

"But you'll stay put here. You won't leave for any reason. You won't use your wrist computer, you won't do anything to draw attention to yourself at all. And of course you won't make any calls on interspatial holography."

"But I want to call my parents!" Asher said suddenly. There was pain in his eyes, but if the woman saw it, she didn't care.

He just couldn't hold her gaze. He looked away.

"Idiot!" the woman exploded, spittle in the air. For the first time, Asher realized that her Basic accent was not among those that he had heard before. He wondered suddenly what planet she was from. "Call your parents," she brayed scornfully, "and they'll know what cabin you're in and who you're with. You'd better forget about your parents, boy. Do you think that the Guild wants anyone to know what they had in mind for you, least of all them?"

Agony was in Asher's mind, but the woman went remorselessly on.

"You think about it, boy. You can die by the Guild, or let us get you out. There's no third choice; you know the rules. Oxygen breathers can't get off the ship through the chlorine or methane or water sections, and vice versa. The lifeboats are out, and the Skill would only attract attention. It's us or nothing, kid. You'd better get used to it now, because I don't really care. I'll just chuck you out of here, and not alive either. I'll not have you blabbing to the October Guild about us two."

There was something about the way she said "October Guild." Fear?

"I don't care if you like me or not," she said. "I have a use for you. That's all there is to it. You use your brain. It's us, or die. Enough said."

She rose and headed to the door, while Asher sat dumbly. The Digger ran a clawed hand over the place on his head where her feet had rested, and clattered behind her without a backward glance. Asher watched them as they passed through the doorway. It closed with a quiet hiss.

His mind settled down after a time. He fingered the place on his cheek where Kerla had slapped him. Thought, his mind said. It's time for thought—for careful, meticulous consideration with as little emotional overlay as he could manage. To put the flaw aside. Events were sweeping him along, and he didn't like it.

He especially didn't like Kerla. For the first time, he wondered what "use" she had for him. He wondered whether it was preferable to death by the Guild.

Emotion kept trying to rise within him. Mostly it was the pain of the idea that he was cut off from his family in a way that might be permanent. Because if he could escape the Guild's attention now, then the only way they could find him among the thousands of inhabited planets in the Galaxy would be to keep watch on his family and wait for a holograph call or some other contact. With all the Skill at the disposal of the Guild, even a second- or third-hand message would provide an open backtrail to wherever he was.

Also, though, he resented the woman. Anger had always been his biggest problem, and it was a problem now. Yet he could see that she was right. His only chance of getting off the *Pride of Caldott* was to play along with the woman and the little alien.

But once off the ship . . . It would be time for another escape, Asher decided.

Emotion struck him again, and Asher tried to keep from feeling loneliness and fear.

# Interlude

Sim Ban-Gor was bored. The vast, milling throng in front of him held no interest. His mind was only slightly engaged in the effort to maintain the President's appearance. High up on the wide palace stairs, he could see the gigantic crowd pressing forward against the force barriers defining the street.

Down that street came the President at a dead run, hundreds of legislators following closely behind.

This annual run was a key event on Aero. The original human settlers had been part of the Perfectionists cult—people who were looking for a healthy way of life. Like most of the human worlds in the galactic arm, Aero had first been settled during that chaotic time just after humanity had discovered interspatial drive. Starships had suddenly become not only available, but cheap. Every little cult and club and interest group that wanted one, got one. Each took off to find an empty world on which they could do their thing, and because there were so many stars and so many planets, enough Earth-type worlds were found to satisfy all of them and then some. Once settled, the cult or club or group faced the problems of government and population growth, one way or another.

So by the time humankind came to the attention of the Galactic Council, there were hundreds of human worlds with all sorts of political and social setups. Aero was only one.

The Perfectionist creed called for healthy food and exercise for all. Anything opposed to health was banned. Someone caught smoking a cigar on Aero, for example, would be exiled from the planet, if he weren't lynched first by a maddened, health-conscious mob.

That's why Sim Ban-Gor was so bored this day. After a decade on Aero, the sight of so many healthy people nearly made him sick.

There was a rule in Aero's Constitution that no one could hold the Presidency who could not run 15 kilometers in the same time or faster than the original founder of the cult, the legendary Calvin Senna. The test of this ability took place once a year at the start of Aero's legislative session, when the President and legislature indulged in an official run before the inauguration speech.

It seemed to Sim that half the population of the planet was surging around him on the steps of the Presidential palace. Actually, he knew, most were watching the holographic image of their President on home receivers all over the planet, for the run was taken very seriously indeed. Failure to run the 9.3 miles in the required time was a sure sign that the mind was sick, along with the body. Perfectionists would not allow a sick mind to rule them. And they were right, in their way: a certain decadence was settling in on Aero.

The trouble was that the present President was inclined to fat. It had been ten years ago, after puffing through a run and barely meeting the time, that the President had hit upon an idea to spare himself this annual ordeal. He would hire himself an Adept of the October Guild, and . . .

And now Sim Ban-Gor was controlling the image

of the President that everyone saw. Instead of the overweight slob that was really there, Sim projected with his mind a distinguished athlete of respectable build and stamina. Instead of gasping out an eight-minute mile, the President had Sim propel him along with levitation, scant fractions of an inch from the ground.

The spectators commented at the President's amazing fluidity of motion. Certainly he was easily surpassing the speed required.

That the October Guild was being paid, and handsomely, for this deception, was no great comfort to Sim Ban-Gor. He was bored, and wanted to be somewhere else. His highly developed Skill was being wasted here on simple imaging tricks.

The milling crowd kept pressing closer around him as more people streamed onto the steps, waiting for the President to come around on his second lap. Sim's four bodyguards fidgeted. They were well-armed, with needlers tucked up their bodice sleeves, but security guards never like crowds.

A young woman, pressed backward by the crowd two steps below the Adept, tripped as she hit a step and fell backwards at his feet between two of the guards. Amused, Sim bent over to help her up. Out of the corner of his eye, he noticed a man pointing a holographic camera at him. Curious . . . The woman glanced gratefully over her shoulder at him as he pulled upward, and he saw pale blue eyes in a fair, freckled face. Then she drove her elbow deep into the pit of his stomach in a movement of blinding power.

The breath left Sim's body in an explosive cough, and he went down. The guards, highly trained, reached as one man for their weapons, but the woman was in motion. In a sequence much faster than it takes to tell, she slammed her right fist against the temple of the guard to her right; caught the arm of the guard on her left in a lock and, in a sudden movement of her head, lashed his eyes with her streaked brown hair; bent slightly forward and snapped a backward kick into the chin of the guard to her right rear; snatched the weapon from the sleeve of the guard she held and propelled him headlong down the stairs; and shot the remaining guard high in one shoulder, then, more deliberately, in the other.

Sim, mouth open like a fish, gasped for air, but it would not come in. His chest was paralyzed, stomach heaving in ineffective gasps. His mind lost interest in the world. He gasped for life.

A roar rose from the crowd as the President stumbled forward and fell in a scraping slide on his knees and elbows, the levitation gone. A dozen legislators tried to come up short, but tripped over him and each other in a tangled mass of arms and legs. The woman brushed her brown-blond hair from her face and eyed the guards she had attacked. The one she had punched was huddled on a step, holding his head and moaning. The man she had kicked was spread-eagled, jaw probably broken, unconscious. The man she had shot was sitting, unable to move his arms. The one she had pushed down the stairs was in a fight with someone he had knocked over on the way down.

And Sim . . .

The crowd roared again as the tangle of lawmakers drew apart and the President clawed his way to his feet, elbows and knees bleeding. This was a President they had never seen—an out-of-shape, fat . . .

"This is the wizard," the woman said in a clear, level voice to the holographic cameraman pressing forward. Sim's muscles suddenly relaxed in a tremendous gasp. The woman leaned over him, hypodermic jet-sprayer in hand. "He, of the October Guild, who controlled your President." All over the planet, people were watching a split image—the President in his real form, the wizard gasping for breath.

"And now sleep, wizard-man," the woman said. She pressed the sprayer home, and Sim Ban-Gor passed into sleep, breathing then easily.

It made the news all over that arm of the galaxy. The October Guild was in disgrace. Worse, it was laughed at.

# Chapter 4

The dark man in Asher's cabin was the only October Adept on the ship, the Digger and Kerla had hounded out at last. So Kerla undertook a project.

"There's your pigeon," Kerla hissed. Asher bent around the corner and looked. A fat, balding man leaned against one wall of the starship, chewing something like gum.

"Go," Kerla said, prodding him sharply with her thumb. Asher was propelled forward into the main corridor, back arched in pain. If the Digger was somewhere around, he couldn't see him.

"Use the Cloak, you idiot!" Kerla's voice hissed. The man had seen Asher's movement out of the corner of his eye, and was already glancing in his direction.

Asher threw the Cloak around him. The man blinked and straightened up, rubbed his eyes and looked again. He had seen something, he was sure, but he noticed nothing there now.

"The Adept . . ." Asher mouthed at Kerla.

"On the other side of the ship," Kerla whispered back. "Trust us, you little fool."

Asher recalled the Digger's Sight, and was somewhat calmed. The alien seemed to have the ability of shielding them from the restless Adept outside. But Asher's mind still held unease; he hated the turmoil inside him, the uncertainty, the fear. He also hated what he was about to do.

"Your life is the most precious thing you possess," the Guild training had taught. "When it is threatened, do anything, short of the Three, to save it. Lie, cheat, steal, bribe, deceive, injure, destroy—anything to stay alive. Life is hope. Nothing can be done without it; everything is possible with it."

He was about to cheat and steal, for fear of the ruthless woman behind him.

Under the veil of the Cloak he sidled up to the man. The latter's teeth were a sickly black from whatever he was chewing. Behind him was a row of vending machines, any of which a wrist computer could activate by passing money from one's own account into that of the ship.

This was the third-class part of the ship, at least for oxygen-breathers. Yet the man, Kerla had told him, was one of the richest of all the passengers. He certainly didn't show it.

Kerla had prearranged the meeting. She had sensed this man's furtiveness as she circulated around the ship and used her Skill to probe him.

Asher waited until the corridor was empty. Then he faced the man and said loudly:

"Money!"

The man looked wildly around. He wore a black, pencil-thin mustache, straight as a ruler on his upper lip. He was a short man; Asher felt tall next to him. Could this, Asher wondered, be a subchieftain of a criminal syndicate that spread across forty planets? Kerla had said so. Asher was amazed.

"Money!" Asher shouted. The man jumped as if jabbed with a pin.

But then he seemed to take control of himself. He shrank down, muscles relaxing, and then he spat black spittle onto the deck.

"Reveal yourself, wizard-man," he said then. His voice

had a sort of badgering quality, as if he were used to pushing people around.

Asher dropped the Cloak. To the fat man, it seemed as if he popped into view out of thin air. The man scowled angrily.

"I don't like that," he said. He took one long step and his nose was less than a centimeter from Asher's. In later days Asher would know this as a way of intimidating someone, a movement into someone's space. Now he felt the effect without knowing why, yet he wanted to maintain his ground at all costs.

"Look," he said. He brought what was in his hand slowly up between their bodies until it forced their faces apart.

What he held was a four-sided plastic chamber, transparent, with a conical top and an opaque black base perhaps two centimeters high. The whole thing rose in height to perhaps ten centimeters, and inside it was a crystal.

It was not just any crystal. It drew fire from the ambient light around them that showed images within—hypnotically moving images, wisps of figures that could only just be recognized. Almost . . .

That's how it looked to the fat man, anyway.

He held a long silence, while Kerla somehow closed off both stretches of corridor with a psionic wall that made people and alien alike uneasy and inclined them to head the other way. Far across the ship, the Adept named Ghulag roamed restlessly forward, sensing Asher's use of the Power.

Finally the fat man spoke:

"I didn't believe it," he breathed, the badgering quality gone for a moment from his voice.

"I trade you it," Asher said formally, "for fourteen million credits in irrevocable transfer into the account I designate."

"If it is a Captor Crystal," the man said, the badgering note returning, "you have a deal. If not, no wizardry can protect you . . . now!"

The man's hand slapped forward and Asher felt the slightest pinprick on his arm. He recoiled backwards.

"Whaa . . .?" But then, in a flash, he knew what the man had done. He had heard about such things.

There was now a little machine in Asher's blood. Not sticking in his skin where a razor might dig it out, but thrust into his bloodstream, floating down through his veins, through the capillaries, upward along the arteries to the heart, pumped through the lungs . . .

"What is it?" Asher quavered. In most stories he had seen, the tiny machine was filled with some sort of poison, set to be released within a certain number of hours if the host didn't or did do something, whatever the blackmailer demanded. If the deed were done, a signal on a frequency known only to the blackmailer would be sent, and the machine would become harmless, to be ejected from the body with other routine wastes.

The man smiled, black teeth making his mouth look empty and old.

"It puts out a signal," he said. "We'll find you then, as easy as finding a dog in a flea circus."

The man chuckled. He held all the cards, he thought.

"In fact," the man said, "I think I'll just take the Captor Crystal now. No point in wasting credits . . ."

Then Asher let the man see the crystal as it really was. To the fat man, the image wavered and changed and, all at once, the crystal was a cube of ice, melting obscenely in its plastic housing.

"No!" the man screamed.

"I herewith overlay that image on top of the crystal. Not even the October One Herself can break it," Asher Tye said.

"Bring it back. Bring it back!" the man wailed, black spittle spraying from the corners of his mouth. To such as he, a first water Captor Crystal was worth at least fifty million credits. No treachery was worth losing a profit such as that.

Asher brought it back. The man mopped his forehead

with a red and white handkerchief. "Don't do it again,"
he said. It never occurred to him that the overlay image
was what he was now seeing.

It had been a stroke of unbelievable luck that this
man was aboard the *Pride of Caldott*, Kerla had told
the Digger, with Asher looking despondently on. What
could be more normal than a fugitive from the Guild
trading something valuable for credits with which to
flee? And who would care how unlikely it was that a
failed Apprentice held something so valuable as a Captor Crystal? It was the "reality" of the crystal that would
impress the fat man beyond all else, she had argued.
They were the only ones in the Guild of Thieves who
could put this over, she had urged—the only ones with
psionic power.

"What? What did you say?" Asher had demanded.

Kerla had looked at him with hostile eyes, but the
Digger had known what he was asking.

"The Guild of Thieves," he had burbled.

"But what . . ." Asher had begun. Kerla had moved
as if to slap his mouth closed, but the Digger's voice
had stopped her: "We will talk of it later," he had said.
And Asher had shut up.

The Digger had turned to Kerla then and argued.
With Loblolly only two days away, he had said, why
cause the enmity of another power beyond October—
the sheer physical power of the interstellar underworld?

"But we are also of the underworld," Kerla had said.
"Why else do they call us the 'Guild of Thieves'—among
other names?"

Asher had made as if to speak, and then had stopped.

And so we pit one thief against another, Digger had
buzzed bitterly, ignoring him.

"Yes, and it's beautiful," Kerla had said, "because
this guy is a hired hand, albeit an important one, and
when he finds out what a fool he has been, he won't be
running to Security, you can be sure. He'll have one
thing in mind, and that's how his boss is going to react
when he finds himself out fourteen million credits.

Once that thought sinks in, he'll be thinking how to get away, and squealing on us will be the farthest thing from his mind."

Oh, she was a persuasive arguer, was Kerla; and besides, both the Digger and Asher sensed that she was going to barge ahead regardless of what either of them had to say. Indeed, when she came to Asher, she put it very simply: do it, or we give you to the October Guild. And with that Guild, Asher would die.

"We are obliged by our own Guild's laws," the woman had finally argued to Digger. " 'When thief faces thief: Steal little, steal big, but at every opportunity, *steal*.' " And Asher had shuddered. The Guild of Thieves. He had never heard of it, and now he had to find some way to escape it.

Now the fat man drew from his cloak a small instrument and pointed it at the plastic box. The instrument began to whir.

Asher felt his mind enter the instrument. No, not his mind alone, but that of himself and the Digger, with the woman hovering behind and feeding them energy and power. The visual image in the fat man's brain became the actual light photons striking the instrument's sensors, the actual molecular vibrations setting up harmonics within the device. Never had Asher manipulated something so delicate.

When it was over, his own face was drenched in sweat, his body shaking, all his Power fed into that one, rigid hand holding a box with a cube of ice, while inside him, a machine swam and sang. He wondered why he was bothering, with such a fail-safe mechanism at work on the fat man's behalf.

The sensing instrument sent the right message to the fat man's wrist computer, which in turn reported into the man's ears. The pencil mustache seemed to relax as the lips smiled.

"The account number . . ." Asher said, and recited the number that Kerla had given him.

The man whispered into his wrist.

"Done," he had said at last. "Done and irreversible."

Asher checked with the wrist computer he was wearing; it was Kerla's, borrowed, while his own sat in the woman's cabin, turned off and inert against a security check. The transaction had been recorded. The account was fourteen million credits richer.

Asher was momentarily staggered. That much money seemed impossible to grasp. What would anyone do with so much, other than give it away?

He left the fat man gazing rapturously into the plastic case at the melting cube of ice, and wrapped the Cloak around him. Although he did not know it, Ghulag was still some distance off. The Adept felt the tremor in energy that the use of the Cloak entailed, and knew that Asher was active somewhere ahead, but by the time he reached the area, there was no trace of Power anywhere.

In Kerla's cabin, the Digger traced down the tiny machine in Asher's blood and squeezed it into slag.

In another cabin, a fat man saw a puddle of water in a plastic case and screamed.

# Interlude

The October One spoke. It was always unnerving, that flat, roughened voice. Cor-Reed stood before her as he had four hundred times before, and still, it was as if it were the first time. He looked into those yellow eyes, shining with a sort of background glow, and feared.

"Sim Ban-Gor barely escaped with his life," she said, her voice grating, "but he will regret it. He was careless, to expose himself to the mob." She seemed to draw inward, brooding, her eyes almost golden with the flame behind them. "Yet who was she?" she breathed through her semi-vertical, lipless mouth. "Who was that woman who moved like a machine, and held October up to the laughter of ten million worlds?" Cor-Reed could feel the electric tension in the air. He was, all at once, afraid.

"Ghulag Sor-Tee has reported," she said finally, facing him, her hair writhing slowly. They were in her chambers. Only the One herself ever ventured beyond the outer rooms. It was something like a medieval castle, something like the mist-filled glade of a swampy and oozing primeval forest. Tapestries hung on the walls, with patterns that attracted the eye and then deceived, shimmering into inexactitude. Images appeared

55

and were transformed, as if animated by someone with a broad, wispy, indistinct brush. Behind them, glimpsed like ornamented frames in an ancient gallery, was stone, grey and weathered, fitted to such fine detail that the mortar, if it was there at all, was not visible to the naked eye.

Even here there was the yellow line beyond which no one could approach the One and live. From her first arrival, the October One had cast the image of the line around her, wherever she was; she had not had physical contact with any living being for nearly a millennium.

Cor-Reed stared fixedly at her. He had learned long ago that to look around these rooms was to invite fascination, obsession, a kind of brief and awful madness.

He said nothing, as protocol demanded. He waited, breathing in slow, measured, disciplined intakes, his mind still, without thought or reaction or emotion, except for that thin thread of fear. Other, untrained men would have panicked, screamed, gone mad, and fled. But he was trained; he stood, and listened, and waited.

The dark hair writhed. He heard faint snappings as the static flickered and burned above her face.

"Asher Tye cannot be found," the woman said. "He has vanished from the public deck of a passenger ship as if never there. Ghulag Sor-Tee has left no technique available to him unused. He flushed him out, lay in wait, and Tye never came. No one came. He eludes an Adept of maximum skill, almost equal to you, Cor-Reed—almost equal to me."

"He is trained well," the rodent-faced man murmured. Soft as it was, the October One picked it up and hissed at it, spitting it out like the pit of a prune.

"An Apprentice overcomes a full Adept? Is that your suggestion, Cor-Reed? And is the ancient knowledge so fragile, so limited, so simple that the most inexperienced beginner knows enough to deceive the most advanced in Skill, in Power itself?"

She let a silence fall. With her unnatural tallness, and

draped in garments of deep, nonreflecting black, she seemed to tower over him, a pillar of nothingness in a background of confusion. The walls mocked him. Out of the corner of his eyes they oscillated and coalesced and retreated, daring him to look and then to stare.

Hypnotic. But no form of hypnotism could touch Cor-Reed. He was an Adept of the October Guild. Nothing and no one, save perhaps the October One herself, could pierce the defenses that years of painful training had provided. And she was not intent upon overcoming him. Rather, she seemed to seek something from him, some knowledge of the boy who had so lately studied with him.

"Do you assume, then," he ventured to say, "that Asher Tye has somehow resisted the Psychic Probe?"

Her face was finely chiseled, etched by a thousand lines, ageless and fair, compelling to look upon, attractive in an alien, feminine way. He loved her and feared her. She drew him to her like a magnet, not merely physically, but mentally. He wanted her wisdom, yet at the same time, desire was tangled by the very insights that he pursued.

She spoke. Even in the near-perfect passivity that he cultivated so carefully, that formed a foundation of his training, he jumped inside. The voice wrapped around him, pierced through him, took him.

"For a hundred years I have sent failed Apprentices home with watching Adepts in attendance, for in theory, the Probe can be resisted; yet never have we observed it to happen. You could break the hold of the Probe, and I, but we have known of none outside of October who would have such Skill. Now . . .

"Have you trained him too well, Cor-Reed?" she spoke, the hiss pronounced, air forced through her teeth from lungs that seemed to need no air. "Can he take Ghulag and use him, twist him at his will, skewer him on a spit of knowledge that you taught him?"

She answered herself, then. He didn't dare to—he,

from whom the face of death itself would have drawn but a passing glance.

"Nay," she said. "This I cannot believe. Power—in its ebb and flow I feel, and have felt Asher Tye, and even were the flaw not there, he would still be as nothing or next to nothing. No, Cor-Reed, there is Skill at work here, beyond that which Tye has learned, beyond Ghulag Sor-Tee. Skill that is the equal to yours, at least, and you only barely pass beyond Ghulag himself.

"You know little of our history, Cor-Reed. We are not alone, yet the October Guild is few in number, spread thinly across the hundred billion inhabited planets of the Galaxy. In oxygen, methane, chlorine, even ammonia and vacuum itself, creatures live near ten billion stars, and only one star in ten has planets at all. And we do not touch more than one planet in ten million."

Cor-Reed was startled. It was the first time that he had heard even a hint of how many of the Guild there were among the stars. He had known for a long time that theirs was not the only October One. But he could not at first believe that the October One's species was spread so thinly as the analogy she presented. There were rumors that the Ones came from outside the main part of the Galaxy itself; the satellite galaxy known as the Sculptor, eight thousand light years from the main wheel of the Milky Way, was sometimes mentioned, but it was only one of twenty known lesser galaxies in near-eternal orbit around the Milky Way—the Magellanic Clouds, the Draco, Ursa Major and Minor, Sextans, Pegasus, Fornax, and Leos I and II, among others.

"The point," he heard himself saying, "is that the Skill may not be unique to the Guild? That there could be, even should be by all the laws of mathematics, other places where a variety of Skill may have formed that may equal, may even surpass, that of the October Guild?" It was almost heresy. He felt his fear leap up, and only the long years of intense training allowed him to fight it back down again.

But . . .

"That I do not believe," the October One grated. "Were there a race of such Adepts, I would long since have felt their stirring. Nay, this is a freak occurrence, Cor-Reed, one that will never happen again. For from now on, I will not Probe those Apprentices who fail."

The October One turned. It was as if she pivoted on a sphere, a gigantic ball bearing. There was no movement under her dead-black robes, as of legs maneuvering. A cold, yellow eye looked straight into his, and static crackled in her hair.

"In the past, I would avoid the public screams of relatives, but no more," the October One said. "For this is a danger I cannot abide. Rather than one Rogue—one failed Apprentice still holding to his partly trained Skill—spreading chaos among those who would have turned eventually to October, I would have ten thousand die."

"If Tye be such," she hissed, sending ripples of cold agony up his spine and into his mind, "he must be ended. And if he has been seized by another Power, we must know what it is, and meet it, and defeat it."

He waited, knowing the words that were coming, and terror mounted in him—a man who would face the empty void itself without a tremor or doubt.

The October One spoke.

"You will find him," the October One said in a voice without breath. "Go, and bring him to me. I will take his mind first, to see how this thing was done.

"Then he will die."

# Chapter 5

For two days the Digger ran an increasingly exhausted Asher through a series of mental and psychokinetic tests. It was obvious early on that the first purpose
was to find out just how advanced Asher was in the use
of the Skill. He shot green flame around the room,
disappeared into the Cloak, and moved physical objects
with his mind, the very definition of psychokinesis. He
faded into Shadow, conjured up images of people and
glowing objects that hung in the air and then faded
away, and filled the room with a miasma of shrieking
terror that made even the hardened Kerla flinch. At
one point the Digger made Asher levitate a shoe, then
a suitcase, then a chair, and finally a cubic foot
of yellow bricks, which Asher discovered later were
gold from one of Kerla's recent swindles. The latter
was too much for him; although he was able to make it
shudder, and shook off the top bars, he could not lift
the immense inert weight against the ship's artificial
Earth-normal gravity.

Kerla was often absent. When she was there, she
grumbled and paced and cursed, muttering under her
breath words that Asher did not catch and that, indeed,
might have been in some other, arcane language. The

alien seemed to tolerate her with sharp good humor. One time, the Digger was crouching in front of the door and watching Asher juggle green balls of fire with his mind, when the fat woman came striding through the quickly opened door and tripped against the smooth, diamond-hard shell of the Digger. She staggered with amazing quickness for one so fat, although if the near wall of the cabin hadn't been there, she would have fallen on her face. She delivered such a round of loud cursing that Asher began to feel defensive on the alien's behalf, until he recalled that the Digger could see through walls. And doors. Had he been distracted by the flying green balls? Wasn't Kerla's mishap an accident and no more? Kerla didn't think so, and even Asher wondered.

Working with the Digger was an interesting experience, so much so that for a time, Asher forgot that the little alien was in cahoots with the offensive fat woman. Through all the tests, Asher sensed a tremendous power buried somewhere inside the repulsive alien body—not a physical one, although the alien was plenty strong and tough, but a power of the mind and will and Skill. Sometimes Asher thought that the alien was holding it back somehow, playing it down for the benefit of the loud and shrill Kerla. But as the latter browbeat and cursed and insulted the alien, Asher began to think that the Digger was afraid of the woman, just as he was. If so, why would he do something like trip her, if in fact he had done it on purpose, if . . .

Asher shook his weary head. The fact was that he had gotten little sleep in the last two days. The alien had wakened him at least a dozen times in the middle of each night to test the speed of his transition from sleep to wakefulness. At one point, Asher was sure, the alien was somehow testing the psychokinetic power of his dreams.

Toward the end of the two days, the alien reported in his ciliatic voice to Kerla, who snorted and cast a baleful eye upon Asher.

"He says you're just a beginner," the woman said, scorn in her voice. "He recommends that we turn you over to the October Guild and be done with you."

Asher, who by this time had mastered the Digger's speech from the long hours of test and retest, had heard no such thing come from the Digger's mouth. He was too tired to fear the woman. Instead . . .

He attacked her. He did it without thinking, all the contempt for her and the pent-up anger from the entire ride on the ship, from the Probe itself, rising in him and taking him over.

He used the Glance of Command. It was something more than a glance, however—a narrowing of the eyes, a blasting forward of the will, a grasping of the other's mind and pulling it in. He reached for her mind and took it, intending to bring her to her knees. And then . . .

She shook him free. It took an effort, which he felt clawing up in her. It heartened him, even as reason penetrated his mind and forced the anger aside. Was she so weak that even a pre-Initiate of the October Guild could threaten her, who had called herself a Rogue Adept?

Then she picked him up by the feet with her mind. He fought, trying to bring to bear all the power within him, but nothing worked. Everything seemed to be turned off, the plug pulled. He dangled in the air by his feet, head a few centimeters from the floor.

She kicked him. He never forgot that kick, for he carried the mark with him to the end of his life. Her foot crashed into his nose and broke it; blood spurted outward and dripped onto the deck below. His head rang into unconsciousness for a moment, then cleared. He swung like a pendulum from his feet, and his blood made a line on the floor.

She drew back her foot for another kick, words melting out of her into one long, obscene curse. Then the Digger appeared between Asher's head and her foot, and her kick bounced off his hard shell. She yelled at him, and he hissed at her—not a laugh this time, but a warning.

He fell suddenly as her mental grasp released him. His head hit the deck, not hurting much from such a short distance up, but matting immediately in the blood that pooled there. His backside and feet, falling from a greater height, slammed onto the deck with bone-jarring force. He lay there, brought two fingers up to grasp his nose and pinch off the blood, and waited for his head to clear.

And he knew hate. Hate was something that he had thought he knew already, a major part of his Flaw. The Guild had called it a circle with no end, a self-feeding fire, a crippler of the Power. But now he felt it far beyond anything he had felt before, in all its immense ugliness and force. He fought it, but he felt it anyway.

When he finally stood up, shaky and messy with blood, he turned toward the cabin door and found that the woman was gone. The alien crouched there, looking at him with eyes in which there was no expression that he could see.

"She has the Power," the alien finally said in his blubbery rasp of a voice, "in greater measure than you. Obey her, or in her madness, she will kill you."

"But why!" Asher said, sudden tears making rivulets in the blood. "I didn't ask for her. I don't want her!"

"We saved you for a purpose, Asher Tye," the Digger burbled. "You must abide by us, or die."

"Then I will die," Asher said, and stumbled blindly for the door.

It would not open.

"Wait," the Digger said. "I will tell you why she, we, are preferable to death."

Asher leaned against the door, head bowed, saying nothing.

"Her mission, by the Guild of Thieves, is to watch for such as you, and then see you safely to a planet ahead. There you will see her no more. It will be forty days—

days that you will not enjoy—but she is ordered not to harm you . . ."

"She has harmed me!" Asher snapped. His nose was still dripping through the pinched fingers.

"Not irrevocably, and neither she nor her superiors would consider you damaged."

Asher's spirits sank.

"It is not a mission she enjoys, for it points to the fact that once she had potential in the Guild of October, and failed; then she had potential in the Guild of Thieves, and again she failed. For when she came out of Erasure, she and I sought out the Thieves, but neither of us could teach them what they wanted and needed to know—how to fight October on its own abnormal level, with mind as well as body. She has not the temperament of a teacher, as you have seen, and that only makes her temper worse. Pity her, Asher Tye, for she could break the evil cycle of failure and self-pity and more failure caused by self-pity—she could do it in theory, but trips herself up when she tries. And so the Guild of Thieves sends her on missions that skirt around October, keeps her away from those Adepts who would sense her activity instantly and, if she sustained it, track her down. You saw the captor crystal incident, which is typical. She steals from the criminal underground with amazing ability, but October she cannot touch. And, too, she is mad in some ways," the Alien said, his ghastly voice almost inaudible. "She despises herself. She hates her body, and inside it, she hates what she has done with her life—hates that despite a Skill unique among the Thieves, she is yet an unimportant part of their Guild."

Asher knew then that the alien was telling him her weaknesses. If he could exploit them . . .

"The Flaw," the Digger said, and Asher started. "The Flaw makes you see her now as an enemy. Yet she has saved you from the Guild. Consider. You have only forty more days with her, and then she will be gone. Would you not have pity on one so flawed herself?"

Asher said nothing. Feelings raged in him for which words could not be found. Hate struggled with emptiness.

In it all, he forgot to ask the alien where the little creature himself would be after the forty days.

# Interlude

The remorseless tentacles of the October Guild, grasping and seizing control of powerful human beings on dozens of planets, were being tweaked. For the first time, the "Subtle Guild" was being challenged, as if someone, somewhere, knew the inner purpose of the October One, knew that it was more than the mere selling of occult powers on the commercial marketplace. The chance that someone had penetrated her designs caused the One to writhe in her mile-high fortress, the dark corners of her mind alive with the banked fire of purpose and arrogance.

On the human planet of Sutton, the national assembly was about to meet. The annual event, which dragged on for four days of exhaustive speechmaking by every political party represented in the legislature, was watched intently by the entire planetary population. So many and so diverse were the views of the parties that rhetoric would regularly reach a fever pitch, and there would be rioting in various cities, which died down after a few weeks only to await the next year's kick-off. And yet the government of Sutton had survived the process for eight hundred years, and was known for the wisdom of its policies, hammered as they were on the anvils of dozens of interest groups.

But Sen Trevor was tired of all the talking. She led the biggest party, and was prime minister as a result. She wanted her policies in place and for everyone to shut up.

She had hired a member of the October Guild, for a fantastic amount of money, to work on the minds of her major political opponents, to bend them subtly to her way of thinking. It was a clean way to total power, she thought; it did not occur to her that the Guild member might influence her, too.

There would be no riots this year, she publicly proclaimed. How she would create this miracle, she would not say. But if she could swing it, her prestige would rise to heights above which her opponents could not climb. She would have wrought a political miracle.

And so the speeches began. But something went wrong. Sen Trevor's scientists eventually found a drug in the legislature's water supply that would effectively block the release of controlled psychic energy. But the target could only be the one individual on the planet who could exert such control, an October Adept, and no one knew about that individual except Sen Trevor . . .

The speeches went on, flaming with passions even greater, if possible, than the planet had seen in recent years. The cities erupted into violence. The government was forced into harsh and unpopular methods of repression. Sen Trevor's standing in the polls plummeted.

As she threw the Adept off the planet, she raged that he had somehow leaked the plan to her opponents. He had not and, his access to the Power still blocked, could not probe for the answer. For obvious reasons, she kept the expulsion quiet. But for equally obvious reasons, she ordered the drug distributed throughout all the water supplies of the planet. At least no one could come after her using the October Guild as a weapon, as she had planned to do to them.

No one, including now, the October Guild itself.

\*   \*   \*

For many years, the feelers of the Guild had extended deep into human space. Thousands of planets, independent of one another, linked only by the tenuous policing of the Galactic Council, felt the presence of October, although few people on those planets knew it, and far fewer still what it implied. Tiny voices in the wilderness cried out against manipulation of the mind for any reason, by anyone. Cranks and crackpots, many were, and no one listened, because things were not bad, and not getting worse. Until the publicity began.

The exposure of presidential fat on Aero had been powerful because it had made people laugh, and since people like to laugh, the news had spread over the interspatial channels, and soon even some nonhumans were laughing—those that could laugh. But as they laughed, the image of October was before them, an October that tricked citizens and propped up corrupt rulers. It caused people to think. Above all, the October World did not want people to think.

The Sutton incident did nothing to enhance the image of October, but it did not overtly harm it in the popular mind, for it was hidden from public view. But Sen Trevor was a planetary leader, and as such, she was visited frequently by colleagues from other planets in the near stellar vicinity. She herself was reclusive, never traveled off-planet, so she was comparatively safe from October reprisal. With all incoming beings ingesting or inhaling or absorbing the anti-psychic drug, which could be effectively carried by the humidity alone in a human oxygen-breathing environment, there was little chance of an Adept reaching her. And even so, she was relatively discreet, dropping just enough information before her visitors to raise vague alarms in their memories when the word "October" came to their attention on their own worlds. But the effect was felt, and finally the One's lieutenant, Cor-Reed, sent in a non-Adept member of the Bodyguard Guild to deal directly with Sen Trevor. Even then, Sutton remained closed as Trevor's successors followed precedence, carefully passed on in official succession instructions.

There were other incidents too within that decade of fire for the October Guild. On Wytopitlock, for example, there was an assassination attempt against the chairman of the board of the corporation that ruled the planet. She had been entering a large, classroom-style auditorium for her monthly press conference, when someone in the back raised a hollow cane and flicked it at her. There shot from it a long stiletto of sharpened steel, flung like a lance, with no sound of compressed air or fire or any other propellant other than the muscles of the attacker. Yet, as the holographic replays showed, the aim was uncannily accurate for such a weapon at such distance. Had nothing interfered, the stiletto would have transfixed the chairman precisely in the center of her forehead, without a millimeter of deviance to one side or the other.

What interfered was the lightning response of the chairman's bodyguard. Replays showed it clearly. The blond woman, who everyone had thought to be a minor press liaison, had entered considerably behind the chairman, along with a gaggle of corporate officials. Suddenly, she straightened from a slouch just as the attacker was throwing. Analysts guessed that she had sensed, with her paranormal powers, the murderous mind of the assassin. Then—the replays had shown it clearly—the space between the eyes of the bodyguard and the streaking stiletto had shimmered, as if invisible lightning had warped the air, and the stiletto had been flung upward as if it had hit steel plate, to bury itself in the corporate seal on the wall above the chairman's head. The huge room had exploded into uproar, and in the chaos the attacker had disappeared as if never there, either merging into the crowd or sneaking out somehow—no one ever knew which.

What they did know was that something abnormal had saved the chairman, and it did not take long for news reporters to link the event to the recent outrage on Aero. Magic, they announced to a horrified planet, had saved the chairman, and afterwards it seemed as if the people would have preferred to see her transfixed, rather than protected by and—who knows?—perhaps under the control of a wizard.

That news spread, too. And on her arid world, the October One hissed and brooded, her slowly widening control over the human universe now slipping. There are too few of us, she thought, and too many worlds; countless trillions of people. And even as her Guild concentrated on the key people, she could not train students rapidly enough to make her domination grow in any but the slowest crawl.

But patience she had. She had worked for decades already, and centuries awaited her, and she had not been in a hurry. She and the other Ones had the Galactic Council, at least, well in hand, and its police, which, if not yet an arm of tyranny, was growing at a satisfying pace. Given the span of her lifetime, even such snail-paced progress made the goal quite reachable: power over and control of the universe—the human universe for her, other lifeforms for the others. Progress . . . but a progress that presupposed no effective interference.

Now, however, interference had come.

"The mind will triumph," came the whisper, floating like the wind across the trackless reaches of space, where dead stars passed among the living in loneliness and indifference. "Who is it that challenges you?" came another thought from somewhere else. "Who can come against mind with fist and steel?"

The ten thousand, on their separate worlds, communed silently, withered female bodies wafting like dead leaves, slow movement inside their ebony robes. Since the time they had fled the Sculptor and gone their separate ways, to work on separate species and take dominion over them, the Ones had touched at the odd moments, sharing triumph, insight, and Skill.

Earlier, Cor-Reed had reported to the October One after studying the Aero and Wytopitlock incidents, and now the October One, projecting her mind outward, repeated what he had said: "The two events have in common only skill of the body," the October One thought to the emptiness. "They could be two random attacks by political forces on Aero and Wytopitlock respectively, but there are in common two things: the uncanny swiftness with which the attackers moved, and that the effect was to reveal an October operative to the public at large. We might see these even yet as coincidence, but for the common effect: they both caused the Guild to be ridiculed, feared and hated. The Sutton incident did the same at official levels, and such identity of result cannot be accident, in our opinion. There must be planning behind it, and that planning must know of October far more than we can permit."

Like a wave beating at a rocky beach, the thoughts poured into her. She sorted them and digested them and responded to them, all in a fraction of an instant. Usually the communing was nearly random, the reception and sorting of disparate thoughts, no common threads tying them into unison. But now she felt concordance from the Ones, a closer concatenation of thought than any she had experienced since that long-ago day that she had persuaded them away from their Teacher and into the void.

How could such knowledge of the Guild exist, unless passed on by one Guild-trained?

It could not be their Teacher, who had closed the Sculptor after their flight and whose presence in the universe they could feel no more. But what of their own students . . . ?

Had one ever resisted Erasure before? It was to guard against such a thing that they all watched the failures after Erasure, even as Ghulag Sor-Tee had watched Asher Tye. But none had ever been detected. Some believed it to be impossible.

Yet whoever had been at work on Aero and Sutton

and Wytopitlock . . . Either it had been random, or someone, somewhere, knew more about the Guild than had ever been made public. In those seeds of exposure were danger for the October Ones who, despite their Power, could never succeed against the might of the galaxy. Only by keeping the myriads unaware might the Ones someday succeed in taking absolute control.

The discordance in the October One's mind increased another decibel when Ghulag Sor-Tee, on the *Pride*, still headed toward Caldott, beamed on scrambled interspatial holography to the October One his report about the captor crystal incident.

And now, she thought, the underworld itself has turned against us. It will agitate on a thousand worlds to break us, for now it will believe us to be rivals, instead of tools that it might use.

The bigger fear was there, too. Did Asher Tye indeed have that much Skill, to pull such an incident off unaided? If so, was he some kind of mutant, able to go far beyond what Cor-Reed had trained him in only a few weeks? Had Erasure triggered the reverse of what it was supposed to do, instead increasing Asher Tye's grasp of the esper Skill of the Guild?

Or was some new and unknown Power at work?

"You must find Asher Tye!" she hurled across light years of space into the shaken mind of Ghulag Sor-Tee. "And then . . ." She left it unsaid. But Ghulag Sor-tee was sick at the image she raised, and sick with terror at what she might do to him should he fail.

# Chapter 6

Asher now realized that he would not be landing on Loblolly. Up to that moment, he had assumed that they would make planetfall at the first opportunity, methane planet or no. Now . . . forty days? That would bring them to the end of the ship's run, to Caldott itself.

Somewhat later Kerla came back in. Asher had washed himself, changed his clothes, and he and the Digger were watching a holographic view of the oxygen-breather's exit port. The ship always broadcast on-the-spot scenes of new passengers coming on board, and other ones getting off.

Asher shot a fearful glance at Kerla, but she seemed set on ignoring him, and he felt relieved. Then the scene from the holograph caught his full attention.

Something odd was happening. Five or six passengers were getting off the *Pride*—oxygen-breathers carrying large, bundled satchels with the equipment that they would need when they landed on the methane world of Loblolly.

The odd thing was that they all looked like Asher Tye.

Asher gaped. Then he saw the Adept, looking wildly around the debarkation gate. The dark man mumbled something, and the Asher images rippled and fixed again. The Adept said something else, louder this time, and the passengers all of a sudden turned blank, their faces indistinct to the Skilled watchers. Through it all, the passengers themselves remained blissfully ignorant that anything unusual was in progress around them.

"Are any of them Asher Tye?" Kerla said, quietly for once. "He cannot tell, and won't be able to until his methane-breathing agents on Loblolly can examine each visitor in turn. By that time, we'll be halfway to Caldott, and will have stopped at a half dozen other planets in the meantime."

"Will he get off the *Pride*?" Asher wondered out loud.

"Not likely," the woman said. "The Digger's tricks are puzzling him now, but the very fact that there are tricks going on will cause him to stay on board, just in case."

And so it proved to be. But life on board the *Pride of Caldott* was chaos for the Adept.

For a while, every passenger on board, alien and human alike, took on the image of Asher Tye. Once the Adept broke through that technique of the Digger's, the latter came up with another one that rendered all the passengers invisible, so that the Adept found himself wandering through an apparently empty ship, except when he bumped into someone and had to apologize to the empty air. The Adept eventually figured that one out, and then the Digger arranged it so that the image of Asher's face alternated with a long series of other faces on each of the passengers, two faces a second, which would have sent a lesser man into screaming madness. Breaking through that finally, the Adept encountered a nothingness penetrating the ship, such a complete lack of rippling of the Power that the average Adept would conclude that the manipulator of the Skill had left.

In the meantime, Asher held to the cabin while Kerla and Digger carried on their guise of innocent passengers.

The *Pride of Caldott* stopped at Ramana, 'Arabi, Hayyim, Clem, and passed by several other planets. At each stop, dozens of Ashers would pour off the ship like ants, sometimes scrambling over each other and cramming the corridors, false images surrounding the regular passengers, themselves carrying the appearance of Asher Tye and oblivious to the scenes that the Adept was seeing all too well.

When at last the Digger employed the nothingness, they were four planets out from Caldott. All at once, the ship returned to normal, insofar as the Adept could see. No more spurious Ashers, no more madness, no rippling of the Power.

"They got off at Clem," the Adept relayed to the October World, his tachyonic image betraying agitation and confusion. "Or maybe they stayed aboard. Or maybe they shipped Tye off at any of the previous worlds we've passed, while their Adept stayed aboard to bedevil me. And the worst thing is, I can't detect the source of it all. There is someone here who can use the Power in ways that only the October One herself could defeat."

When at last they reached Caldott, there were at least thirty members of the October Guild circulating around the ship, having come aboard at various of the planets at which they had stopped. But not the faintest sign did they find.

Caldott was the last stop. All the passengers disembarked, including the Digger and Kerla. Fifteen members of the October Guild, wrapped in Shadow, stayed aboard and waited.

But such extensive use of the Shadow rippled the Power into chaos. No longer could the Digger's activities, much less Kerla's or Asher's, be separated from the general confusion.

The Digger and Kerla rode the shuttle down to Caldott, the impossibly numerous stars in this central region of the galaxy blazing around them like coals from a blast furnace. On the planet, they climbed into an air car and sped out of the central city.

When they were sure that no one was following them, the fat woman relaxed the grip she had had on the spell cast by the Digger.

The Digger changed. On the floor of the air car in front of her, the hard shell shimmered and melted. All at once, there leaped into view the occupant of the space where a Digger had been seen moments before.

A human on all fours.

Far above them, the real Digger cast fifty Shadows around the ship, causing consternation when they disembarked like disembodied souls, one by one, with the Adepts. By that time, the Digger himself was on one of the water-breathing shuttles, heading for Caldott's great inland sea.

Water, oxygen, methane, chlorine, ammonia, vacuum. It didn't matter—it was all the same to the Digger.

# Chapter 7

If he had been aboard, Cor-Reed could have tracked Asher down on the *Pride of Caldott*. He had been so close to the boy that he could distinguish the tiny effect of his personality on the Power. But there had been no way for Cor-Reed to reach the *Pride*. And now Asher Tye was lost among the billions on Caldott itself, or on one of the lesser planets that the great ship had visited on its way in.

Yet Cor-Reed was a Hounder, a more advanced Adept than Ghulag Sor-Tee. He could follow someone that he had met before like a bloodhound on a scent. The scent was not a smell, but a mental taste. It was a Skill effective in a range of no more than four light years; most stars in the galactic arm were much farther away from one another. So it meant visiting the planets, a long, slow ride along the spacelanes, stopping over while the visiting ship went on, waiting for the next one.

The fastest way was backwards, from the planet most likely to hold the fugitive, to the one just before it, and so on.

Two planets in from the October World, Cor-Reed was able to catch an express ship for Caldott. He arrived no more than two days after the *Pride*, and immediately felt the aftertaste of Asher Tye. There would be no need to retrace the route of the *Pride*.

But in a way, the worst had happened. Even as he felt the ripple that Asher had left, he knew that Asher was no longer in the solar system. But Caldott was the nearest thing to a sector capital that there was. Ships leaving it went to any of fifty thousand common destinations, and several million uncommon ones. Unless by some incredible chance he were able to find the same ship that had carried Asher, he would have to send agents outward at vast expense to the Guild, to comb the most likely planetfalls first, then the less likely.

The only good thing about it was that Caldott was the easiest place to quickly gather members of the Guild, precisely because it was so central to galactic transportation.

So Cor-Reed put out the call. When he had a few hundred agents on hand, he gave them the mental taste of Asher Tye, and sent most of them off-planet, leaving a few behind to pass the information on to the several thousand Adepts he had called in.

But after communicating with the October One, he caught a ship, too. He had a hunch, for on Caldott, he had done what Ghulag Sor-Tee was not skilled enough to do.

He had caught the aftertaste of one other, an Adept with a strange flavor, yet familiar in a way that disturbed dim traces of memory without bringing them to light, as if he sensed something from his childhood, or something from a time when his Skill was in its infancy. It was no Guild member that he tasted, and he carried within his cunning brain the imprint of them all. No present Guild member. The implication sent a shiver up his spine. He guessed that it had done the same for the October One, if she had a spine.

But there was a clue. The taste had a certain womanness to it that could not be mistaken. He retrieved by transmission from the October World a list of all female Apprentices from the past, those who had failed the final Test and had been erased. If one had had the same resistance as Asher Tye . . .

Forty-three names. But he could narrow it further, for the taste bespoke a certain range of ages, and many on the list were too young.

Perhaps eight good possibilities, then. He would start with the most likely, and work down the list.

A Hounder of great Skill, he set off in search of Kerla Cwan.

# Interlude

Neither knew that the other was on board the *Augusta*, although one of them should have. Dru-Thun was an Adept of the October World, and she had studied the other passengers on this luxury cruise with all the Skill at her command. They all seemed to be what they claimed—the idle rich, elderly mostly, who had bought onto this special cruise to visit the Roil.

Abner Caldon was a thief of the Guild of Thieves. He had no psychic defenses, and he was masquerading as Bluet Canfield Wingate, very rich and younger than most of the thirty-odd passengers. He affected herbal smokeless cigarettes in long holders, and a lisping speech that delighted the older ladies who made up most of the tour.

Dru-Thun had probed "Wingate's" mind and had found nothing odd there. She should have, and her failure was abnormal.

The October Guild, and through it Dru-Thun, had been hired by the cruise agency that had arranged the tour. Foiling thieves was only an incidental part of her job, which was mainly to act as the ultimate protector against pirates. Buccaneers trying to board the *Augusta* would have no chance against an Adept. She would simply blast their minds into unconsciousness, and then the *Augusta* would take the pirate ship, rather than the other way around. Another Adept had done exactly that a year earlier, and word was reaching business ears around the galactic arm that the October Guild offered highly reliable, even profitable, insurance—expensive insurance, to be sure, but worth it. The cruise agency had heard of heavy pirate activity around the turbulent area of the Roil and was taking no chances, even though the October fee had been very large indeed.

One of the old ladies was a Mrs. Dherkin, kind and sweet, with an air of befuddlement that fooled everyone. Dru-Thun had seen through it, of course, but was not interested in smugglers; her job was to protect the ship itself, not to do off-ship police work. Maybe that was the whole trouble.

Abner Caldon was intensely interested in Mrs. Dherkin. She was the reason he was aboard. Mrs. Dherkin was smuggling seeds, from a plant that was the core of a company's secret process for making ding syrup, a sweet that was making the company rich. People tasted ding syrup, and after that they bought nothing else.

Maple and corn and cane and f pur syrup companies didn't like it. They decided they would make ding syrup, too. They went to their syndicate, which sent Mrs. Dherkin in. She had pretended to be someone's mother—she was good at it—and wrangled her way to the company planet where the particular plant grew.

It had taken her a long time to set up a tour of the fields. The company began to suspect her when she showed too much hurry in leaving the planet. They would have caught her, but she had flashed money at the cruise agency's office on the first planet she came to, so they had switched her onto the cruise ship and not told anyone about it. Now she was chattering about the mysteries of the Roil, and feeling very safe. She didn't know about Abner Caldon.

Caldon had been keeping track of Mrs. Dherkin for months. He could not touch her as long as she operated on the company planet, and his Guild cared nothing for the ding syrup company. But the Guild did not like the syndicates; it was time to frustrate them again.

They had visited the Roil, a strange region of space in which dozens of stars and planets—and, some said, a dwarf quasar—were crammed into a tiny cloud of rainbow-colored dust which no instrument or ship had ever penetrated because of the fantastic gravitational forces and radiation that prevailed within. The cruise was almost over; they were a few days away from the ship's home planet when Mrs. Dherkin suddenly screamed. A few moments later she was with the captain; Dru-Thun stood in Shadow just inside the door, listening.

"Someone stole my jewels!" Mrs. Dherkin screamed. "They were in a little brown box in my cabin, and now they're gone!"

"You should have registered them," the captain murmured. But he was not happy. He tried to soothe the old woman.

"I'll have the ship searched," he said. When the old lady had gone, he snarled at the corner where the Adept stood.

"No problem," the disembodied voice of Dru-Thun said—and then went through the worst two days of her life.

She knew, of course, that there were no jewels in the box. But the captain thought that there were, and Dru-Thun was not about to disabuse him—to accuse the old lady of seed smuggling when there was no proof at hand. Finding the box, or the seeds themselves, should be little problem. She merely had to scan all the minds.

One by one she did so. With increasing panic she did it again, and again, digging deeper each time. Caldon was completely unaware; if she had known, he would have despaired. He had no defense against an Adept.

He knew that the crew was searching the ship. They were very careful not to let the passengers see it, for the passengers were very rich and could make immense trouble for the cruise company if they were offended. But Abner Caldon could see it; he was a thief, after all. He sat in the passenger lounge and puffed on a cigarette, hating it, sipped on a drink, and lisped witty comments to the old ladies around him. He was not worried at all, for he had tossed the box of seeds into the garbage chute in Mrs. Dherkin's room the minute he had found it. No doubt the box and seeds both had been atomized with the rest of the trash, and turned into stardrive fuel.

Circulating among them, in Shadow, was Dru-Thun. She couldn't believe it. *Someone* had stolen that box. But there was no trace of it in any mind she scanned.

"We dock tonight on Machias," the captain had yelled at her. "We paid your Guild a lot of money for you, and you had better find those jewels. Mrs. Dherkin is a paying customer. You don't find them, and I'll see to it that you and your entire October breed are never hired on the spacelanes again, I'll tell you that."

But she didn't find it. Something was interfering with her Power, and it wasn't Bluet Canfield Wingate or Abner Caldon.

As the captor crystal incident had turned the underworld against the October Guild, so now October was disgraced among legitimate businesses, too.

# Chapter 8

Kerla looked at Asher Tye sourly and turned away. Asher neither waved nor said goodbye. He felt a wave of relief.

Asher and the Digger climbed aboard a journeyman passenger ship. They walked up a long ramp and worked their way down old, shabbily kept corridors to a central viewroom. There they relaxed on recliners and watched as the old ship spun out of orbit and fled away from Caldott.

"She's gone," the Digger burbled. Asher didn't visibly react.

"I won't miss her," he said at length.

"I told you that hatred stands in your way," the alien said. "Having her gone makes the hatred fade, but you yourself must drive it finally away by your own will, or it will always be there in some back corner, ready to spring out and devour you."

Asher said nothing. He heard what the Digger was saying, and yet felt the rage inside. He still felt the kick to his face, still felt his nose bleeding and dripping on the deck.

"You have to let it go," the alien persisted. "It comforts you, and gives you ego, but you have to let it go."

Asher was momentarily startled. Hatred giving comfort, supplying ego, for heaven's sake? He was about to protest that he didn't *like* hating, but some inner sense told him to hold off. The Digger was rarely wrong.

So Asher said nothing, but this time, instead of badgering him further, the Digger subsided into vague bubblings and rumblings, as if the point had been made, or as if the pupil were so obtuse that the point could never be made.

"You are to go to the Warrior Planet," Kerla had said when the Digger had finally joined them at the cheap hostelry they had found on Caldott. She had left him alone in the plain room; Asher guessed that she had gone to meet with her superiors, whoever they were. When she came back, she had seemed both happy and annoyed.

"Blast you, you're the cause," she had said first thing as she came through the door. "I lose the best assistant I ever had, and all because of you. I should have killed you back on the *Pride of Caldott*."

Asher had tried to turn her attention elsewhere. "What did they think about the Captor Crystal trick?" he asked her.

She threw back her head and brayed the overly loud laugh that he had come to loathe.

"They loved it!" she shouted, "Fourteen million credits!" But then she had scowled again. "Maybe that's why they want the Digger to go with you," she said. "It was mostly him and you pulled that one off. Maybe they want to team you up." She had suddenly slammed her fist down on the table between them. "What can you do that I can't!"

She had still been fuming when the Digger clattered through the door. He had seemed to bring some calmness to the scene, though Kerla remained unhappy for the rest of their stay together.

"The whelp is needed on the Planet, and so am I,"

was all the Digger had said about it. It hadn't been enough.

"When I first presented myself to the Thieves," the Digger said, "they wanted to know how I had found Kerla, and then how I had found them, the Thieves themselves. As to Kerla, it was a providential accident; I had been scouting some of the planets taken early in the October web, and Kerla was there. It was easy to sense her training, even buried as it was beneath the effects of the Probe." (I would have missed it altogether, thought Asher.) "But once I had released her mind, finding the Thieves was something else. It took us many months, but among other techniques we left an ambiguous message in the online personals, figuring that an organization such as the Thieves would maintain a continuous database scan. Indeed, it was so; the Thieves found us, so to speak, and studied us carefully, and finally took the great risk of inducting us into their Guild. If we had been October spies, then the Thieves would exist no more; October would have wiped them from the Galaxy.

"The Nin sent us out in between other missions to travel the ships that visited the October World, to catch failed Initiates just after Erasure. I could not seem to teach these warrior thieves even rudimentary forms of the Power. Perhaps one of the failed Initiates could. They would be of great use to the Guild of Thieves in any event."

"The Nin?" Asher asked.

"The ships were few," the Digger said, ignoring the question, "at least those that were not wholly owned by October. They all followed routes outward from Caldott and back, with many gaps in between—the October World was a backwater, regularly scheduled but not a place where ships stacked up in the sky. During those gaps, I was on various missions for the Nin, some with Kerla, some without."

"The Nin???" Asher said plaintively.

"The Leader of the Transfer Guild," the Digger said.

"The . . . Transfer Guild?" Asher said, word by word.

"The Guild of Thieves."

"Oh," Asher said.

"There are other Diggers—a planetful of them—but we tend to like tunnels and dislike the open sky. Few will travel as I do, and none have the Skills I possess," the alien said immodestly. "I joined the Thieves because they fight the corrupt, and because they do, they will eventually fight October. And I, with what little Skill I have, abhor the way that October uses the Power for evil ends, with death often following their presence on some hapless world.

"The Nin has formed the Thieves in direct reaction to October, I believe. Lacking Skill, the Warriors seek to maximize other talents. And still they seek a handle from which to gain some advantage over October. As now it stands, the Thieves can only skulk in the background, undertaking surprise forays against October interests, but little else. If the October Guild ever finds out that the Warrior/Thieves are among its hidden enemies, then they will use their superminds to track the Warriors down, and nothing and no one could save them then.

"You are about to go to the Warrior Planet, where you will learn to hone both mind and body, for the two, they say, cannot be separated. Your body will be transformed into a fighting machine. Your mind will take in the knowledge of the laws and practices of a hundred cultures on a thousand worlds. You will learn how to dominate people in normal, everyday settings, even how to intimidate them to give you what you want, gladly, gratefully. Your psionic powers will be tested and, if it can be done, shared. You are a remarkable find for the Guild, Asher Tye, and it hopes to use you well."

"But they are thieves!" Asher whispered. "By definition they are evil and they do evil." The alien looked at him penetratingly, out of his round, yellow eyes. Asher felt something driving him to continue:

"The flaw is better dealt with by death than by serving masters such as those." He looked morosely away, hoping that the self-pity was convincing.

It wasn't.

"You do not know them—not enough to come to such a conclusion," the Digger said in a hiss that was not a laugh. "I can read that you yourself see hope in all this, else you would have activated that Adept back on the *Pride* and let yourself be taken. Ah . . . I feel your surprise," the alien said as Asher's mouth dropped open. "I can see it in you; it is my job. You weighed the yeses and the nos back there, and decided that Kerla and a little alien were a safer bet than the rigid law of October."

"You wouldn't have let me free the Adept from the Time Stop," Asher said feebly.

"On the contrary," the alien said. "I may not have been able to stop you, and I would not have, nonetheless. You had to come with us willingly, or you would have died."

Asher could find nothing to say to this. Instead, he said: "Why are you coming with me, then? I would go to your Warrior Planet if you just showed me the way. Kerla certainly didn't want you to come." His voice was bitter, and he wasn't acting.

"Because there may be more Adepts," the alien said. "And because we couldn't trust you all that much. And because I, with my alien psionics, will be useful in translating your October skills for the Guild. And also because I like you, Asher Tye."

Once again, Asher could find no reply.

Asher and the alien changed ships twice during the voyage, both times at oxygen worlds around which ship transfer was common and routine. The ships that they took were always run-of-the-mill, nondescript plodding workhorses that had made the particular runs a thousand times and would a thousand times again. Asher saw a bewildering array of oxygen-breathing aliens come and go.

Finally, the two found themselves leaving a way station, orbiting around another oxygen planet, this one a beautiful ocean world with but one small continent, squarely astride the planet's south pole.

"A haven for both water-breathers and oxys," the Digger muttered, more to himself than to Asher. "Beautiful. I have heard of this planet. I would like to see the color of the sky, the mile-wide hot springs bubbling in great concentric gatherings on the planet's north side, the incredibly large sea creatures, with arms a hundred feet long . . ." So surprised was Asher at this glimpse of another side of the Digger, that the implication of his words took a moment to sink in.

"Wait a minute," Asher said, looking quickly around. "Isn't this the planetary shuttle, on its way down?"

"It surely is, Asher Tye," the alien said. "But here we are not staying. Come."

Wheeling, the alien clattered out of the private room they had engaged, and down another dingy corridor until they came to a hatchway. Deftly, the Digger reared up and opened it with hands that Asher had never seen.

They passed through two airlocks, and Asher gasped. They had just gone from one ship to another.

"Alarms will be going off all over the shuttle!" Asher yelled. "You can't just open an airlock when the outside door is already open . . ." He was silenced by a look from the Digger.

"No alarms, no problem. The captain is bribed, the circuits turned off. Already the shuttle is far away, hatches closed."

Asher spun around. The hatch behind him had slid silently shut while he was yelling at the Digger.

They were in a much smaller vessel. Who manned it, Asher never knew, for the Digger took him to a small cabin and locked them in. Asher noticed that there was no viewscreen of any kind.

"Ah, I understand," Asher said. "No clues to wherever the Warrior Planet might be."

The alien didn't reply. Instead, he dialed for food. After a moment, Asher did the same.

And then the Digger recommenced Asher's training.

At night, Asher's mind began to feel bruised. The Digger was relentless, and Asher began to worry about exactly what the Digger was preparing him for, what he might find on the Warrior Planet. "They will ask you to teach them how to block access to their minds," the Digger burbled briefly at one point. "You will try."

"Will I be able to do it?" Asher asked doubtfully as he tried to hold the image of eighteen snarling Murrainian swamp devils who seemed to have replaced one wall of the cabin. Vibrating the air to make the sound was the hard part.

The Digger said: "They hate and fear October above all else. Before they found Kerla and you, they had no defense, and Kerla cannot teach Skill—she has tried, but she has not the patience."

"What about you?" One of the swamp devils wavered and its snarl became musical. Asher wrenched it back into shape desperately, juggling all eighteen at once with a painful effort.

"You are my only pupil," the Digger said.

"But why?" Asher whispered, most of his mind engaged on the wall.

"You are my only pupil," the Digger said again.

"But don't the thieves resent it? I mean, they must have asked you, too . . ."

The Digger hissed and Asher, startled, saw that one of the monsters had taken on the face of a kitten. He yelled, and the eighteen images dropped into nothingness like balls from a juggler's hand.

And another time, the ship passed into real space for a few hours to cross from one jump point to another. Asher went into a deep trance, preparing to cast his mind with the Digger to the nearest star system, a red giant with several attendant dwarfs. For a long moment, Asher seemed to hear a voice from far away, without any garble, deeper, clear and distinct. It was teaching him something outside his awareness, giving him some tool for the future, yet what it was and what for, Asher could not seem to grasp. Something very short, but very deep somehow, as if all the mysteries of life and death had been condensed into a single word.

For long days, far into the ship's artificial nights, the alien kept up Asher's training, until he felt ready to collapse.

And then, one day the Digger suddenly threw wide the cabin door and walked out, leaving it open behind him. Asher, in the middle of juggling a dozen silver bars with his mind (for so far had his power increased), hesitated while the bars wavered in their paths. Then in a rush, he released the bars and ran after the alien. The silver landed in leaden thumps behind him.

He caught up, and they walked back to the same hatchway they had used to enter the ship. The Digger cycled it open. Again the outer door was ajar. But this time, Asher stepped not into another ship, but onto the surface of a planet.

The Warrior Planet.

# Part II:

## SEARCH

# Chapter 9

The sky was purple. That's the first thing that Asher saw. It was as violet-hued as a grape. Through the dark sky there were stars. It was either twilight, or . . .

His breath caught. He tried to breathe harder, and found himself gasping. He reeled and fell heavily against the ship.

"Here," the Digger said. From somewhere he produced a trickler. His vision darkening, eyes popping, Asher grabbed it and thrust the nozzles to his face. Oxygen poured into and around his nose.

He fitted the trickler around his head, little tank of supercompressed liquid oxygen hanging down his back. He tightened the strap across his chest that held it in place. The nozzles fitted exactly now over his nose and mouth.

His vision clearing a little, Asher sucked in oxygen and looked around him. His eyes still felt as if they were popping out of his head.

"You'll get used to it," the Digger hissed, reading his thoughts. "The body will adjust. It can adjust to many things." The Digger himself was apparently wearing no trickler, nor anything else.

"The sky!" Asher said. Now that he could look fur-

ther, he saw the hard light of the planet's sun, so
blinding that he couldn't look directly at it. The sun was
almost overhead. It was nearly noon on the Warrior
Planet.

"The atmosphere is thin," Asher said, his voice penetrating the trickler and sounding faint in the air. "That's
why the sky is purple."

"Aye," the Digger said. "Thin, but not poisonous to
you or me. There is oxygen in it, but it would not
sustain you. Remember this, Asher Tye: on the Warrior
Planet, you must always have a trickler and enough
oxygen to get you where you are going, or ten minutes
after you run out, your brain will begin to die. You can
hold out that long with the help of the oxygen in the
air, but after that . . ."

"And it's dark," Asher muttered.

The harsh sun was bigger and redder than the one he
was used to, but the tenuous air did little to scatter its
light. The Warrior Planet was a world of purple shadow,
blue fading through violet to black, a world without
bright yellows or whites. A gloomy and depressing place,
thought Asher, though to its natives it might appear as
a paradise of bright beauty—if it had any natives.

There was plant life, anyway. They were on a hill
covered by a sort of clover, but purple clover with
flowers deeper, almost black. Just down the hill some
kind of forest started, blackish trunks of celerylike trees
poking squatly into the sky, with purple tentaclelike
fronds on top that seemed to wave on their own, without the help of any breeze. Smaller growths wove among
them, almost choking the spaces between and making a
vegetative wall that looked impenetrable. Asher saw
hundreds of birdlike creatures wheeling and soaring
about the tentacular trees, creatures as large as small
dogs, but with detail blurred by distance and the dark
background of the sky.

From where they were standing, gentle hills swept
away into the violet darkness, one after another like
marching soldiers frozen in place, all covered with the

same vegetation, all looking just about the same. Asher could see no lights, no buildings, no air vehicles, no sign that human beings or any other intelligent life stood on this planet under its bright red sun. In the air there were the birds and, buzzing around, what might pass for insects. But no . . .

"Goodbye, Asher Tye," he heard the Digger say. Asher whirled and looked wildly around. He caught the briefest glimpse of the alien's bizarre form as the airlock cycled him inside.

Asher flung himself at the now featureless side of the ship, pawing frantically for the switch that would let him in. There wasn't any there. Then the little alien's burbling voice came to him, inside his head, all around him.

"This is your first Test, Asher Tye," the voice said. Asher thrust his fingers in his ears and still heard it. The alien was sending his message telepathically.

"Stand away from the ship," the voice burbled. "In thirty seconds it will rise, and if you are too close you will be torn apart by the gravitational effect.

"At this moment twenty warriors are two thousand meters to your south, heading toward you. They intend to kill you. Your task is to elude or defeat them. You have all the time you need, until your trickler runs out. Good luck, Asher Tye."

Asher stood there aghast, gaping at the closed ship. Then he heard the beginning hum of the wail that would signal the rising of the ship. Frantically, he turned and ran down the hill, straight at the forest. When he reached the first tree he stopped and looked back.

With a wailing roar the ship leaped off the ground and flashed into the air. The trees bent as the displaced air rushed by them. In a flash of light, the twinkling of an eye, the ship shot into the sky and was gone.

Air gusted into Asher. He staggered against a tree and yelled. Sharp spines stood out from its trunk like needles; half a dozen of them were in his side, his left arm. He tore away and the spines came with him, breaking away with brittle snaps from the parent tree.

Two thousand yards away . . .

Whimpering, Asher grasped the first spine by its end and pulled it out of his skin. It tore out like a porcupine quill, rings of barbs lacerating his flesh. He gritted his teeth and pulled the second one out. He hoped there were no poisons in the wicked quills.

The third one. It was as he wrenched it out that he realized, through a haze of pain, that the flaw had dominated him from the moment that the little alien had spoken here, on the Warrior Planet. If he had any chance of escaping this peril, he had to climb on top of the flaw and dominate it.

He knew how, too. It wasn't that he didn't know how to overcome it. It was just that when it first came on, it always took him over, carried him away in a period of panic, clouded his mind with fear and emotion and anger.

He took hold of the fourth quill, halfway up his side, and pulled savagely. The pain was enormous. His fingers, slippery from blood and sweat, lost their hold and the spine stayed in his skin. He grasped it again, and concentrated within himself. He was his head; his body was just a tool, like a hammer, being damaged, but under control . . .

He yanked. The barb came loose, and he threw it away. The pain was there, just as bad, but he was above it now, and it was more a datum to consider, rather than a power over him.

The fifth and sixth ones were in his upper arm, right in the middle of his triceps muscle. The angle was bad. How close were the warriors to him now? How much time did he have? For a moment he considered moving off and leaving the last two. But no; they would fester and hurt and he would be distracted by them. Gritting his teeth and again bringing his mind into itself, he pulled, then grasped and pulled again.

The last one was out.

Gasping, he wiped sweat away from his eyes and looked around him. Two thousand yards to the south—probably half that now. The south . . . where in this featureless, high-noon place was the south?

Then he did what he should have done all along. He sent out his mind. Just a little, a gentle sweep in a large circle around him, not far enough at first, then farther. An elementary October skill—reckoning danger, finding it, identify it . . .

There. Facing the hill, directly to his left. For a moment he lost them, then bore down harder and found them again. A few seemed to recoil instinctively at his mental contact, but their Skill was so primitive as to be almost nonexistent. It was not a mental contest that he wanted right now, so he did not press further than he needed to locate them.

Close; very close. His Skill could not tell him just how near they were, but he began to move away to his right in an awkward, shambling run, side and arm numb but still hurting with every step.

What kind of warriors? Members of the Guild of Thieves? Or natives of this purple planet? If the former, why did they want to kill him? If the latter, why again, and what kind of beings were they?

One thing was certain—they had a tremendous advantage over him. If native, they would not need a trickler. If of the Guild, they would have spare bottles of oxygen aplenty. No matter; he would be in serious trouble even if he got away.

And yet, why were they on foot? Why not send an air car, track him with heat sensors, and then blast him out of existence?

He didn't know. And yet he sensed danger in them.

It was then that he noticed a break in the vegetation. No, many breaks, dozens of breaks. Perhaps his eyes were getting used to the pervading gloom. Perhaps too he hadn't been looking carefully enough. He began to get angry with himself, and then cut it off as a bad idea.

The vegetation under the trees was hollowed by hundreds of tunnels, heading off in all directions. The bushes just seemed to grow that way, bending up and over.

There was a shout behind him. Asher looked around and saw nothing. Were they there, just beyond the edge of the trees, snaking toward him like rabbits through the brush? Or were they almost on top of him, right there behind him but in Shadow? No. He felt no exercise of Skill anywhere near.

He bent and plunged through the tunnel nearest him. It was just over half his height, and he could move at an awkward running shuffle, alert for the trunks of the wicked trees. It wasn't much darker among the bushes, for light worked its way through the thin tentacular branches of both trees and bush. But it was still shrouded in that purple gloom that seemed to characterize the planet itself. Asher could not move very fast without running the risk of impaling himself on one of the trees.

In a moment he was hopelessly lost. The maze of openings gaped around him in stupefying sameness. He had a solution for that, but did not know in what direction he had turned since entering the forest. Now that he was aware of the need, he could lay a psychic trail behind him, a kind of ghostly reminder hanging along the path he had come. But if he did that, could the warriors behind him follow such a trail? He did not know, and he did not want to find out.

He decided to use a variation of the idea. He shot ahead of him an arrow-straight aura of mental power, a thin line stretching out before him. He did not want to double up upon himself and run right back into the arms of his enemies.

He followed the mental trail, keeping as close to it as he could. As he passed along he dissipated the traces of it that he was leaving behind, ordering it to wisp away like tendrils of smoke. Adepts would still have been able to follow the tiny, lingering traces of his passages, as they could those of an unaware mind, even an animal's. But Asher had to assume that his followers were not Adepts; otherwise, the Digger's comments about his own value to this training planet of the Guild of Thieves would have been meaningless.

He started to take note of his body, left to itself since he had pulled the spines out. As he shambled, bent over, through the forest, sweat streaming down his back and around the edge of the trickler, he felt his breath gasping at the exertion. His left side and arm were beginning to cause more serious pain from the still-oozing wounds. His legs were beginning to cramp at the unaccustomed movements and position. His feet—they were soundlessly breaking the soft, dry, thin fallen leaves from the trees and bushes, leaving distinct footprints from his passage.

Footprints!

His mind screamed danger and he threw himself to one side, through a tunnel that opened there. Something long and sharp flew at incredible speed through the space where he had been—an arrow? To use such a weapon in this age of technology would be beyond easy belief . . . They were right there, behind him. He threw himself into Shadow.

He ran. Behind him he heard voices. Some were human, some were not. "That way!" a few of them said. He was still making footprints in the forest, even if the Shadow prevented them from seeing him.

Levitation. He was not skilled at it, but could use it somewhat. On the October World he and the other trainees would sometimes slide up and down the sand dunes on invisible toboggans made from their own minds. That was a kind of levitation, and here he had a thousand tunnels to choose.

But levitation would leave a distinct psychic trace behind.

It was a chance he would have to take.

He made the toboggan, flopped down on it, and shot off through the tunnels. He let his mind feel the trees in front and to the sides of him, sensing their massive-ness and directing the mental sled around and past them. He slid centimeters from the ground, not touching it, not disturbing it, flowing like a living carpet up rises and down their other side. It took intense concentration, mental work of a high order, and Asher Tye was exhausting himself more and more with every meter he gained.

He was still casting his mental track ahead of him to prevent himself from circling aimlessly in this dizzying maze. The purple leaves and black trunks shot past him. His body jolted as the fluid toboggan shot over dead logs and rocks and bumps of all kinds. His side yelled at him inside, and then again, louder and louder.

Another shout behind him, much farther away.

Asher kept it up as long as he could. Through an increasing agony of body and fatigued mind he rushed on his belly through that spiny forest, careening from one tree to another without ever touching them, roaring down one gentle hill and, without slowing, up the next. Endless masses of tendrils hung over and around him, not moving down here as they did up above.

It was his side and arm that finally stopped him. He hadn't left the place of the arrow more than half an hour before, but his mind was reeling from exhaustion, his mental powers were fading, and his body was screaming pain at him. He tried to isolate his mind from it, but he was engaged in too many things, thrusting the thread ahead, feeling for the trees, maintaining the toboggan, and thrusting his body forward . . .

His concentration slipped for an instant and he crashed sideways against a fallen tree. Its spines were gone, rotted away, but its trunk was still heavy and massive. Asher hit it on his left side, and all concentration passed from him. He cried in agony at the purple around him.

As he lay there, toboggan gone, body throbbing, he rolled over on his back and looked into the sky. A hundred tendrils obstructed his view, but still the sun appeared to be at zenith. It hadn't seemed to have moved at all.

There was a sudden deeper shadow over the sun, and at the same moment the tentacles of the tree under which he lay lashed upward. Loose spines rained around him; there was a high-pitched scream, then a struggling shape was engulfed by the tentacles and dragged downward, to disappear in the crease of the tree's trunk.

One of the "birds" had flown too low. Asher shivered.

He wasn't in good physical shape. That was one of his problems. The October had never stressed it. They had allowed recreational periods, trained him in various breathing techniques, but had never forced a physical fitness regimen on their Apprentices and Initiates.

He lay there gasping, and tried to uncover the lucidity of his mind from the fog of physical and mental fatigue that enveloped it. Yet it was long minutes before the random thoughts flitting through his mind settled down.

Then he sent his mind out again, to find his enemies. He closed his eyes and shut out the sunlight, cast behind and around him. Yes! There they were. Far from him now, milling around where he had been, trying to pick up his trail. He had eluded them for the moment.

He rolled over, and all at once he was in a little clearing, one of the few that he had seen in this world of spiny trees and tendrily bushes. The trees still rose about him, their bizarre topknots writhing in the nonexistent wind. Asher wondered if they caught the insects, too; he rather imagined that they did.

Why were the Warriors after him? He could understand their testing him before letting him into some select group of trainees. But that arrow, if that's what it was, had been lethal, and the Digger had said that it was his death that they wanted. Had the little alien taken him all this way merely to kill? Or was he himself an agent of the October Guild who, for some reason, had waited all this time to bring him to his death? Was he merely an interesting exercise for the student killers of the Guild of Thieves?

He could elude the strangers behind him. He could perhaps blast one or two of them with the Green Flame. But he hadn't the Skill to overcome twenty at once.

An animal moved into his clearing. For a moment, Asher was too stunned to react. It was big, bigger than he. It seemed to be spiked all over with dirty, savage-looking spines. The planet seemed to be alive with things with spines. It had a mouth, too, with tearing teeth gaping, and a tongue that shot in and out, blunt and blue, tasting the air. It was something like an armadillo with pins stuck all over it, and a badger's jaw.

Asher was about to leap to his feet when he froze. He was still in Shadow, after all. The beast could not possibly see him.

It snuffled the ground, bothered by something. Its nose was bright red, the first bright thing Asher had seen on this odd planet. The eye was red too, not so bright, and it stared without blinking all around the clearing, casting over Asher many times and not noticing him.

Yet something was bothering the beast, and it began to systematically scour the clearing with its snuffling nose. It had four legs, all ending in pads that might or might not conceal claws. Its spines quivered all over its squat body. Asher sensed a hollowness at their ends, not like the barbs of the trees—hollowness that could carry poison.

As the beast approached, Asher crawled away, keeping himself carefully in Shadow, but not entering the main part of the forest where he would have little room to maneuver. He would not make the same mistake here that he had made on the October World. He would not attack this animal with a blast of Green Flame that would alert anyone within ten kilometers.

The beast snuffled over the spot where Asher had fallen. Suddenly, it raised itself up on its hind legs, pawed at the air, and roared. The roar, with a whistle and shriek built in, rose up the scale and keened into ultrasound, shaking the trees above it and causing their tendrils to thrash wildly as if in mortal fear.

The beast had smelled Asher. It turned its nose and stared directly at him, not seeing him, but smelling him.

It flicked its tail, and a cloud of spines hurtled at the air. No porcupine could do that, even a giant one. But Asher's training was in him, and without conscious thought, he whipped up a shield of mental force that took the spines and held them, quivering for a moment in the air, some sort of pale liquid seeping from their tips, before they dropped harmlessly on the ground.

The animal screamed in rage and drove at Asher, not seeing him but knowing where he was. Had been. Asher skipped out of the path of the beast. But when the animal reached the point where Asher had moved aside, its nose sensed it and, once again, it threw a cloud of spines toward him.

This time, Asher caught the spines in midair and held them there for a moment, then gently lowered them and placed them, points upright, on the ground.

The animal charged toward him and stepped full on its own weapons, piercing its paws and driving the spines up through them.

A scream unlike any Asher had ever heard filled the clearing and reached up into the sky, until Asher had to cover his ears and close his mind against it. The animal stood on its hind legs again and tore at the spines in its paws with its jaws, shaking the paws and then biting at them with teeth that were cut and needled by the spines they touched.

The animal stood on its legs like a bear and shuddered horribly, and then fell forward heavily, inertly, all animation gone, on the leaf mold of the forest floor.

Was it dead? Asher touched it with his mind, shaken as he was by the scene he had just witnessed, and found no heartbeat, no movement. He had guessed that the spines held poison, but had not guessed that it was so lethal.

He was shaken in more ways than one. He had just killed another animal. Could he have avoided it? Maybe, but he doubted it. The animal had been coming at him, Shadow or no Shadow, and he had had little mental energy left with which to protect himself. He had done what made sense at the time.

Asher reflexively cast his mind in a great circle while his eyes stared at the body of the animal. His mind touched those of his enemies.

They were close. They had heard the beast.

# Interlude

The *Augusta* incident threw the October One into a near frenzy. She had thought that she had conquered fear long before, but for an instant the tiniest whiff of it disturbed the hard composure of her mind, and her recognition of it caused fear of another kind. She mauled and shredded both fears—fear, and the fear of fear—and then sent the shreds reeling into the unconscious. But it worried her. She wondered if she had destroyed it all, or merely pushed it under darkness, from which it could rise again.

For now she knew that another user of Power was moving in her sector of space. She knew not whether it was Asher Tye with vastly increased Skill, or a new Power altogether. Another Power . . . it was the worst of all thoughts. For if it were not another October One—and she knew all ten thousand intimately, with the certainty of mental contact—then it would have to be someone with training outside of theirs, and she knew that her Teacher had worked with her own species and no other. But there had been many incidents now, enough to suggest more than one hand and mind at work. The implication was staggering: another Teacher somewhere, perhaps another race of beings with access to Power, through methods that could be alien to October. Never among the millions of races had there arisen one with more than the most rudimentary Skill. Only in the Sculptor subgalaxy had a Teacher arisen, and taught the October. And then they had closed themselves to the Sculptor, and he to them, when they had fled to the central Milky Way, wanting to exercise their Skill, wanting to control.

Yet . . . yet . . . she had sent her mind on timeless journeys through the galactic arm, with no hint anywhere of a new Presence. Were Power in use anywhere in her sector—indeed, anywhere in the galaxy—either she or her sisters would have detected it with the precision of eagles spotting mice.

She had to have Asher Tye! When she had him, she would take him apart and know, one way or the other.

# Chapter 10

Asher did not run. He was too tired to conjure up the toboggan again. Besides, he was losing the fear that had held him so tightly when he first found himself alone on the Warrior Planet. Maybe it was fatigue that had subdued the fear, or maybe just time. In any event, Asher Tye's fear was rapidly being replaced by something else.

Anger. Not hot, wild, irrational anger, but a cold sort of anger that left his mind clear and lucid, his thoughts quick and pointed. Fatigue and anger. He was tired of running, and he was angry at it. His body was exhausted, and he resented the wounds in his side and arm. He was so sore that he could barely move. He blamed the warriors for his killing of the animal.

He huddled down in one of the tunnels leading out of the clearing, lying on the ground, facing the opening, still in Shadow. He brought his breathing to steadiness and stilled his mind, preparing to battle the warriors of the Warrior Planet.

One by one, they filed into the clearing. Asher saw them clearly through the shadowy high-noon light.

The first one was a human boy, not much older than himself, but blond, bigger, smoothly muscled. He stepped quickly and softly, like a cat. His hair was long and bound in the back by a black ribbon. He wore a loincloth and nothing else, save for a hissing trickler. In his hands he carried a crossbow, bolt cocked and ready, finger gently on the trigger guard. A crossbow! Asher would have been just as surprised by a homemade stone axe.

After him came a . . . It rolled, like a ball. It was furry, mostly tan with a large yellow circle on one side. It came almost to the boy's neck, which meant that it weighed far more than he did. It rolled quietly and smoothly, thrusting itself with nothing that Asher could see.

Behind it Asher could see the outline of a Ghiuliduc, and over its head something else, maybe another human. But the leader had seen the animal, and with a gesture brought the group to a halt.

The round alien rolled soundlessly over to the beast, while the boy stood tensely, rifle ready, scanning the forest all around. Time and again he looked straight at Asher, but did not see him.

Asher waited for the other warriors to enter the clearing, but they did not. He couldn't see the Ghiuliduc anymore.

The blond boy spoke through his trickler.

"Roller?" he said. Even in that one word, Asher could hear the strangeness of his accent.

The Roller had been very close to the animal. Now it moved a half-turn backward, toward the boy.

"Quite," it said, and Asher was startled to hear clear pronunciation, coming from somewhere in the alien's body. "Poisoned with its own venom."

"How . . .?"

"Oh, it's quite common," the alien said. "Venomous creatures can often swallow their own poison, but rarely survive when it is injected into the blood."

"He's clever and skilled," the boy said, looking around the clearing.

"Yes," said the alien, "but not experienced. He's watching us right now."

A thrill of fear ran through Asher. How could the Roller know? Was he Skilled, too?

"Come out," the blond boy said loudly. "You've proven your point." They waited. Asher crept, inch-by-inch, deeper into his tunnel.

"He's moving away," the Roller said.

"Wait!" the boy yelled. "I mean it. We won't hurt you."

Asher stood up, still in Shadow.

The Roller somehow pointed toward him.

With stunning fluidity, the blond boy whipped up the crossbow and fired straight at Asher Tye.

If the bolt had hit, it would have driven through his chest and out again. The barb would have torn his lungs and heart, and he would have died in seconds.

Instead, it hit his Shield, long since up, deflected upward and buried itself in one of the trees, which reacted by whipping fronds down and around it—fronds that were covered, now that Asher could look at them, with needles sharper than those of its trunk.

Asher was, oddly, feeling a queer sort of mental detachment. He had expected the treachery. Nothing would surprise him anymore. He just did not know how the Roller had sensed where he was.

He slipped deeper into the tunnel. The boy was fitting a new bolt onto the crossbow. The Roller had moved until he was in a direct line between Asher and the blond boy. Where were the other eighteen?

In a flash of logical insight, Asher realized what the Roller was doing. He was pointing Asher out to the unseen warriors around the clearing. They would know that their enemy was directly along the line that the alien and the blond boy described.

Asher decided to use the toboggan again, fatigue or no. He dropped to his knees, intending to form it. Something flew through the spot where his head had been. Something else shot out of the Roller. Gaping,

Asher saw a hand of some kind, attached to a thin, stalky arm. The hand was holding a crossbow bolt; it had plucked it out of the air.

"Clemmy, you idiot!" the blond boy screamed. Asher turned his head and looked incredulously behind him. A girl, no older than thirteen, was fitting another bolt into her own crossbow. She was almost crying.

"He's there, I know he is!" she whimpered. "There wasn't anything between you and me, and I couldn't see you. There had to be something in the way!"

Asher sidled into a side tunnel and the girl brought her crossbow up, pointing toward where he had been.

The boy was running toward them.

"Don't shoot again, confound it," he yelled.

Asher was behind the girl now. He reached out and yanked her trickler off her head. She dropped the crossbow; her hands flew up to her head, and she screamed. But at the same time, she did something that Asher had not expected. She pivoted on the ball of her right foot, and her left slammed into his stomach.

He gasped and fell backward, clutching her trickler in his hand. He landed heavily on the leaf mold, just missing the trunk of a needle tree. For a moment, his control slipped, and he heard a shout: "There he is!" Then, even as he gasped for breath, he brought the Shadow up again and tobogganed through the tunnel opening, slipping a dozen feet from the girl before he had to stop for fear of hitting another tree. He had to take a breath, and his breathing was caught in his chest, just above where her heel had hit him.

A dozen forms snaked through the forest toward him. He finally gasped oxygen in, and his eyes cleared enough so that he could slip even farther among the trees. He saw the girl, on her knees, one hand to her throat. A boy that Asher had not seen before was holding his trickler out to her. Behind her, a Ghiuliduc was pulling another tank out of her backpack.

Asher heard a great crashing. A Roller tumbled out of the tunnel nearest him and roared down upon him. He raised his Shield. The alien crashed its full weight upon it and bounced right over his Shadowed body. It careened full into the trunk of one of the trees. Spine-studded tentacles shot down and wrapped around him. Asher heard a low gasp of agony; the Roller quivered all over itself, and Asher could see by its darker brown that it was not the one from the clearing. It seemed unable to tear itself off the tree's spines, and they seemed unable to lift anything so heavy. Asher saw then that none of the tentacles was long enough to reach the ground. That's why he hadn't been impaled long since. If they had, they would have wiped out animal life here long ago, Asher thought.

Asher tobogganed deeper into the forest, and this time he kept going. He clutched the extra trickler to his chest, and after a moment, realized that it was still turned on, sending oxygen out uselessly into the purple-tinged air. He thumbed it off and sped on, again using a gigantic portion of himself in maintaining the sled, avoiding the trees, watching for danger. He couldn't keep it up for even ten minutes.

He found himself gasping among the trees, no one in sight, hearing nothing around him through the sound of his own breath. Now he was really lost, but he had extra air. How, how, how had the first Roller been able to point him out? At the time Asher had felt for a psychic probing from the alien, as he had felt from the Digger. But nothing had been there, and Asher had no sense that the round alien knew anything about the Power.

He lay there for a few moments, gathering strength. He could not go on for long like this, tremendous bursts of energy with too-short rests in between, each burst shorter and weaker than the one before. And he had no idea how long the tricklers would last—how much oxygen remained in his own, how much in the girl's.

For the first time, he confronted his immediate future, and found nothing there. The warriors were out to kill him, so he could not join them. Yet without the touch of civilization, he could not survive on a world that demanded tank after tank of oxygen. On his own, he would suffocate inevitably. And that left only a few grim choices.

He had to join the warriors somehow, either by their accepting him, or by him overcoming and ruling them.

Or he had to find another way, native to the planet. Perhaps there was a plant that sprouted oxygen. All plants release it; maybe there was one that could support him by his nearness to it, by placing his mouth over an opening and breathing . . . Or perhaps there was intelligent life beyond the warriors, aliens hidden deep in their jungles who would succor him, protect him from the outworlders, find a way for him to breathe.

Idle fantasy. Garbage of the mind. Hopes replacing reality. Asher brought himself to the cold realization that there was only one choice, in the end. There would be no oxygen superplants and no native aliens. How could he find them if there were? There was only one way.

To use the warriors. To follow them home and sneak in. To capture one and force him or her or it to help him. To talk them into accepting him.

Acceptance. That was the best way. Then he would no longer be struggling against something or someone. Then he wouldn't have to sneak around in their settlement, wherever it was, or somehow dominate them, which he doubted he could do for long. He had to sleep sometime. The twenty warriors had come close to killing him already; what could a town full of them do?

But acceptance would be difficult, at best—perhaps impossible. As far as he knew, the warriors of this planet intended to hound him until they had either killed him, or the planet did it for them. Other than a vague understanding that this was a training planet of some kind, he had no grounds to suppose that they would ever befriend him.

Lying there, blood seeping from his wounds, muscles

and mind aching in ways that he had never known they could, Asher Tye brought his mind to its clearest focus and faced squarely the only two choices that he had control over, that would follow from his own actions and not from some hoped-for fantasy. He put them into perspective, weighed them, chose—and took a long step toward defeating the Flaw.

He could overcome the warriors.

Or he could die.

He chose to live.

# Chapter 11

As if to offer a counterargument, his trickler ran out.

One moment he was smoothly sucking in air; the next he felt the freshness leave it, and he was breathing only the planet's gases. Hastily he sat up and, pulling off the empty tank, he yanked the girl's tank away from its harness and snapped it onto his own. Life-giving oxygen began to flow again.

Holding the empty tank and the useless harness, he looked around him. He did not want to carry anything that he didn't have to, but he could not leave the two items for the pursuers to find. He had to keep them guessing.

He scratched at the leaf mold with his fingers, but it was only inches deep and revealed an interlocking network of roots that resisted his efforts to pull them up.

He looked up. The tentacles waved dreamily above him, only fifteen feet or so up.

Now there was a way to hide something! He grasped the harness in his right hand and, with an underhanded thrust, threw it upward into the trees. It rose smoothly into the air, and then . . .

There was a whipping sound. A dozen tentacles lashed

out and spun around the belts of the harness. Asher saw the leather pierced by a hundred spines.

It happened that two of the trees had been in reach. There followed a tug of war of such fury that Asher quailed away. The celerylike, needle-covered trees quivered and shook, their free tentacles waving wildly, and dislodged spines rained around Asher and onto the floor of the forest. Those that hit his skin just bounced off; they were not heavy enough to penetrate.

Asher staggered back nonetheless, away from the convulsions. The contest had been decided from the first, Asher saw. One of the trees had eight or nine tentacles embedded in the straps of the harness; the other had only a few. With a jerking wrench, the winning tree tore its opponent's tentacles out by their roots, brought them and the harness upward in another blinding whip, and thrust it all into the very center of the tentacular mass on the top of the tree, where Asher could not see. Meanwhile, the vanquished tree vibrated in apparent pain, spines falling like scales around it.

It had been a bad idea; if the warriors were close enough, they could not fail to have heard the noise of the two combatants. But Asher went through with it, and threw the empty tank at still another tree, this time taking care that only one could reach it. At the same time he cast his mind outward, seeking the enemy.

Tentacles lashed around the tank and it was hurled into the maw of the tree. Perhaps it would prove indigestible; Asher did not wait around to find out. His mind touched those of the assassins pursuing him.

They were not far away, but Asher guessed that they could not have heard the trees. Still, they were closer to him than his ten-minute flight would have allowed, so they were still on his heels, following him by some method that he could not divine. Certainly it was not psychic. Although certain of them quailed unconsciously at his mind touch, he could sense that none of them were truly adept at psionics, none a threat to his own use of the Power. Yet they were following him nonetheless, and even as he sensed them they quickened their pace, as if they did indeed hear the thrashing of the trees.

Asher had dropped Shadow when he had collapsed under the trees, but now he drew it about him again and moved quietly off in an oblique angle, not toward the warriors, but circling around them as they raced through the jungle. Instead of a toboggan, Asher strode on a sort of psychic snowshoe that moved from one foot to the other as each was about to touch the forest floor, preventing footprints in the soft mold. He knew that the process left psychic traces, but he judged that the pursuers were incapable of following them.

After a few minutes he was well to the side of the warrior party. Now he began to approach them, in deep Shadow.

A worry was growing in him, and he tried to file it into a conscious thought so that it would not distract. It was that the girl's tank would soon run out. He had no idea how long ago it had been that she had first put it on, but it had not felt much heavier than his own when he obtained it. He did not want to die gasping his life out on the floor of an alien forest. Only the warriors could save him from that.

Then, a few feet ahead, he saw one. It was a human he had not seen before, a man older than the blond who was the apparent leader. The man was short, stocky, and black, and was not looking toward him. He did not notice the slight disorientation of the air that Asher's presence in Shadow caused.

It was a question of focus. Asher had never been able to learn how to use the Skill to disable someone he couldn't see with his eyes. It was an ability that an Adept routinely possessed, that he would have learned eventually as an Initiate of the October Guild. It involved subtle probing of the victim's mind, for there were natural defenses to be gotten through, defenses that could ward off a sudden hammer-like mental blow but could be wrinkled aside by a skilled mind so that the inner consciousness was exposed. Asher could do it only if his target were within view, so that he could focus on the head and use the victim's mental aura to advantage. Some Adepts could fell entire groups with a massive mental hammer blow; Asher wished he had that Skill now.

Still, he would do what he could. He walked quietly forward, analyzing the man, moving aside his defenses, probing for his mind. It was relatively easy; this was not a complicated man, but one of determination and bravery nonetheless. He did not sense Asher coming, did not see him or feel him with his mind. He held his crossbow at ready, and kept walking in intense alertness, oblivious to the danger at his back. On his belt swung three oxygen tanks among the various weapons.

Asher was only a few feet away now, and his probe had broken through. Gently, as if handling a baby, Asher took the man's mind in his own and squeezed it, and blanked it out.

The man collapsed as if the life had been whisked out of him. But it hadn't been; he would be unconscious for an hour or two, and that was all.

Asher unsnapped the man's belt, drew it off, and wrapped it around himself, then hefted the tanks to make sure that they were full ones. They were.

One enemy was down.

The entire operation had been done in near-total silence, but suddenly Asher heard a heavy body moving his way. Alarmed, he scooted backward, away from the fallen man, and tucked himself into a narrow opening between two needle trees.

A Roller approached the fallen man and nuzzled around him. It was the lighter one. Asher realized that the one he had impaled on a tree might be entirely out of the action.

Then the Roller spoke. Asher nearly jumped out of his skin. He probed at the alien's mind; it was shut tight to him.

"Give up," the alien said. It rolled a few feet toward

him, showing Asher that the Shadow was not working somehow.

Asher looked around. His mind still had some of the calmness that had been settling on him during all of this alien day. There were no other warriors in sight. That meant little. Still . . .

"No," he said softly. "I will stay alive."

The alien moved a foot closer.

"You injured———," he said, sounding an unfamiliar and almost unpronounceable name. It had to be the darker Roller that had bounced off Asher into the tree.

"He wanted to kill me," Asher found himself saying. He began to back away.

"No, listen," the alien said, moving tentatively forward, then stopping as Asher reacted by hurrying backward. There was a note of desperation in the Roller's oddly cultured voice that made Asher pause.

"We know we cannot take you. Therefore, our orders now are to bring you in . . . alive." The alien's voice was rushed, as if he wanted to get it out before Asher faded away.

"I don't believe you."

"Believe him!" the blond boy said, as he strode into view and stood next to the Roller. He glanced down at the fallen man, and stiffened.

"Is he . . .?" he asked the Roller.

"No, just knocked out," the Roller said.

The blond boy wiped a hand over his face, as if to drive away his rage.

"If you had harmed him, I would kill you whatever the orders said," he snarled into the air. Asher noticed that he was not looking directly at him. He could not see into Shadow, as the Roller somehow seemed to.

Asher began to wend his mind into the blond's. He found strength there and . . . fear?

"Your crossbow bolts would have torn me apart," he said aloud. The blond boy's head spun toward him, but still could not find him.

"But they did not," the Roller said. "And by that, you proved that you are worthy to become a Warrior."

"A thief, you mean," Asher said. He was through the boy's defenses now. He wrapped his mind around the other's—and recoiled from the evil he felt there.

"We're tired of chasing you around the jungle," the blond boy said. "Our orders are to save your neck. We . . ." Then Asher took mental hold again and squeezed. Consciousness went out of the startled blue eyes, and the boy fell on his face on the forest floor.

The Roller moved back a little. By this time, Asher sensed several more of the warrior party nearby. But none were behind him, none had a clear shot at him.

One of the Ghiuliducs came into view, and Asher found its mind as open as a vast, deep lake. He plunged his mind in like a hot iron. The Ghiuliduc spun on its axis and fell.

Three, maybe four down . . .

"No more," the Roller cried.

A blond-haired teenage girl bounded out of the forest, past the Roller and the two fallen warriors, straight at Asher Tye, her face contorted with fury.

Asher conjured up the same animal that had attacked him earlier, and placed its image between himself and the girl.

The Roller moved backwards again, and the girl skidded to a frightened halt. She raised her crossbow and fired. The bolt hit Asher's shield and ricocheted upward to disappear among the trees. He had to push aside a number of unconscious defenses before he made it into her mind. She had fitted another bolt, while the phantom animal seemed to wave its tail toward her. Then, even as she raised the weapon to fire, Asher squeezed.

"Please . . ." the Roller said. Then it shouted. "Warriors, listen to me. I am now in command by our prior agreement. You will lay down your weapons now, where you stand. You will stand still and you will not move."

Asher touched some of the minds around him. He found another Ghiuliduc and ended its consciousness without its being in sight, and then was amazed that he had been able to do it. He found some human minds, and their owners were not coming nearer. The Roller's orders were being obeyed.

The jungle leaned over him. He obliterated the image of the beast.

Blood still seeped from his puncture wounds. He was still exhausted. But he knew that he could defeat most of the warriors eventually, with his mind. He could avoid the Rollers, too, he thought. He could win.

"Offworlder," the Roller was saying. "How can we convince you that you are safe with us now?"

Asher considered. The lucidity of his thoughts intrigued him.

If he conquered them all, there was endless trouble ahead—with oxygen, with the real possibility that some of them would die as their own tanks ran out. That would weigh on him for the rest of his life.

And if he believed . . . Then he would be a fool. There had to be some middle ground.

"Lay down your weapons," he finally said. "All of them. Come into this place and lay down all your weapons, all of you."

There was a horrified silence. "Do not ask them to do that," the Roller said, desperation there again.

Asher had found another Ghiuliduc. Revelling in his own strength, the ability to disable this class of aliens without having them in sight, he plunged his red hot mental poker in.

"No more!" the Roller thundered. Asher was taken aback. How had the alien known?

"All your weapons," Asher demanded. "Or I will take you all."

And then the miracle happened. He heard a few clanks in the jungle, and then, one by one, they filed into view, alien and human alike. The darker Roller came too, moving unsteadily. Asher counted them; they were all there. He sped his mind around the jungle. Nothing.

The humans looked unhappy, the aliens inscrutable.

"Take me to your leader," Asher said airily, and stepped out of Shadow.

# Interlude

Cor-Reed communed with the October One, remote and far away on her world at the fringes of the galaxy. But he did not do it as did the other October Ones, who poured out their power from their various worlds around that spiral disk of stars.

He communed instead by common tachyonic holography. His lifelike image appeared in the October One's chambers; hers, in his hotel room on the planet Leah, in a globular cluster of stars deep in the Draco Sector.

"We have traced down every Erased woman Apprentice in the appropriate age range." Cor-Reed cleared his throat. It had depressed him, seeing those failed ones. "There are three, on separate planets, who cannot be accounted for." The October One scowled.

Cor-Reed went on. "The pattern was the same in every case. Each lived a routine life after Erasure, until suddenly, at different times within a two-year span, each up and vanished. There had been nothing paranormal about them before that, as far as anyone can tell. But the aftertaste in each case troubles me, as if after the long delay, something retriggered the Skill. But I have probed the minds of all who knew them, and none know what happened, or where they have gone.

And there is no common denominator among the three, except that they had once failed the Guild; none knew, or had even met as far as I can tell, any of the others."

The image of the October One held steady before him. She was in profile, her yellow eye staring in his direction. He could not hear the snapping her hair, but from time to time he could see the tiny flickering.

"Three," she mused in a voice like a dying serpent, "are too many for random chance. Something is at work here, Cor-Reed. Name the three."

He did so; and he could see the static in the hair of the alien woman flare for a tiny moment, as if she correlated the names with every bit of knowledge that she had ever taken in, whether through mind or body or soul.

Finally, after a long, cold moment, she spoke:

"She on whom you will concentrate," the eerie voice came, "is the last of those three failed: Kerla Cwan."

Cor-Reed's wonder ignited for a sharp moment, and he would have asked: "Why her, and not the other two?" But it would have been an impudent question. For she had, he knew, some measure of clairvoyance, among her many talents. The name had set up a psychic resonance of some kind. And in any event, Cor-Reed had known Kerla Cwan, for a while, long ago.

Kerla had entered the October Guild at the same time he had; they were classmates, as it were. But she had been willful and headstrong, he subtle and obedient. When the Test had come, she had failed, and been brought to the psychic probe. But obviously the Erasure had failed after many years.

"I believe," Cor-Reed said carefully, picking every word, "that she hated herself. One cannot go forward if there is hatred for oneself. The beginning of wisdom is to know that there are better than you, and worse than you, and that such is true for all."

The October One said nothing, and Cor-Reed was satisfied. If he had uttered something moronic, she would have told him.

Identifying Kerla had opened up a new approach for them. If they found her, they might not need Asher Tye. If Kerla were resistant to the psyhic probe, they could analyze her instead, and then take steps to make certain that those who could not be erased would be neutralized in some other way.

By death, for example, thought the October One.

"Your plan, Cor-Reed," the October One said, her voice like gravel. Even from this tremendous distance, Cor-Reed could feel her strength rippling through the Power around him. Not for the first time, he wondered if there were any limit to her Skill.

"Already I have passed the aftertaste of her onto our Adepts," Cor-Reed reported to her. "As they are looking for Asher Tye, now too they are seeking Kerla Cwan. It is only a matter of time."

The October One's eye stared at him, unblinking, like a reptile's. Again Cor-Reed felt that thrill of fear that he had never entirely understood. She had never injured him, and yet he feared her as he feared nothing else. And there was love there, too, in a strange way. How could he fear and love the same individual at the same time?

"There are billions of planets, Cor-Reed," the October One reminded him gently, "and only a few thousand Adepts."

"I know," Cor-Reed said somberly. Was it another Test? If so, he was ready. "Therefore," he said, "I will pursue her in two ways. First, I will station Adepts at the major crossroad planets, the ones she has to pass through eventually when taking commercial starships. Second, I will take every incident from the past years in which our plans have been frustrated, and visit those planets myself, or send another Adept in. Some of those incidents may well have been Kerla's doing—at least the recent ones. We will find her mental aftertaste, trace a pattern of her movements, find out where she has been and where she is likely to be going next.

She has been on Caldott several times, for example. If she comes again, we will take her."

"She is the equal of some of our lesser Adepts," the October One growled. For an instant she had felt a surge of elated hope. What if there was no new Power moving in the Galaxy, but merely a rogue Adept? But if so, how to account for the remarkable increase in her Skill that the incidents seemed to suggest? No, all was confusion still.

"We will not move in on her, until I am there," Cor-Reed said. "And, of course, the same goes for Asher Tye.

"And finally," he said, like the trusted, ruthless adjutant that he was, "I will cause some Adepts to look into the whereabouts of further Apprentices who have been Erased. Because our candidate selection is so thorough, most make it through, and in all the history of our Guild, less than two hundred have failed, if I recall aright. I will seek to discover if others beyond these three have disappeared, and what became of them."

Cor-Reed paused, and then said, as a matter of form: "End of report."

And, just as abruptly, the eerie figure of the October One went two-dimensional and then faded from view. Cor-Reed could barely hear her last words, yet somehow felt them in his mind.

"You do well, Cor-Reed."

He felt a flash of sheer joy, something he had not felt for many years.

# Chapter 12

"Why didn't we see him?" the thirteen-year-old Clemmy wailed. "He's right here—he must have been in sight the whole time."

"Aye, he used some psychic trick," one of the other humans muttered.

Asher looked them over, standing in front of them, hands on his hips. He was feeling wildly lightheaded, powerful, shakily strong.

They dragged the fallen—three humans and three Ghiuliducs—into the tiny clearing. Besides them, Asher counted eight other humans, including Clemmy. Two Ghiuliducs were standing, their foot-high bodies spindly and still over their fallen friends, and Asher felt hate pour out from them. There were the two Rollers, and the last two were . . .

There was alien life in bewildering diversity all over the galaxy, on millions of planets, oxygen and chlorine and methane and ammonia and water breathers, and breathers of gases even more exotic, and even a few who liked vacuum itself. They all sped across holographic images on entertainment programs that every house received on demand, and most citizens of the galaxy figured that nothing could surprise them anymore. But when his eyes fell upon those last two warriors, Asher felt surprise rise in him as if his stomach had been kicked in—surprise that gave way to horror and then to fear. For these were the most awful nightmares come to life, lumpy pus-yellow bodies covered with splotches of green ooze, raw redness here and there, ghastly snaky motions of muscles under it all, five feet high and three hundred pounds on massive, elephant legs—three of them—and . . .

Asher tore his eyes away as his concentration wavered and the Shield faltered. The group was looking at him with varying expressions, some curiously, the aliens inscrutable except for the tangible hatred of the Ghiuliducs. Clemmy did not look happy, her face pinched behind the trickler.

"What are those?" Asher croaked, gesturing at the horrors.

The Roller said: "I beg your pardon?"

It was the height of rudeness, Asher knew. Among the chaos of races around the galaxy, it was offensive to call attention to the physical differences of anyone, but he couldn't help it now.

"I, er," he said, gathering himself, "I am not, uh, familiar with . . . those. What is their race?"

One of the lumps spoke then, in a voice that reminded Asher of the hiss of steam.

"Are we the first Therds, then, that you have ever met?" Through the hiss, the tone was formally polite. Asher forced his eyes to look at them. If there were eyes or ears or a mouth or arms, he couldn't detect them.

"Yes," he managed to say.

"Ah, we are not common in this sector," the hiss said. Meanwhile, Asher probed at them with his mind and encountered . . .

Nothing.

Nothing? But there was always something—resistance, confusion, shields, openness, but never nothing. Even animals registered something to one October-trained.

He drew his mind back, as if it had touched something dirty, even though it had seemed to touch nothing at all. He didn't understand this.

"You have tried to probe us," the hiss said calmly. "This cannot be done by a human Adept. The minds of our races are unlike one another."

Unlike one another! But there were common rules among sentient beings. Asher had never heard of any instance wherein October training would find . . . nothing. Except, perhaps, for the Digger.

Suddenly his own mind leaped to an idea. What if such as these were sent against October? They would be immune to psychic detection. Perhaps the galaxy was not completely at October's mercy after all!

The warriors had set to work reviving the fallen ones with medicines from their kits, and it didn't take long for the three Ghiuliducs to rise shakily to their feet, and the three wobbly humans to crawl upright and lean against each other and the Roller, shaking their heads and drawing deep upon the oxygen in their tricklers. Asher found the eyes of the blond leader focusing on him, and he didn't like the expression in them.

"Is everyone all right?" the leader muttered to the Roller.

"Egos bruised, nothing more," the Roller said impasssively.

The leader grunted. "My name," he said to Asher, "is Teel. Follow us." Turning on his heel, he led the warriors off into the forest, following no particular path that Asher could see. Asher waited until the last one, Clemmy, had passed, and then fell into step behind her.

It was hard going, and Asher felt once more the wounds on his side, the soreness everywhere on his body, the mental and physical fatigue that was the result of the incredible effort that he had had to expend from almost the moment he landed on the Warrior Planet. He tried to hate these warriors who had tried to kill him, but it was hard—they had merely been following orders. He couldn't even hate the Digger, who had gotten him into all this. Treacherous, yes, the alien had been, but he had taught Asher many things, and one of them was how not to hate, and that lesson was a direct attack on his flaw.

Now what? He was marching these warriors back as virtual prisoners. That would go over big with the leaders of the warriors, whoever they were. Maybe they'd respect him for what he had done. Maybe, like the blond boy and the Ghiuliducs, they would hate and fear him for it.

A sense of massive power grew in Asher. And if they feared and hated him? He would defeat them all. By all accounts he should be torn and beaten, dead on the floor of this forest, and he was alive and well. He was battered, true, bruised, with wounds festering in his side. Yet he felt an odd exhilaration. He felt lightheaded and alive, and the pain and wounds were almost interesting, instead of crippling. They were in the remote "out there," only incidentally linked to him, and he felt great, better and better every staggering step he took.

In front of Clemmy he caught glimpses of the two Therds. Good, he thought. He hardly ever saw the rest of the band because of the twists and turns of the tunnels they crouched through. But he didn't much care if the others tried to sneak around on him; he would catch their minds with his if they tried. The Therds were the only ones who might have succeeded. But even then, there was his Shield.

"Hey, kid, I'm sorry I took your tank," he found himself babbling to Clemmy's back. "I mean, don't hold it against me, all right? You were trying to kill me. Kill me. I had to defend myself, didn't I? And it worked out, didn't it? You're alive, and I'm alive—boy, am I alive—and you feel great and I feel great." Asher felt this odd compulsion to talk, on and on. Thoughts were tumbling over themselves in his head. He had to let them out. For a moment, he felt a shot of alarm. Was he drugged or something? How? But his pain lessened, and he reveled in it. "And once we get to wherever we're going—where are we going, anyway?—then I'll show you a few tricks and make up for it, and maybe you can show me how you kicked me. That was something—I didn't even see it coming, and the Shield was down. Why did I leave it down? I don't know; stupid of me. I'd like to learn to kick like that. That's one thing the Octobers never really got into, is physical defense. They always figured that the mind was enough, and I guess it was today since I beat all of you, but you almost got me that time . . . ha, ha, ha, ha, ha. Almost got me!"

Clemmy cast a puzzled glance behind her and Asher felt his mouth running on, playing with words, having great fun, making him laugh. That little pinprick of alarm was buried under hilarity. He stopped and doubled over, laughing into his trickler. Clemmy stopped too and came back to him.

"What's wrong with you?" she asked sharply.

"Ha, ha, ha, ha, ha, ha, ha," said Asher. Everything was terrific. Everything was great. "Everything is terrific. Everything is great!" he shouted.

"You're crazy," Clemmy said, her pinched little face calculating behind her trickler.

Asher staggered again and almost fell. "I'm not afraid anymore. Don't you get it, girl?" he said, laughing uncontrollably. "I'm not afraid and I'm not angry and I'm not sad and I'm not bad, I'm not sad or bad or mad, or even glad, or unclad." The latter idea struck him as the most hilarious thing he had ever heard. He clutched his belly and roared.

Clemmy regarded him with analytical concern.

"I'll show you that kick now," she said softly.

"Sure! The kick. The hick, the kick, oh boy, let's do it," Asher yelled, dancing from one foot to another.

"It has to be as it was," Clemmy said.

"As it was!" Asher shouted.

"Drop your Shield," Clemmy whispered.

"As it was!" Asher screamed. And dropped his Shield.

Again he didn't see the kick coming. To the side of the head, this time.

# Chapter 13

Asher came to slowly. His head hurt mightily. When he moved his body a thousand pains lanced through him—from the spine wounds, from the cuts and scrapes he had gathered in the forest, and from the unaccustomed muscular effort he had undergone.

His eyes opened and he looked up at the ceiling of a room. It was grey. He looked around and realized that he was on a cot, and that the room was small, with no windows, one closed grey door, speckled grey walls that looked like glassy granite, and no other furniture except a tiny table holding what looked like a large glass of water.

It took him a long time to sit up. The first time he tried it, so many pains shot through him that he cried out. He rolled over onto his unwounded side and then onto his stomach, and slid his legs off the side of the cot so that he was kneeling on the floor. The uprightness caused his head to spin dizzily; he clung to the cot as if it were a rowboat in a violent storm.

"All things end, all things end," Asher thought, over and over, and they did. The dizziness subsided, leaving behind a sharp ache in his head, thoughts muddled and confused. Then, with a massive effort, he stood up and swayed uncertainly, afraid the dizziness would come back, afraid to turn his head. When he turned toward the door, he moved his whole body like a turntable, not twisting his neck at all.

It was locked. He pushed weakly at it, pulled on its handle, placed his palm against what was obviously a palmprint lock. Nothing.

He sat down heavily on the cot, feeling haggard. All at once thirst assailed him. He seized the glass of water and drank it down. Then he realized that there could be more than water in the glass, and fear ran through him. Poison? Did the warriors bring him here just to trick him to his death?

But pain was passing from his legs and arms, and his side was beginning to feel far away. As the moment passed, he felt traces of the dizziness fall, and decided that if there had been anything in the water, it was a painkiller of some kind, not poison at all. Still, he shouldn't have drunk it without at least smelling it. His judgment was shaken by that blow to the head.

By a thirteen-year-old girl! He still could not believe the incredible speed at which she had moved. What had been wrong with him? But even if that babbling jag hadn't come over him, he didn't think that, even in the best possible shape, he could have stopped that blow with anything other than the Shield.

And then he realized that there wasn't much to his fear. He scarcely cared anymore, and it was not resignation that he felt, but acceptance. He could accept and survive anything that came to him. He would work to affect it, to change it, and whatever happened then, he would not agonize over it. He would always do his best, and that doing was what was important, not the outcome. Good results often come when you do your best, Asher thought, but not always, and that doesn't mean that you should stop doing your best, because then good results would never come.

And so Asher Tye took one more giant step in conquering the Flaw.

* * *

The door slammed open, startling him out of his reverie. Asher looked, and shuddered with the memory of the evil mind he once had touched as he now saw the blond boy Teel standing there, two Ghiuliducs barely visible, low on the floor behind him. But Asher noted that the Ghiuliducs carried needlers scaled to their size—little guns that would poke holes in him just as effectively as their bigger cousins.

"Come," Teel ordered harshly.

Asher sent a thought probing toward the boy. Nothing happened. His mind touched nothing—it did not even seem to reach out.

Asher tried to bring himself into focus. Nothing came. His mind was refusing to work. His Skill could not be brought into plan. Power was not accessible to him.

Something was interfering with his Skill.

He felt, all at once, as helpless as a baby. Now he was truly at their mercy; he had no special resources to fall back on.

He stood up and swayed, then gained control. Teel watched him cynically, a bitter smile on his thick lips, which sat like rubber worms on a face that Asher could fully see, now that they were not wearing tricklers. It was a handsome face, but not a face of character. He stood aside as Asher came through the door, and pointed him down the corridor, falling in step with the Ghiuliducs trailing close behind.

"Where?" Asher asked wearily as they came to a place where the corridor came to a tee, one arm heading off to the right and one to the left.

"Right," Teel said.

Now Asher's befuddled consciousness was beginning to see how strange were the corridors through which they walked. They were almost round, except for the flatness of the floor, and glazed like glass. Convex doors, set in the sides, followed the shape of the corridor. The color was almost black, lighted by light strips running just over a tall man's height. It was as if a blowtorch had blasted through a tunnel of sand and left tubes of black glass.

At length they came to a wider door, one that was open. It was almost as wide as the corridor itself. Teel motioned Asher in, and he walked through. He had expected nothing, moving in a calmness born of recent decisions and experience, and abetted by whatever drug was in him. So he reacted to the scene before him not at all.

It was a large room, apparently blasted out of rock just like the corridor itself. There was color here— a long desk of light maroon, soft chairs in front of it, space for maybe thirty people. A Roller was there. And behind the desk was a woman.

A woman such as Asher had never seen.

Perhaps Asher had been cloistered too long on the October World. But this woman was, if anything, as tall and powerfully built as any man he had ever seen. She was woman-shaped in every way, and yet her body, even sitting down, bespoke strength far beyond Asher's own. And now she rose, as smoothly as a sword coming from a sheath, and stood before Asher clothed in a scarlet tunic belted black at the waist. Her hair was a mixture of blond and brown, strands apparently alternating colors with one another, and it was cut short, so that it distracted nothing from her face. Asher could see no weapons, but wondered if this woman would need any, ever.

"Welcome," the low voice came. "Welcome, Asher Tye, to the Warrior Planet, to learn the ways of the Guild of Thieves. My name is Nin Tova. Sit down."

Nin, Asher thought. Nin . . .

Numbly, he stepped to a chair in front of the desk and sat down. She slid softly back into her chair, and regarded him with a half smile on a face that was faintly lined, and competent, and deeply intelligent.

"You did very well," she said. "You are the first recruit ever to overcome a party of warrior trainees, even if it did not last."

Asher could find nothing to say. Somewhere behind him sat Teel and the Ghiuliducs, and Asher did not need to be psychic to feel the hatred emanating from them.

Teel's voice came then. "He cheated," he said harshly. "How can we fight the tricks of a wizard?"

"The girl Clemmy found a way," the woman spoke softly. "A warrior always looks for a way. Defeat is never permitted."

"With all respect, Nin Tova," Teel's voice came back, "I would learn how. If we would release his mind, you would show us ways of defeating him."

For a moment, Asher saw anger in the woman's eyes. Nin Tova—an interesting name.

"Perhaps I will," the woman said. "But later. First I will train him. His body is a disgrace to his mind."

Sudden rage flooded Asher. His fear might be gone, but his self-respect was still there, in force. A disgrace to his mind!

"I will train him," Teel said evilly.

"Silence!" said the Nin. She said it softly, and yet it seemed to Asher as if an arrow had pierced the air.

Finally, Asher found his voice as the flaw raged in him, unabated.

"You were going to kill me, all of you. And now you probably will in some other way. Why am I here? What does the Digger want with me? Why that big chase to kill if he wanted me dead? Why . . .?"

"Stop," the Nin said, no more loudly, but the arrow sharpness was gone.

"I will answer your questions to a point," she said then. "But part of what you will do here is to discover answers for yourself.

"As to what the Digger wants, that is not a factor here. It is what I want, what the Transfer Guild wants.

"As to the chase, I will say only that it humbles the new recruit, few of whom have faced death in any form before."

Hysteria rose up in Asher's gorge; he remembered

the animal in the October Test, and he remembered Kerla Cwan. He laughed, and even he heard the wild edge in it.

"You would have killed me," his voice came, shaking. No answer.

"You would have killed me!" Asher said, shouting now. The Nin, though, said nothing, regarding him with a quizzical little smile on her square face.

When she finally spoke, it was in that same soft cadence that, despite himself, caused Asher's tumult of uncontrolled emotion to seep away, like water out of a paper bag.

"What you should know of these things," the Nin said, "you will discover in good time. Were life so valuable, then people would not have killed one another with such ease and with so little regret over the centuries of humankind. And yet, if life were not so valuable, then you and I would not be here."

The door behind them opened again. Asher turned his head and saw Clemmy walk in, carrying a trickler in one hand. She settled on one of the rear chairs, not saying a word, her small body dwarfed by the room. Her narrow face, not under a trickler now and fully revealed, was more relaxed, but there was no real expression to be seen on her; she was like a monk in a world of silence.

"Digger has sponsored you to us," the Nin's voice came, and Asher turned back toward her, "in the hope that you might teach us while we are teaching you, as Kerla Cwan could not. If you could teach us to block the probes of the October warriors and nothing more, we would be well served. If you could teach us to see through their illusions and pierce the fabric of their magic, all the better. And if you could teach us active magic, as you used on the syndicate fat man on the *Pride*, we would push October right back to its barren world on the Outer Arm. And we will teach you . . ."

"Pardon me, your Ninness," Asher interrupted with an edge on his voice, and heard a gasp from those behind him. But Asher was tired of being led and used and ordered around. From Cor-Reed on the October World, to Kerla on the *Pride*, to the attacks from the warriors, Asher had not controlled the direction of his own life. Perhaps it was time that he began. "You are the Guild of Thieves. I am not a thief, and do not want to be. Taking something that someone else owns is wrong to me. I don't want the galactic police taking a mind probe and wiping a part of me out. Guild of Thieves! The carrying of a name like that would make me ashamed."

Nin Tova seemed paler than before. Those behind Asher were dead still, as if not daring to interfere with the Nin's rage. The Nin leaned intensely forward, palms on the desk, and looked deeply into Asher's eyes. She spoke, her voice grim:

"Do not speak of things about which you know nothing, O stupid one," she said, still speaking quietly, but with controlled anger. "That name was not ours, but was placed on us by outsiders. And even a name like that can mean many things, as you might have guessed from the one incident you know, when we stole from a criminal group far larger than we."

She called to the room's computer one word: "Starscene." The wall behind her dissolved into a panorama of the galaxy, spiral whorl clearly visible, although from an oblique angle. Twisted spiral arms of billions of stars turned like a wheel, so slowly that it always seemed to the limited sight of man to be eternal and still.

The Nin did not look at it; instead, she continued to fix Asher with her gaze.

"Billions of planets, thousands of races, governments growing heavy and oppressing people, syndicates robbing on a scale that we do not even imagine. Until we arose, Asher Tye, there was nothing to balance the corrupt and crooked wheel—government linked with crime syndicates which paid off and supported businesses and governments alike. The October people might have done it, but they move as passive errand-runners for the highest bidder, hiding their Skill, never acting for any abstract good. Or worse . . . they move for the mental control of the galaxy. And meanwhile, the common people struggle, and of the trillion trillions and more, very few ever rise above the morass of crime and taxes that hold them down. Those few are almost all the pirates of business—the few among the armies of honorable businesspeople who take over honest companies and squeeze them dry.

"There must be a balance!" the Nin cried suddenly, banging her fist on the tabletop with a blow so hard that Asher saw the desk jump. "I have formed the Guild of Thieves to provide that balance, Asher Tye. We are only a few yet, but we steal from the corrupt and most of the money returns to the honest."

"Like Robin Hood," Asher muttered.

"What's that?" the Nin asked sharply.

"A thief from the Old Planet, who robbed from the rich and gave to the poor, as legend tells it," Asher mused. "I have seen the old stories . . ."

"Even so. Even so," the Nin said. "We keep some of the money, I admit, for it takes many resources to maintain this world in secrecy, and to send our forces where they are most needed throughout the galaxy. But we harass the syndicates and bedevil politicians who are corrupt, and we cause headlines in the news media, and people begin to think about what we have done and why we have done it. We are heroes to some, Asher Tye." She said this last with a loud voice now, as if speaking to a large crowd. Suddenly she seemed to catch herself, and settled back in her chair. "And yet, we are but a pinprick on an amoeba the size of a world. We are too few, and barely felt as yet. It is the structure we are building that is our main task, and in the course of the universe, I, or even Clemmy there, may well not live long enough to see that pinprick become a comet, even if we live to the ripest old age."

"But the name!" Asher cried, recapturing some of her intensity. "How can you call yourself thieves and

expect anyone to listen? They will fear you, not honor
you; they will fear that you will steal from them, as well
as from the bad ones."

"Aye, there is that," the Nin said thoughtfully, her
brow contracted. "It was not the name I set out to
use—that was the Transfer Guild—but a nickname that
sensationalist newscasters invented and that finally captured even us. But maybe it is not so bad; it has an
exciting sound to it if nothing else, and stirs the imagi-
nation of some, especially when they see what we're
about . . . you can make any word mean anything,
Asher Tye, if you repeat the new meaning often enough
and loud enough."

"But," Asher pursued, surprised at how things were
beginning to fit together, "under the old meaning you
will attract rogues and cheats, people who do not share
your view, but want only your skills so that they can
gain loot. Such a one as Kerla." Now here was sweet
revenge for the heavy woman who had handled him so
savagely—to speak of her to her Master! "Such a one as
Kerla, who never seemed to me to be anything but a
thief, and a mean one at that."

"I will judge that," the Nin said sharply. "Kerla Cwan
has been valuable to me. She and the Digger tracked
me down, moving like fugitives through the darkest
parts of the human universe. She lacks certain qualities,
but she is after all like you, Asher Tye. The October
thought they had Erased her. Until you, she was the
only such among us."

"Then have her teach your warriors, or have the
Digger teach them as he taught me," Asher said. "I do
not want to teach killers such as Teel skills that could
make his killing sneakier and safer."

"Sit!" the Nin commanded, sending the sound over
his head. Asher had heard the angry stirring behind
him, but did not look around. He waited until there
was no sound back there, scarcely any breathing. He
wondered then if anyone had ever talked to the Nin in
as sharp a way as he was now.

"Nay," the Nin said then, "she cannot teach, for her students hate her and she hates them. And as for the Digger, he claims that he can teach only those already inducted into the Power— that he has not the authority to induct the unskilled himself—though what he means by that I have never been able to fully probe. Do you know, Asher Tye?"

The sudden question caught Asher flat-footed, but he recovered swiftly.

"He taught me, but then, I was already trained," he said, and then a thought came to him. "Perhaps there is a Master involved here—the Digger's own teacher—for there is always a teacher. Were the Master to order that his students not teach the unprepared, one like the Digger would not do it. Maybe there is something about the Digger that would damage a new student; perhaps the Digger cannot control his Power at certain critical times. I don't know. It could be that, or something else. The Digger was always controlled when I saw him."

"It bears considering," the Nin said thoughtfully. "And now, Asher Tye . . ." she began.

Asher heard a sound behind him. Glancing around, he saw that Clemmy was holding the trickler to her face and breathing deeply. Puzzled, he turned back. Was there something wrong with the air here? If so, why then were the rest of them not supplied with tricklers, too?

He caught the Nin's gaze, and the powerful woman had a grim smile on her face. "Now," she said softly, "do you understand?"

Understand what? Asher wondered, confused. Why would Clemmy need a trickler, and the others not, including himself, unless. . . .

Unless! Unless she needed an air that was somehow different from what the rest of them breathed . . .

That was it!

"What is it?" Asher croaked. "A bit of nitrous oxide, perhaps—laughing gas? Or some complicated drug evaporated into the air of the planet from which she comes?" He remembered the giddiness, the hysteria, the dizziness. No wonder—it had been Clemmy's air that he was using then, stolen from her back in Asher's first theft on the planet of thieves!

"Just oxygen," the Nin said, smiling. "Only a little oxygen."

Only a little—a little more than he was used to! Clemmy must come from a planet with more oxygen in the air than his own, or most humans'. No wonder he had felt giddy—his brain had been saturated with oxygen, the calories burning too rapidly. He would have passed out in a few minutes more, if Clemmy's foot had not kicked the sense from him.

That explained, too, the narrowness of her chest. It was not just that she was slightly built; it was also that she came from a planet on which the lungs did not have to be as large as those of most people, for they took in oxygen easily and needed less surface to do it. Here, in a normal human atmosphere, she was probably working her way up to breathing unaided, as a long-distance runner would—practicing, gasping, expanding the lungs, causing their surface to grow. Only occasionally now would she need to use her trickler while inside, Asher could see. It was his bad luck that he had picked the one human whose trickler air could poison him.

"As I was saying," the Nin said, "you can stay with us and teach and learn. We always offer choice to our people, and you are one of us now, if only for a short time. Your other choice is to die—we could not risk the October One learning of our planet from the description that you could now give, not to mention the galactic police. We have many principles, but we will kill, Asher Tye. Choose."

To die, or to learn to steal—when held up to the light, it was not a difficult choice. He had stolen twice already: once from the fat man, and once from Clemmy.

Each theft could be a choice, too; but if he were dead, there would be no choosing, ever again.

But yet at the mercy of others . . . it rankled Asher. He wanted to be free, and alone, to make his way back to his family. Could he find some way to flee the Warrior Planet? He doubted it, but it deserved a place in the back of his mind.

The Nin could see the resignation in Asher's face. She beckoned to Teel.

"He is assigned to you, Teel. This is a test for you. You must learn to master others without crushing them. Go!"

The others rose, but Asher, transfixed in his chair, exploded: "No! I have felt him inside. Teel is a killer; must you be psychic to see it in him? Please keep him away from me!"

It was a mistake; he had not yet learned the code of the warriors, who never argued with the Nin, and never begged for anything.

The Nin regarded Asher, the grim smile back on her lips.

"Welcome," she said, "to the Warrior Planet."

That night, Asher lay alone in his granite cell. He was tired and bitter and sore. And ready. He thought.

# Chapter 14

"Hit me," Teel commanded. It was the next day, and Asher was in a great underground hall, burned out of the soil and rock by whatever process had hollowed the tunnels. Around him were dozens of trainees, alien and human, in little groups of five to ten, scattered across the large floor that somehow had a little bounce to it, like not-quite-hard rubber.

Asher swung his right arm at Teel's contemptuous face, fist balled, arm traveling in a great looping arc. He guessed what was coming, and threw all his speed and strength into the blow.

It didn't do any good. Teel waited until Asher was sure his fist was going to connect on that sneering jaw, then his arm shot up and swatted Asher's fist away, and his leg swept Asher's feet out from under him. Asher landed heavily on his backside.

"Get up," Teel said. Asher's Skill still eluded him. He suspected that everything he was fed was drugged.

Every muscle sore, Asher clawed his way to his feet. He was wearing a white tunic in the same style as the Nin's, belted white at the waist, very short, not quite reaching his knees, white leggings underneath it. It was all he had on; even his feet were bare. But it was the

146

same with every human in the great hall. The differences were in the colors of the clothes themselves.

Teel wore a black tunic and green belt. His large muscles showed clearly as he moved, with the grace and speed of a dancer. But dancing he was not.

They had been there for hours. In their group there were five, all human. Clemmy wore a beige tunic with a green belt. There was another white-tuniced and belted trainee—the blond girl from the forest whose name was Tawna. The black man he had felled in the forest was there, shorter than Clemmy, round of face and body—almost fat, except that he moved like an acrobat, and when he hit the floor he bounced back up like a rubber ball. His name was Ran; his skin was very black indeed, and he smiled a lot and wore a beige tunic with a yellow belt. The two others were Dov and Rasha. The first was as tall as Teel but skinnier, with red hair and pink tunic and blue belt. Rasha had the face of a rat: long nose, narrow head, and was a little taller than Clemmy. He wore the same outfit as Ran, and it was well used, spotted here and there with brown.

Teel was the teacher here, and the subject was defense and attack. The training was unrelenting. They had started the morning by running around the hall fifteen times, with Asher staggering far behind the others. Then stretching, then basic movements, then this free-form series of commands by Teel, and responses by his students.

Somehow Teel seemed more professional here, less beset by hatred. Perhaps it was the one place he felt that he was valuable, teaching others the things he had learned himself.

"Kick me," he said to Asher. And oddly, Asher didn't feel singled out. Teel would not damage him here, in front of a hundred trainees.

He kicked at Teel with a vengeance, knee straight as a ramrod, aiming at Teel's crotch. Again the blond boy seemed to do nothing about it, and again, at the last possible minute, he deflected it. He simply took a half step back, so that Asher's foot shot harmlessly upward, and with a smooth movement, cupped both hands under Asher's heel and heaved. Asher's other foot flew out from under him, and again he landed on his backside with bone-jarring impact.

From the floor, Asher saw Clemmy and Ran throw themselves at Teel; evidently there had been some kind of signal he had not seen, and Teel was now fair game for his students. There was a confused blur of black and beige, arms and legs banging against each other. Teel blocked Clemmy's kicking attack by bringing one leg up so that Clemmy's foot hit his knee instead of his stomach. Ran's fist almost caught Teel on the side of the head—they all wore headguards—but was snapped away by Teel's block at the last second. In amazing coordination, the blond boy snapped his upright leg out and caught Clemmy in the pit of the stomach, and his blocking hand chopped down on Ran's exposed shoulder, a blow deliberately stopped the instant before the collarbone would have broken.

The encounter put Teel facing away from Asher, and he launched himself off the floor onto Teel's back, wrapping his right arm around his throat. At least he tried to; Teel had whipped one fist up to touch his own chin, and Asher's arm crossed his. With a convulsive judo movement, Teel bent and flipped Asher over his back, and Asher landed with a hard whack. Tawna and Rasha had not moved, but Dov had chosen his moment well, and had swept one leg against Teel's knee as Asher was in the air. Teel landed on his backside. Dov was in the air to stomp him, but Teel let his shoulders fall on the floor. One leg shot up and caught Dov in the side with rib-cracking force.

"Very good!" a voice called. Asher, half dazed, levered his head up and saw the Nin moving toward them. Clemmy, who had caught hold of her trickler and was gasping into it, dropped it as if it were on fire and sprang up, feet together, straight as a ramrod. Asher saw that the others had done the same, and he struggled up, body screaming in protest.

"How is he doing?" the Nin asked Teel, coming to a stop a dozen feet away. She was wearing the same scarlet tunic, and again Asher was struck by the power she radiated, and the determined iron of her face.

"He's as soft as a marshmallow," Teel said, and Asher felt anger. "But he has a will," Teel said grudgingly. "He does not give up; I have not broken him yet."

"And never will!" Asher shouted.

"Silence!" the Nin said sharply. "On this floor you speak only when spoken to by me or your teacher. I warn you this once; if you do it again; you will be punished."

Words trembled on Asher's lips, but he stayed silent. There was no point in inviting pain; he had enough already.

"Line up!" Nin Tova shouted, and around the hall, the swirling combat groups stilled and hustled into line. Asher saw that each race was grouped with others of its own kind, and he guessed why. Even the most uncoordinated human could catch and stomp the foot-high, spindly Ghiuliducs. In their turn, humans wouldn't have a chance against the massive Rollers or Therds, at least in an open area with nothing to hide behind. Each race had its own strengths.

"We will give our new recruit a demonstration!" the Nin called, and many of Asher's guesses turned out to be wrong.

First a Ghiuliduc faced a human—the other in a white tunic, Tawna. It was like an elephant against a dog. Tawna leaped upward, and the Ghiuliduc seemed doomed.

But the little spindly creature skittered away at the last moment, and as Tawna's feet landed, it leaped in, grabbed one of her toes, and yanked upward. Tawna cried out and tried to kick the little being, but it danced away. Tawna crouched down and dove at the alien, trying to wrap her arms around it. But she was poked in one eye, her nose was pinched, she was somehow tripped, and then the Ghiuliduc was on her back in the exact spot that she couldn't reach with any strength.

"If Ghiiip had a weapon, Tawna would die," the Nin commented.

Tawna fell on her back, but the Ghiuliduc slipped out just before impact, and as it did so, it grabbed Tawna's hair and yanked, so that instead of having her chin tucked against her chest in a proper fall, her head bounced off the floor instead. Asher could see that without the headguard, she would have been stunned, at least.

"Enough," the Nin said. Tawna stood up, red with embarrassment. Asher thought that she had nothing to be ashamed of.

The Nin then selected a Roller, not one that Asher had met before, and a Therd. They seemed to be of near equal bulk, and were unclothed in any way. But Asher was not prepared for what he saw.

The Roller thundered down upon the three-legged alien like an express train against a mountain. The Therd's legs seemed to sink into itself, and it sat like a big ugly blob on the floor. The Roller hit with an impact that would have killed a human being, and simply bounced off. The Roller came again, and bounced off again. Then the Roller rolled up and stopped. One of its tentacular arms appeared and poked at one of the raw red patches on the Therd's ghastly body. A cry came from the Roller—something had bit or stung or pinched him. Asher was later to find that the red patches were the Therd's most vulnerable areas, where its mouths were.

Then the Therd rose up and kicked the Roller with two of its gigantic feet. The Roller rose up in the air like a huge basketball and landed with a thud fifteen feet away. And then it thundered in again, so fast that the Therd could not sink down in time. This time, the Therd was thrown off its feet and knocked on its side. The Roller bounced up into the air and came down

upon the ugly alien, but even as it landed, a great cloud
of stinging spray came from somewhere on the Therd's
body and engulfed it. The Roller choked and gagged
and rolled away to the farthest part of the hall. The
Therd stood groggily up, and the odor hit Asher like a
moving wall. He staggered back and gagged, and he
was not alone.

"Enough!" the Nin ordered. She was right in the
middle of the cloud, and it did not seem to affect her.
Quickly, the ventilators drew the smell away.

The last demonstration involved the Nin herself. She
faced a Roller, and this time it was the one Asher had
spoken to in the woods, the one with the cultured
voice. Asher paled. What chance would any human
being have, even the Nin, against this gigantic tan ball?

Like a huge bowling ball the Roller rushed in, apparently bent upon crushing the Nin. She stood there,
magnificent body ready, hands up in front, until the
Roller was on top of her. And just as it was about to hit,
with the force of a safe dropped from a fifty-story building, she stepped gently aside. As it roared past, she hit
it in the exact center of that large yellow spot with a
closed fist, with an impact that everyone in the hall
could hear—like a sledge hammer hitting a steer. The
Roller rolled on, but there was no acceleration anymore. It rolled with decreasing speed until it hit the far
wall, then bounced back leadenly and stopped. It did
not move.

The darker Roller broke out of line and rushed
toward the other.

"Stop!" the Nin commanded, her face dark with anger. "He is out cold, but not hurt. Get back in line!"

The Roller hesitated too long. With one fluid step,
the Nin leaned out and smashed her heel against the
Roller, this time catching the edge of the yellow spot.
The alien screamed. It rolled back, and seemed to
cower.

"Get back in line!" the Nin commanded. The Roller,
whimpering, did.

"Discipline!" the Nin's voice thundered. "You must command yourself. When I speak, you will not think—you will act. When a teacher speaks, you will not think—you will act. Someday you will face danger, out there among the stars. Then, if you think, you will die. You will have to act without thought, with instinct trained into you here, thought so compressed and absorbed that you can meet any variation with the right move, the right defense, the right attack. You can and will do it. You obey me not because I can kill you, but because what I give you can make you stronger and more powerful and better all around. And you may never use it; I hope you never do. But if you need it, it will be there.

"And if you misuse it . . ." her face darkened, anger seeming to enter the body like lava, heating it. "Like any real Teacher of any skill, if you take what I teach and twist it and betray it, I will hunt you down and destroy you.

"Strength!" she thundered, and Asher jumped. The voices of all assembled shook the room as they repeated it.

"Power!" her voice came, and was answered.

"Justice!" the last word came, and was shouted from seventy throats, human and alien, some of the latter with more than one.

Asher shouted it, too, a fraction behind the others. He shouted it, but he did not yet understand what it really meant.

# Chapter 15

That night Asher thought: "It wasn't so bad." When he woke up the next morning and swung his feet to the floor, the muscles of his thighs and calves screamed. He moved around that day with awkward sensitivity, grimacing as his underdeveloped and overused muscles complained bitterly. The morning after that, much of the immediate soreness had subsided, and it was a good thing, for the exercising began again.

Asher's soreness was an every-other-day thing, exactly in tune with the exercise schedule, subsiding as time went by. New muscles were constantly challenged, let go, and challenged again days later. Asher began to sense a certain rhythm to it, but he did not see it right away. He saw little he liked, at first.

For the first week he said almost nothing to his companions and they said almost nothing to him. A kind of perverse pride kept him functioning, going through the motions—pride, and the lack of any plan. He did not know what else to do. There was no way off-planet as far as he could see. And he could not let them see his pain or his aimless sadness; he just could not show his insides to them. It seemed to him that he had no goals anymore, just a role that he didn't want, assigned by the Digger: to teach these warriors mental skills if he could, and for them to teach him the craft of thieves.

Grueling as the training schedule was, though, the physical part of it took place only every other day, for four hours in the morning. The days in between were spent in learning the arts of thieves: pickpocketing, sleight of hand, scams and tricks as old as the human race. There were some skills involving muscular effort here, too: one day they practiced what Asher thought of as the human fly routine, learning to climb apparently sheer walls with suction cups, fingers and toes, nail-like spikes called pitons, or grapples—it depended on the type of wall.

On the seventh day they rested, and gave themselves over to study and talk. Asher realized dimly that the alternating of the days gave bodies a chance to rest and heal; there were fewer ripped muscles and torn ligaments than there would otherwise have been.

He was soon moved into a room with Ran, and found the powerful little black man full of smiles and jokes. It took him a long time, but he began to respond; he couldn't help it. Not responding was like ignoring a bowl of ice while walking through a desert. Across the hall lived Clemmy and Tawna, and next to them, Dov and Rasha. Teel lived somewhere else in the nest of corridors—the place was like a rabbit warren of hollowed-out passages, level upon level, with aliens and humans in close proximity.

In the afternoons there were classes. They were taught by dozens of different teachers, each one with a specialty. They learned practical things, such as how stardrives worked, how to disable an air car or a starship in a dozen ways, take them apart and put them back together, how to program robots and computers and anything else. They were taught techniques of survival on alien worlds, game-playing that they were stranded on this or that world with this or that equipment. On some worlds they "died," on some they survived. Once an Andalian teacher suggested to Asher that he was on a water world in a spacesuit; there was oxygen aplenty, but the sea was wracked by continuous storms. Asher cracked open his faceplate, just enough, he hoped, to let some air in. Instead, the faceplate was torn from his hands by a wave and he "drowned." Ran, presented with the same problem, learned by Asher's error and did not open his faceplate, and so suffocated when his bottled air eventually ran out. Clemmy, though, opened her air tank valve a little more than was normal, and the suit ballooned so she rode higher in the waves. The multiband antenna in the suits was a typical telescoping rod of metal, as portable antennae had been from time immemorial. Clemmy snipped the tip off and telescoped it as high as it would go, so that it rode above most of the spray. Then she hooked its end into the intake pump of her suit, and fed new air into the tanks. She survived.

Asher was shocked by the social relationships he saw around him. The October World had represented an almost sexless environment, desire dampened by the grim presence of the October One, the sexes rigidly separated and, even then, watched. Now, he saw informality. It wasn't that there was overt physical contact, it was just that the human men and women there treated one another with casual friendship, and it troubled him. Long-suppressed desire began to stir.

At night some of the recruits talked, some watched holographic movies, some read as their inclinations led them. Asher did not often leave his room, though Ran urged him to. Instead, he spent a lot of time with his wrist computer, tying into the local database (which Nin Tova had brought in a long time since) and probing where his thoughts led him, for he was beginning to realize the importance of time. It could be wasted, or used. While some watched movies, Asher read. Sometimes he watched movies, too, or talked. But most times he read, and learned.

His Skill still eluded him. At the simple breakfast on

nonmartial arts days, or the more elaborate lunches, or the open-ended snack that stood for supper, Asher ate first one food and then another, trying to stay off each one long enough to find the one that was drugged and let the drug wear off. But either everything was drugged, or he was being watched carefully and the drug switched around, for when he reached into his mind for the Power, it stood tantalizingly out of reach, dimly sensed but ungraspable. It was maddening, and here the Flaw raged in all its force, the fear part mostly gone, but the anger still there.

Teel was professional as a teacher, nasty outside of class. Of the Nin, Asher saw little, and he heard that she was often off-planet, looking to the interests of the Guild of Thieves.

"The Guild of Thieves," Asher read one night from the database. "Rumored to be in existence in the outer spiral arm of the human sector. Claims to itself an idealistic goal of despoiling persons it sees as dangerous to society. Outlawed and pursued by Galactic Police, who have not yet identified the home world. Thirty-six incidents now attributed to this Guild, others rumored (description follows). Guild condemned by all recognized planetary authorities as vigilante group breaking any law it wishes in pursuit of stated goal. Only two possible Guild members apprehended; both died by suicide. Autopsy revealed unusual physical development. See also *Nin Tova*."

Under "Nin," Asher found this: "An honorific title of Tau Cetan origin, referring to a master with no known equal of a particular discipline." Under "Nin Tova": "The possible Guildmaster of a suspected Guild of Thieves, which see. Nothing further is known of her origins or present activities." Asher looked under "Warrior Planet," and the database said: "No entry in recent thousand-year scan." Then a moment later it said: "The name of a video movie from the Old Planet, not now extant, referred to in Simon Hughe's massive committee study, *The Old Planet: A Compendium of Names, Fea-*

*tures, and Everything Known about the Home Planet of the Human Race."*

"That's certainly not what I wanted," Asher said to himself.

One time Asher told Ran: "Training with kendo sticks? One needler or blaster and the greatest stick master in the universe is dead." And in the next class, the Nin addressed them all, and said: "The weapons are just tools to teach quickness and thinking so fast it is no-thought. We will teach you needlers, too, but if you have to use them, you have failed. It is not an army we are training here; it is an underground force of spies and weapon-masters." Asher had resented at first the obvious fact that Ran had passed on his gripe; later he saw that it had given the Nin a way to teach them all something without singling him out. His resentment passed.

Early on, the new recruits had a tour of the underground passages of the Warrior Planet. Rashid Kalani, second-in-command and a formidable warrior himself, led them. He was short, massive, and dark-skinned, brown rather than black. Asher thought that it would take a dozen Rollers to overcome him.

"Corridors, whole place, blasted out of solid rock by disintegrators," he said in his strange, clipped accent as they walked from passage to passage. "Robot controlled; expensive. Backfield of disintegrator slowly disintegrated robot; disintegrated anything of metal or rock. Had to replace many robots. Would disintegrate bone, too; nothing alive can handle. Many robots needed, mostly plastic. Plastic too disintegrated, but slowly. Robots expensive. Glassy walls caused by disintegrators' heat. Look." They had walked into a large room, and there were glassed-in cases all along one wall. Asher saw weapons of all kinds, from samurai swords to needlers to blasters to bazookas.

Then, looking into the glass cases in the little museum, he saw little flare-nosed things that looked like hair dryers, but bigger and uglier. They seemed to be made of wood, though Asher guessed it was something rare and impossibly expensive. "Mostly iridium," Rashid said then, referring to one of the rarest and most valuable of all elemental minerals. "Disintegrates self, very slow. Cannot build iridium robot, too expensive even for Guild."

Asher gazed in awe at tools that had carved up part of a planet.

"No one would ever steal," Rashid said. "Would turn body into blob of jelly. No more bones. Ha!"

They saw the hatches that led up to the surface of the planet. Each one debouched through a false exit made to look just like one of the millions of spiny celerylike trees. They also saw the underground gardens, where food was grown by nuclear light, an art developed by ancient humanity in its later years on the Old Planet. They saw where quiet humming motors sucked air from the planet's surface, selected out nitrogen and oxygen, and fed it into the underground. And for the first time, Asher realized that the Warrior Planet was restricted to oxygen breathers. There were no chlorine or methane or water breathers in the Guild of Thieves. "Maybe day will come," Rashid told them. "Should expand. Must start somewhere. Starting here."

Asher felt empty and alone still. He missed the Power. During the years of training on the October World he had felt it more and more, growing inside him as he had opened to it, and now he felt like a ship without motor or sail. Sometimes he sat in his room and reached for it, probed and prodded in his mind, and felt it pulsing somewhere out of reach, blocked by a veil of greyness. What Skills he could teach these thieves! he argued to himself, as if someone inside could say, "Okay," and release him. Ran would sit cross-legged on his cot and watch him, flexing his dark muscles against each other so that they bulged and rippled.

Another night, Asher lay back on his cot and gazed up into the darkness, sore all over, head aching, listening to Ran's breathing as he slept across the room, and hearing the sigh of the ventilator set into one wall. The darkness reminded Asher of space, but in this tiny little bit of space there were no stars. There was nothing but a glassy ceiling, and a hundred feet of rock. It was space as he had seen it that first day, long ago, when his parents had sent him to the October World. He had hugged first the one, then the other, a little boy, crying, his father crying, too, his stoic mother trying not to, and his sisters letting it come, matching tear for tear. Eleven years old, and he was being sent away. He didn't want to go, and yet he did. Both desires had raged in him—the anticipation of the adventure of it, the fear of the change.

He had the talent, they had said. The shadowy recruiters of the October World had seen it in him, and they had worked on his parents until they had agreed. It would mean a future for Asher Tye, they had said, not the drudgery of the plain world on which they lived with its lack of purpose. It was just a place to work and eat and sleep, with no goals or challenges—a little ingrown place where people talked about each other and got nothing more out of life than that. Asher had seen it in his father's face—it and the weariness—and in his mother's, too, in a stronger way, for they had given up. They wanted only that their children have a chance at something beyond their own horizons, sensing that there could be more to living, yet not knowing themselves what it was or where to find it.

Asher was eighteen now, and only now could he think thoughts like this, yet it still hurt. The little boy was not entirely gone within him—he still hurt sometimes, and missed them sometimes. It was cruel to send me away, Asher thought; I was hurting then, too young. Now I see what I did not see before—that it had hurt them, too. "It's best for you, boy," his father had said, and had believed it. They had loved him, and still probably did, he did not doubt. They had not been perfect; there had been a lot of yelling and fighting that he remembered all too well when he let it come. But they had shown guts in a way, Asher thought. They had sent him away for something better. Had they known about Erasure? No. But they had thought that the mysterious October World offered something more than most people ever see.

When I get out of here, Asher thought, I will go back home.

Another time Ran grinned at him and pressed his palms together, then pushed, one against the other. He said as his biceps went rigid: "I think you don't like Teel, Ash. He's a little crazy, but he knows what he's doing most of the time."

Asher looked up from the "Summary of Knowledge" database.

"He wants to kill me."

Sweat beaded on the little black man's naked arms. "No way. If he killed you, the Nin would use him for weapon practice. You ever see her with one of those samurai swords? She would cut him one piece at a time.

"Tell you," Ran continued, a tremor in his voice matching the rippling of his tremendous arm muscles. "You ever hear of Toby O'More? No? Some say that there was this guy, Toby O'More, that lived down here and was just like us." Ran suddenly sneezed, and his palms, slippery from sweat, slid abruptly apart. He almost hugged himself before he got them under control. He laughed, and sneezed again.

"Allergy," he said. "Anyway, this Toby was working out one day with a little black kid, and he lost control, got mad at something, and gave the kid a karate kick that broke three ribs and nearly killed him. It wouldn't have been so bad, except that Toby didn't care—he thought it was funny. The Nin stood him up before everyone and just looked at him. Looked at him for *half an hour*, man. He shifted and squirmed, and after a while he was crying that he was sorry, and she still stood there and looked at him. Then he got mad, and started yelling that he never wanted to be here in the first place. He said a lot of things, and the Nin didn't move. Finally he jumped at her and you could tell he was crazy, and when he kicked at her she brought her hand up at the last second and caught his foot in it. They stood there for a moment, he on one foot, she holding the other, and then she squeezed. You could hear the bones crack like sticks breaking. He screamed and pulled and fell down, but it was like his foot was caught in a rock. And we never saw that kid Toby again." Again Ran sneezed, pulling out a gigantic red handkerchief and wiping his nose. "Some say that the Nin took him up and pushed him outside, in which case he's dead. Me, I think she just shipped him out, back home—wherever that is. One thing the Nin wants is control."

Control . . . Asher's thoughts flashed to the October World. He remembered Cor-Reed drumming it into him: control yourself, and you control what's around you. Play each situation like a violin. Decide what you want, and make everything you do, from the smallest word to the biggest action, contribute to your goal. In some ways, the training he was getting here, though all physical skill and none psychic, was a lot like the training on the October World.

Ran's voice interrupted his thoughts. He was now pressing his feet against the wall, hands behind his head, palms on the floor, pressing, arching his back. "Now, Teel's good," he said as he panted, still grinning—he was always grinning, "and he remembers how you beat him in front of everybody that first day, but he knows the rules and he wants to be a Warrior. I don't think nothing's going to happen; warriors watch out for everything, but I think you shouldn't worry about Teel."

"I saw inside of him," Asher said quietly.

"What did you see?" Ran said. "Squad leader that failed? That's what made him look the way he did inside and out. He serves the Nin down here. He will do exactly what she wants, and no more."

Ran, though, was wrong.

# Interlude

As he began his long search for Kerla Cwan, Cor-Reed sought out the *Pride of Caldott*. The huge passenger starship had made three more runs to the outer stars, and by the time Cor-Reed was able to return to Caldott, the ship was preparing to set forth again, taking on cargo outbound from Caldott as it refueled and underwent routine maintenance. It would be another week before passengers were shuttled up to the ship. In the meantime, it was closed to all but working personnel.

Cor-Reed, however, hung the Cloak of Unnotice around himself—the spaceport's crew areas were too brightly lit for effective use of Shadow—and waited for his chance. The Spacer Guild's assignment room was a constant beehive of activity as the Guild screened its swarming members and assigned them to this or that outgoing ship. Cor-Reed stood along one wall and watched as men and women saw him and dismissed him as an object of no importance whatsoever.

At length the Guildmaster, doing something a computer could have done better, but secure in her Guild's right to use any method it chose, began to put together a clean-up crew for *Pride of Caldott*. As she, a woman

of enormous width, rapped over the loud-speaker the
requirements of the job, the rodent-faced Adept watched
those coming forward toward the Guildmaster's platform. The dregs, he thought. Old spacers on hard
times looking for drinking money. Cor-Reed stepped
away from the wall.

Five spacers were chosen, three men and two women.
The women were overweight and sour; the men surly.
One of the men was fat, the other two skinny and
dissipated. One was about Cor-Reed's height and weight.

Once they checked in and were approved by the
Guildmaster, they shuffled toward the embarkation zone,
Cor-Reed moving close behind. A guard at the door
counted them as they moved past. Six? She put her
hand on her holster and went after them. But suddenly
she hesitated. They were only a few steps away, but she
noticed only five. Where had she gotten six? Cor-Reed
didn't even bother to erase the confusion from her
mind.

*Hand me your card*, Cor-Reed thought. The man in
front of him drew out his card, and then looked down at
it, puzzled. Cor-Reed gently lifted it from his hand and
blew the memory out of the man's mind. *Now you feel
sick*, Cor-Reed thought. *Your head is beginning to hurt.
It hurts worse and worse. You're afraid. You need
something to drink*. He squeezed the man's brain, just
a little. The man stopped, and held his hands to his
head. He would have moaned and the others, now well
ahead, would have heard him, but Cor-Reed reached in
with his mind and opened his throat, so that the moan
turned into a sigh.

*Go out the nearest exit*, Cor-Reed thought. *Go back
to your bed. Buy Ree absinthe with this; drink the
entire bottle*. And he slipped ten credits into the man's
breast pocket.

Ree absinthe—the man would be lucky to survive.
Cor-Reed envisioned him vomiting out his life. But of
pity, Cor-Reed felt nothing. The October One had long
since purged him of that . . . "flaw."

\* \* \*

When Cor-Reed reached the *Caldott*, he began to scour it with his mind. Hundreds of passengers had been through these plas-steel corridors since Asher Tye. But he was not looking for Tye now. He was scenting out Kerla Cwan.

And he found her, or rather her aftertaste. It was still strong, for she was a forceful woman. And he found something else, which caused him to consult the on-board computer, referring first to the passenger records and then to the database that held the encyclopedia of galactic knowledge. Soon he found his way to the cabin that Kerla had occupied. Here the scent was stronger, both of Kerla and Asher. Of the Digger there was nothing, but the passenger records had shown him.

In Shadow, he moved to one of the on-board tachyonic holographic transmitters.

"She *was* here," he told the October One. "And there was someone with her besides Asher Tye."

The October One was silent, waiting. Her mouth looked like a vertical knife slash.

"The passenger records show a Digger. According to the database, a Digger is a species from a planet on one of the inner arms—a mole-like species with a plain culture, nothing really distinctive except for a little telepathy among themselves."

" 'A little telepathy,' " the October One rasped.

"No recorded evidence of any use of the Power beyond that," the Adept stated. "And I cannot feel his scent, this Digger. It is like trying to read an invisible book. He is very alien. Yet the encyclopedia refers to no Skill beyond minor telepathy—no kinesis, for example, and no foresight."

But the October One's eyes were closed. Far away, another One felt her and entered into communion with her.

"Yes, I know the Diggers," said the Other. "They have a minor importance in my sector for their communication skills. I have met many. They could not function with the Skill that you describe."

The October One considered. Suppose, though, that a Digger linked itself with a failed Adept such as Kerla Cwan. Could the combination raise the Power in a more complete way?

"Perhaps . . ." thought the October One, opening her eyes. Egg-yolk yellow looked out. "Perhaps . . ."

# Chapter 16

The weeks turned into months, until nearly a year had gone by. Asher began to lose his sadness as the routine took control of his life. No longer sore, he began to look forward to the every-other-day physical training, grueling though it was. Friendly now with Ran in particular, Asher was beginning to lose some of the reserve that had closed him off from the rest of the world for so long. He no longer felt that every move he made or word he said was awkward or embarrassing. As his body grew stronger and more confident, so too did his mind.

But his Skill did not return. Once he asked Rashid, who clipped laconically: "When ready." When who was ready, Asher wondered? He was ready; he wanted it badly, missed its power despite his growing self-confidence. No, it must be the Nin who was not ready. Despite their need for what he could teach, they did not yet trust him. And he knew, deep down, that they were right. If he had the Power back, he well might use it to leave the planet. But then again, he might not. In the meantime, his mind was on other things. For example . . .

\*     \*     \*

Tawna was beautiful, Asher decided. He liked the way her hair, dark blonde and almost brown, just touched her shoulders and bounced when she walked. He liked the way her mouth turned down when she smiled. He liked the way she moved; in fact, he liked everything about her.

Their meals were taken in a cramped mess hall in two shifts, and the room was always crowded, especially when Therds and Rollers jostled in. But one day the crowd was thinning out when Asher came in late, and as he took his tray from the line, he spotted Tawna alone at a table, halfway through her meal. He walked over and sat down across from her. She looked up at him and smiled, and Asher's mind seemed to go blank.

After a moment she said: "Are you surviving, wizard-boy?" The nickname didn't seem insulting when she said it.

"Aye," he said, his mind racing. This week he wasn't eating anything that looked like meat, trying to avoid the drug. He picked at the vegetables on his plate, trying to come up with something that didn't sound stupid.

"You had a hard time with that Ghiuliduc," he said finally, and then realized that it was the wrong thing to say, even though months had passed. Her face clouded.

"Thanks for reminding me," she said shortly, and bent to eat.

"No, I mean, you did fine," Asher stammered. "He was an expert, you could see that."

"And I'm not?" she asked, still looking down.

"Not yet," Asher said, "but you will be someday."

She took a forkful and chewed it, scowling. The gently opposing curves of her temple and cheek distracted him. Asher sought desperately for words.

"You couldn't help it!" he said. "Like when I squeezed your mind, that first day. How could you have stopped me? I was skilled in that, and the Ghiuliduc was skilled in . . ."

She was looking at him now, and her eyes were even angrier.

"When you squeezed me, it hurt," she said. "It hurt! I hated you after that. I wanted to forget it, because it wasn't your fault, but I hated you."

"I didn't mean to hurt you." It sounded feeble.

There didn't seem to be anything else that Asher could say, and Tawna didn't seem to want to talk at all. They ate for a moment in a silence that was awful to Asher, whose food could have been slime worms, and he would not have noticed.

"Tye!" a voice rasped. Asher looked up.

"What?" he said.

"You stay away from Tawna," Teel said. His hands were on his hips, balled into fists, and Asher could see them shaking.

"She decides that," Asher said. He knew that Teel had ten times the fighting skills that he had, and even as he spoke, he wondered at his calmness. He felt like a buffoon while talking with Tawna. But not with Teel.

Teel grabbed him by the shirt and hauled him to his feet. He brought his face an inch from Asher's and hissed:

"No, I decide that, wizard-boy." In Teel's mouth it truly was an insult. "I am your squad leader, and you obey me!"

Asher, nose almost touching Teel's, looked directly into his eyes, and said nothing. No fear, no rage, no emotion showed at all. Inside he indeed felt no fear; he felt some rage, but kept it down.

"You have no right . . ." Asher heard Tawna begin, but Teel stopped her: "I will talk to you later." He lifted Asher off his seat and up into the air, Asher resisting not at all, and threw him down on the next table's bench. Roughly then, he lifted Asher's tray and slammed it down in front of him.

"Eat," he rasped. Asher did absolutely nothing, and Teel took a step toward him. Asher did not yet know where Teel's authority ruled, and where it did not, but he would not eat on command unless the Nin herself told him to.

There was a scrape from behind them. Teel glanced around and saw Tawna ten feet away, carrying her tray toward the disposal belt, back stiff and straight.

"Tawna," Teel said, turning abruptly and going after her. As she put her tray down, he took her arm. She shook free. He followed her out of the mess hall, talking urgently. She neither looked at him nor spoke.

Asher watched them dumbly until they disappeared from sight. His emotions had flown into chaos and back, and now he felt empty.

"On Saddleback IV one of our operatives stole a starship," Nin Tova told them during an assembly one day. "It was full of drugs. She landed it right in front of a galactic police station and walked away while the place was in an uproar. The police traced the ship to the owners, and a syndicate drug planet was closed down."

She strode up and down before them as they stood at attention. She spoke as if she were talking to herself, but her voice was clear and strong.

"Then the chief of the drug planet bribed the judge while the trial was going on. The same operative stole the bribe. The judge was furious when he found the money gone, and believed that the drug chief had doublecrossed him. He sentenced the chief to fifty years in jail. The drug chief couldn't believe it. He told everybody in sight about the bribe, and the corrupt judge was investigated and ended up in the same prison with the drug chief. It's all the guards can do to keep them from ripping each other apart."

The Nin was smiling to herself now.

"In the Rubel Sector most of the oxygen planets are inhabited by Singers," she went on. "They are long-legged beings who trade songs instead of money, and their songs have hypnotized humans with their beauty. In that Sector, the sector chief of the galactic police decided that the Singers were easy pickings. He and his men began to squeeze the Singers out of the gold and platinum and rare elements of their planets. They said, in secret sessions with Singer leaders: You dig mines for us, or we break your heads. Their heads are in their stomachs, but no matter. The Singers mined, and sang sadly, but were afraid. But one of our operatives joined the police force . . . he was good with weapons"—they laughed—"and after a time he stole a holographic tape of the sector chief making one of his threats to a group of trembling Singers. Our thief smuggled it out of the sector, and we brought it to the attention of the head-quarters office on Caldott. There was a massive purge in that sector. Now no one threatens the Singers, and their songs are happy again."

As Asher watched the Nin, a fierce joy radiated within him. He realized that he was proud, and yet these people were thieves! And the Nin fascinated him. She seemed to slide across the floor on wheels, so smoothly did she move. He admired her, he realized all of a sudden, in a way that he had not admired anyone before. He had loved his parents, respected and dreaded Cor-Reed, and feared the October One, but he had not admired anyone except possibly the Digger, who was too alien for him to say to himself: "I want to be like him." And anyway, the Digger was of the Guild of Thieves, too. There was reason to be proud.

"And Abner Caldon, whom some of you know, has reported . . ." she went on.

"*Kendo*. An ancient fighting art, an offshoot of samu-rai sword skill (which see). Long, tough, resilient poles are used instead of swords (see holographic image), with very rapid attack and defense." Asher didn't need to see the holography from the database. He had been training with the other humans in kendo for five weeks now. His hands were constantly swollen from being hit by kendo sticks, despite the padded gloves they wore.

Part of the kendo skill was learning how to avoid getting fingers broken.

Ran was skilled with his stick. When he and Asher practiced, Ran grinned when Asher attacked, nudged Asher's hardest blows aside with a bare movement of his wrists. Then his stick would come down in a blur and touch Asher's head or shoulder or side, and the point was scored—Asher was "dead."

It happened that way every time. Asher could not get inside Ran's guard. And he could not stop Ran's stick.

But every day he got better at it. Sometimes he managed to last for a minute or two before Ran tapped him. Then three minutes. He was making progress.

One day he had a chance to speak to Rashid Kalani. Asher was in the infirmary, having his knuckles bandaged again, when Rashid walked in.

"Tye. Found you, good," the short, powerful man said. "Message."

Now Asher had been fretting for days, off and on. No one was telling him the things he wanted to know, such as how long the training would be, when he could leave the planet, what mission he would be on when he did. For the first time, though, escape was not uppermost in his mind. First he wanted to know what they wanted him to do. So when he saw Rashid, he laid it all on him before the latter had a chance to deliver the message.

Rashid heard him out impassively. Then, as Asher's questions ended, he clapped him on the back in a blow that sent Asher off the couch on which he was sitting and onto the floor.

"Answers!" Rashid said jovially as Asher picked himself up. "Two years. Missions decided then. Depends."

Two years! Asher thought, aghast. I'll be nearly twenty-one in two years!

"Message," Rashid said. "Digger say, hi! End of message."

The Digger! "Where is he? Can I see him? Tell him that my Power is gone. Tell him . . ."

"Stop," Rashid said. "Will be here one day; no worry."

"But . . ." Asher's mind veered away from the Digger. "Two years," he said, almost wailing. "How can I teach Skill when I can't reach the Power?"

Rashid put a massive hand on Asher's shoulder. "What you do if off-planet, wizard-boy?" he asked. The doubt came into Asher's eyes; he tried to hide it, but it was there. "Aye, escape, do own thing," Rashid said. "You Power back when you want to stay. No before."

They can't trust me yet, Asher thought dazedly. And they're right—I might flee them and head for home. Not for sure anymore, but maybe. I like what they are doing to the syndicates, but I don't feel a part of them yet.

"Don't you want me to teach?" Asher asked unhappily.

"Aye. But when ready," Rashid said. "Message delivered," he smiled, then released Asher and walked out.

There were ships under the planet's skin. The Guild feared that someday the galactic police would discover the Warrior Planet. Therefore, they had a drill. In an emergency, everyone knew what tunnel to take to one of the escape ships. When they got there, the ship would arc downward through an incredibly long tunnel, and emerge nearly a third of the way around the planet from the Guild's main tunnels. It was hoped that the attention of the police would be concentrated on the central caves, and the escape ships could flash into interspace before the police ships picked them off. They would then rendezvous in a deserted solar system many light years away.

They were in the middle of such a drill one day, when Teel's squad and another were peeled off and sent to the surface. Asher found himself in almost the same group that had come after him on that first day, many months ago.

One by one they emerged from the false tree, tricklers gurgling. There were eighteen of them. The other squad leader, a Ghiuliduc, stood on top of a Roller and addressed them. How the Ghiuliducs breathed, Asher did not know, but they never wore tricklers.

"A new recruit is coming in," the Ghiuliduc said in his thin, reedy voice. "We will take him."

"What is he?" Teel asked.

"A being," the Ghiuliduc said shortly, and Teel flushed. The Ghiuliduc was the senior of the two, and Teel had no authority this day.

They fanned out and headed into the forest. In Asher, a chorus of conflicting thought clashed and banged. Vivid in his mind was the memory of his first day on the Warrior Planet. Crossbow bolts. Death darting in the air. Now he carried a crossbow, and he well knew how to use it from long days of practice.

He found himself next to Ran.

"I don't want to kill anyone," he found himself whispering. The black man grinned at him. "I don't either," he said, and would say nothing more.

Asher found Tawna. "Tawna," he said. She looked at him, and in her green eyes there was wariness and puzzlement. "Tawna, are we going to kill this new recruit?" Understanding flared in her eyes, and she opened her mouth to speak, but then something grabbed Asher's ankle and he fell to his knees.

"Pig!" the Ghiuliduc piped. Actually he named a more disgusting, alien animal. "No noise, no sound. Are you a warrior, or a marching band?" Asher got to his feet and looked at Tawna. She looked back at him with no expression on her face, but in her eyes Asher fancied that he saw laughter.

At length he caught up with Clemmy, who looked over her shoulder at him. On her back were oversize tanks, and in her hands she held a crossbow, cocked and ready. She looked competent and determined.

"Clemmy . . ." he began, but she would not break silence.

A Roller rolled past him, and they came to a clearing.

For all Asher knew, it was the one that he had landed on, many months ago.

No mental probing this time. "His tracks," the Ghiuliduc piped. Asher saw them then, broad impressions in the mold, not human certainly, but what he did not know.

They followed the creature, and in minutes they were back in the forest. The sun blazed overhead, as if it had not changed position since the day Asher had landed. It was hot and humid, but Asher sweated not only from the heat. In his mind he could see himself raising a crossbow and sending a bolt into the chest of a teenage girl, shattering her heart. Somehow he could not shake the girl image away, and when he looked into her face in his mind, he saw Tawna.

But it was an alien they were chasing. Still, what was the difference between killing Tawna and killing this unknown alien, in the larger scheme of things? Asher knew and wanted Tawna, but perhaps someone or something knew and wanted this alien.

Asher prayed then that the alien would elude them. But the warriors moved like shadows among the spiny trees, flitting like ghosts, and at every step the tracks became clearer.

It was something with at least four legs, two of them with large impressions, as if they were chasing a gigantic jack rabbit. It was certainly aware of them, for the tracks twisted and turned through the tunnels, as if the creature was fleeing from them in a panic, dashing down any tunnel it saw.

Asher found, to his surprise, that he wasn't out of breath. He had been loping along with the others, and now he discovered that he was in far better physical shape than he had been when he had landed. The training was taking effect. But his mind was in agony, the Power still apart from him.

Suddenly he bumped into one of the Rollers, the light tan one again. He looked around, and saw that the entire group was scattered around the Roller, dead silent. He looked down, and the tracks seemed to be everywhere.

"He doubled back a dozen times," the Ghiuliduc said, his little black form almost lost beneath the shadows under one of the trees. "Turn off your tricklers, and let the Roller listen."

The humans among them, Asher included, reached up and turned their tricklers off. The sudden silence sounded strange to him. He held his breath for a while, then breathed in the thin air of the planet. It was not enough, but still he stood silent. He heard absolutely nothing. He remembered back to the time of his own pursuit, and the puzzling part the Roller had played then.

A tentacular arm came out of the Roller and pointed. "That way," it said, and then Asher remembered how, during his own Test, the Rollers had always seemed to know where he was despite his use of Shadow. *They had heard him!* They had heard his movement and his trickler. Their hearing must be five or six times more acute than a man's.

Like jungle cats they sped through the trees. Finally Asher heard a crashing ahead of him, and then a whimpering. He burst into a clearing, and the warriors ringed the recruit that they were chasing.

It was a pinkish being, bigger than Asher, almost as tall as a Therd but not as massive. It had seven legs—no, six—and a long snout that looked like a leg. It sat back on the two large legs like a kangaroo, and the next pair, farther up its body, were thinner. The last pair had seven-fingered hands. The face of the being was oddly human, but small and compressed behind that long snout. It was cowering within itself, fear radiating out from it like waves in a pond.

The Ghiuliduc said: "Now!" The warriors raised their weapons. Needlers and crossbows pointed at the whimpering alien.

Whatever the signal was, Asher didn't catch it. He held his own crossbow loosely in one hand, pointed down. He saw a ferocious joy in Teel's face, an impassivity in Clemmy's, disturbance in Tawna's, determination in Ran's. As one they fired their crossbows, and from a dozen directions the deadly bolts transfixed . . .

Nothing.

"Wha . . .?" Asher said.

The needler energy beams seemed to reach a point a foot in front of the cowering alien and dissolve in a shower of sparks. Some of the crossbow bolts vanished in that energy; the rest ricocheted upward and disappeared in the trees, which waved agitated tentacles and showered them all with dead spines.

"A Shield!" Asher gasped. He looked again at Teel, Tawna, Clemmy, and Ran. No one seemed surprised. They lowered their weapons as if they had finished a job well done.

"Aye, a Shield, Asher Tye," a voice burbled, a voice that he knew. And out from the trees there scuttled . . .

The Digger.

They prodded the confused pink alien back to the nearest tree-door.

"It usually ends this way," Ran told Asher, grinning, as they walked back. "We practice killing, but we never kill, unless really threatened. When the Digger or Kerla's on-planet, we rely on their mental shields. When they're not, we just grab the recruit and drag him back, as we did before Digger and Kerla were recruited."

"In your case, the Digger let you put up your own Shield," the Ghiuliduc said. All his anger toward Asher seemed gone now. "And now, another new recruit knows the value of life, for he knows now that it can end at any time. Before, death was just a dim and abstract idea. But, of course, you yourself remember how it felt."

Indeed, Asher did remember. The Ghiuliduc moved away.

"Asher," Tawna spoke softly as they walked side-by-side. "I am a sorry warrior, I guess. I'm glad you didn't shoot."

"He proved he's a pansy," Teel snapped, coming up to them. Asher looked at him.

Teel sneered at him for a moment, then the Ghiuliduc called to him. "Tye, I told you to stay away from Tawna," he rasped. The Ghiuliduc called him again, ordering him. He left them, glaring at Asher over his shoulder.

"He would have killed me that day," Asher said quietly. "And he would have killed that alien today, and liked it."

"I know," Tawna said, looking after Teel, her face unreadable under the trickler.

Asher turned back and found the Digger, and greeted him joyfully; somehow the resentment he had felt for the little alien, for that long ago betrayal, was gone. The gigantic nose looked Asher over and said:

"You are looking well, Asher Tye."

"Yes, but I cannot reach the Power, Digger," said Asher, walking along beside him. "Please, help me?"

The Digger was silent for a long moment.

"No, I cannot help you, Asher Tye," he said at last. "I will defer to Nin Tova. She will release you when you are ready."

"I am ready now!" Asher pleaded.

"You are not," the Digger said.

That was the end of it. Asher walked forward, brooding, and almost walked into a tree.

# Interlude

The search for Kerla Cwan and Asher Tye and the Digger went on. Fifty thousand crossroad planets in the immediate galactic sector had to be touched by one Adept or another, and the search was hopeless if the two had fled to another arm of the galaxy. But at intervals of sometimes weeks, occasionally months, news would come, and it was always of the mental aftertaste of Kerla. She was extensively traveled, and had passed through Caldott so often that Cor-Reed stationed Ghulag Sor-Tee there, hoping to catch her coming through again.

In the meantime, other Adepts had found four more failed Apprentices missing.

Kerla had stopped for a day on Ramban a year before, one Adept reported to Cor-Reed. Another noted her fifteen-month-old scent on Koachish, a gigantic methane planet with a huge spaceport rotating around it like a metallic Earth moon, and almost as big. Yet another sensed her among the sixteen billion psyches on Aryeh, and she had passed only forty-seven days ago. The computers correlated her known past positions and tried to find a pattern, a way to predict where she would likely be next. A little luck, and the pattern could come quickly; otherwise, it would come after two years, or three, or four.

But of Asher Tye, they found no trace.

But the October Guild did encounter luck, eventually. Cor-Reed was passing through Caldott after a frustrating search among the speckled planets, when he decided that he might as well check the central computer of the galactic police. The weak Galactic Concourse of Planets was little more than a federation, and in many ways, less. It had never even tried to identify and keep tabs on all its quadrillion-plus citizens, with their incredibly varied life forms. Even so there were billions of records there, of politicians and con men, of swindlers and soldiers and pirates and criminals of all shapes and sizes. There was a tiny chance that Kerla would be there; at the beginning of the search he had checked without result, but with a stream of data coming in from police stations all over the sector, perhaps there was something new.

So Cor-Reed walked right through the security checkpoint at Caldott's massive information storage complex. No one saw him; he used both Shadow and the Cloak of Unnotice as needed, and his mind was constantly darting here and there, neutralizing this or that mechanical or electronic or magnetic detector that might have told the soldiers that he was there.

When he was in effective range of the databanks, he reached in and sought the file of Kerla Cwan. The computer and its ancient optical and more modern molecular-pattern storage files were both easier and harder to manipulate than a human mind—harder because there was a far vaster store of information there than the human mind could contain, and easier because the logical circuits were in fact logical, and not subject to emotion or disease damage.

And there she was. There had been a complaint against her on Greystoke, not for any wizardry, but for a fistfight she had somehow gotten into. And in her file, there was an entry that brought Cor-Reed up short:

"Consider dangerous. She is a suspected member of the Guild of Thieves."

The Guild of Thieves?

# Chapter 17

He could run forever, Asher thought. His legs pumped beneath him, his breath gasped strongly in rhythm—two steps as he breathed in, two as he breathed out. The glazed rock tunnel stretched before and behind him, Clemmy up ahead, Ran at his back. Fifteen miles now; they reached the turnaround point and started back. Asher's chest began to labor; it was mostly uphill here, where the disintegrator had dipped down in its long run to the far surface of the planet. The air was planet air, and they wore tricklers. This was one of the escape tunnels, and they ran here because there were no trees in the way.

Twenty-eight miles. They walked the last two, breathing easily, light-headed and alive. Asher felt a calmness that he had not had since the October World. For a moment, he did not want escape. He was willing to live this moment all by itself, and the next, and the next. For they are all "now," he thought.

Tawna came up to Asher and smiled at him, and his calmness was shattered. Teel was off-planet on his first mission, and Tawna had turned to him as he so badly had wanted her to. Asher had been on the Warrior Planet now for eight months more than a year.

Rashid stood at the hatch to the main part of the underground. It was set into the side of the tunnel, just before the blunt nose of the escape ship that filled the space farther along. The ship was always there, always ready. They hoped they would never need it.

"You run good!" Rashid hollered at them as they came up, the human squad minus Teel. He cycled the air lock and they stepped in, and emerged from the second door into a storeroom. The hatches to the escape ships were not in obvious places.

"Juggle time!" Rashid said jovially, and Asher groaned. He didn't seem to have the knack for juggling; it was all he could do to keep four balls in the air, or three clubs. He got most of the benefits of juggling in his back, not in his arm muscles, because of all the times he had to bend down to pick up fallen clubs and balls. But once he had the rhythm, he could keep them in the air until, excitement at the length of time taking hold of his mind, his concentration was broken and he dropped one or the other.

That night, in his room, Ran told him something he had not known: "You are lucky, Ash. You have a family to think about. Almost none of the rest of us do."

"You're kidding me," Asher said. "You're not kidding me? All of you are orphans?"

"Or abandoned," the black boy said, not looking at his roommate. "Clemmy doesn't know who her father is, or was, and her mother is dead. Tawna's folks were killed in a pirate raid on Millinocket the last time they attacked a whole planet. My parents died in the Seven-Year Plague. Rasha claims he doesn't know who either of his folks were."

"What about Teel?" Asher looked over at Ran, away from the wrist computer.

"Teel," Ran said, grasping his hands together and pulling hard. "Teel is the only one who is like you. His parents are alive; he knows who they are."

"I don't understand," Asher said.

The black man strained, muscles glistening gigantically.

"Watch it, you'll pop them," Asher said.

Ran let the strain die down, slowly, until the fingers were loose.

"Teel knows who his parents are," Ran said, pressing his toes together and grabbing them with both hands. "They sent him here. They're hard people, Ash. They wanted Teel to be hard, too. So they let it be known that they would give their boy to the Guild of Thieves, and if it didn't come to take him, they would leave him in the streets. They came. The Nin didn't like it, but Teel was strong and smart, fourteen years old, and had potential. The Nin took him, but figure it out, Ash. Your parents don't want you. They throw you out; you didn't do anything, but still they throw you out. How would you feel?"

Asher was used to seeing Teel as an enemy. Now to see him as a lost little boy was hard to take.

Still, he thought about it. Suppose his own parents hadn't wanted him? They had sent him away, but it hadn't been because they didn't want him.

"Always place yourself in the eyes of the other, enemy or friend," the Digger had once said, the positive flip side of the October attitude of doing unto others before they get a chance to do unto you. "Put yourself in his place, for then you have a great advantage. You know what he thinks and what he will do, and can act to meet it." And maybe feel sorry for him, Asher thought, and knew that such an idea would drive Teel to raving anger.

A few days later, Teel was back. Asher first realized it as he was walking down an empty corridor. In front of him he saw the grating of an air shaft, one of the ones that led from the topmost passage through the many levels of the underground, down to the hydroponic gardens where the plants grew and distilled oxygen into the air, and then to bedrock below. There was a huge-bladed fan somewhere down there, which whirled with fantastic speed and sucked air from the hydroponic chambers into the rest of the underground.

The grating that normally covered the shaft was pulled out and was lying in the middle of the corridor. Asher frowned as he approached it. It was a traffic hazard; it looked as if the screws had worked their way loose and allowed the grating to fall outward. Asher carried a pocketknife with a screwdriver blade, as did anyone with any sense, and that would be enough to screw the grating loosely back into place until he could get a stronger tool.

Asher bent to grab hold of the grating. As he did so, something slammed into his backside, and he was flung sideways. His shoulder caught the side of the shaft opening, and he teetered there for a moment, hands grasping wildly on the glassy surface and finding no fingerholds. Then he was falling, and down below he could hear the violent whir of the fan which would shred anything, a boy or an elephant, that landed on it.

Then Asher's body slammed into the side of the shaft, and he realized that he had twisted and his hands had grasped, and he was hanging by both hands from the ventilator opening, feet dangling down the shaft.

"Still with us, Tye?" a voice came, and Asher looked up into the eyes of Teel. "But not for long. Not for long." He raised his kendo stick.

"Tawna is mine," he said, and brought the stick down on one of Asher's hands. Asher felt the pain streak through him, and his hand slipped from the opening, all strength gone. Only his right hand was left now, hanging by four fingers over the death below.

If he could levitate . . . Asher reached into his mind, and the Power was there, but he could not reach it. The drug was still with him, no matter what food or drink he tried to avoid.

He felt something on his right knuckles, and saw that Teel was resting the end of the kendo stick on them.

"Up, and down again," Teel murmured.

"You will be banned from the Guild," Asher gasped.

"I suppose I would," Teel said. "If they knew. Even then, it would be worth it."

He saw Teel's hand tense for the upward movement of the stick; and then they both heard voices, coming around a turn in the corridor.

"Teel?" he heard Tawna's voice say. "You're back!" The footsteps began to run, and even as he hung there, Asher felt a jolt of jealousy—was she so eager to see Teel? There were slower steps behind her.

Teel's head was turned away, staring at the two, and Asher tried to bring his smashed hand up for a grip, but the fingers wouldn't work, and the arm slipped uselessly away.

For a long moment, Teel held the stick against Asher's knuckles, as the girls stepped toward him. Then he pushed it down the shaft, almost into Asher's face.

"Tye nearly fell down the ventilator," Teel said, a frustrated edge on his voice. "I'm saving him!"

"What!" Tawna said, and Asher could hear their feet running, faster now, toward them.

Asher let loose his good hand and, for an awful fraction of a second, felt himself falling. Then the hand was wrapped around the kendo stick, and he felt the three of them pulling him upward and outward. He wrapped his numb hand around the pole with almost no strength, and then found himself lying on the grating.

He sat up, rubbing his numb hand. He looked at Teel, who scowled at him, but in his face there was fear, for once. For this one moment, he knew that Asher had power over him. One report about this, and he would be out of the Guild of Thieves.

And then Asher made a mistake.

"Are you all right, Ash?" Tawna was kneeling beside him. "What happened?"

*I am not a squealer.* "Tripped over the grating," Asher said. "It must have worked loose; it was lying on the floor." Asher looked over her dark blonde hair straight at Teel. Then he saw Clemmy, standing confusedly nearby. There was some hint here that she had almost caught, but not quite.

"I'll get a work crew," Teel said at length. He turned away. Tawna still had her arms around Asher Tye.

"His mission failed," Tawna whispered in Asher's ear, as they watched his retreating back. "He tried to steal a particular piece of paper, and they caught him. It took the Nin herself to steal him back."

Asher said nothing, rubbing his bruised hand. Should he go running to the Nin and tell her about this? "Your Ninship, Teel tried to kill me again!" No, it did not fall in line with the idea of the Warrior Planet, the idea that you learn to take care of yourself.

The icy calm was with him. He would beware. He would not die for the likes of Teel.

It did not occur to him that he was not leaving only himself open to another attack. For all he knew, Teel had further enemies. By not turning Teel in, he might be exposing others to the type of danger that he himself was in. But Asher was not aware enough yet that what he did affected others besides himself.

# Interlude

The October One brooded in her mile-high chamber on the world that was hers. She communed with October Ones throughout the Galaxy, in ways that they had learned from their Teacher so long ago. Across light years they touched one another, crossing boundaries set when they had come from the satellite galaxy that had been the home of their species.

For no October One was a partner with another; each had sole control over one ten-thousandth of the Milky Way. They did not like to share power; it was why none of them had children, or ever intended to. They themselves were products of parthenogenesis, and needed no one and nothing to maintain the race. But they all looked to this One, the ruler of the October World, the planet to which their fleet originally had come, and from which they had divided up the spiral arms of the galaxy. Ten thousand beings, never having children, never growing old, though how old they already were no one knew. All female, all Powers, but so few in the face of the teeming multitudes, the millions of races, life so abundant and spreading that it was the rule among planets, not the exception.

"A Guild of Thieves!" the October One's thoughts

sighed across the light years. "They did not concern me until this day."

"Fewer than we," another One drifted in, "but they cannot last."

"The organized governments will kill them," came a thought from thirty thousand light years away.

"We will kill them," the October One's mental breath whispered.

"Yet it is not well," came another thought. "No thief could have done what happened here, or caused the disaster in Spergeit's Sector."

"Aye, and in mine," came a hundred thoughts.

"Too many," mused the October One. Unexplained failures of the Power. October missions aborted, Adepts captured, Skill rendered useless. Yet there was no apparent single cause. No new types of aliens had been reported; no single type had been detected at enough of the disasters to be singled out.

"We train Adepts, and they sense nothing," another thought came. "We ourselves are never near enough when the incidents occur. We cannot sense a cause even by probing the Adept's mind to destruction."

"Aye, but something is moving in this universe. It may involve this Guild of Thieves in some way." The October One touched the minds of those ten thousand that had come with her out of the Sculptor's eye, one by one. It took only seconds. "It cannot have been Kerla Cwan alone. Yet other failed Apprentices are missing. And what of the combined minds of Tye and Cwan together, perhaps, and this Digger? Or another force, another Power? Whatever it is, it will destroy the October Guild, unless we stop it."

The October One fell into musing again, hair crackling softly, yellow eyes now closed, lying stiffly on her settee, withered legs concealed under a gown that was too long for a human being. The galaxy grew alive with October thoughts as she mused, the others intermingling like hints of rain, one to another, tangled nets of thought without passion or liking or love or even much hate. Perhaps they were coming together at last, to fight the common enemy. Information passed and opinion exchanged. It did not take long for all interest to be squeezed from the news of the ten thousand.

At length her own thought drifted across the uncountable miles, touching the remnants of her race, bringing them all to new attention:

"Somehow, somehow," the noiseless voice said, "this new Power must be brought forth, and examined, and ended. One way or another, we will track down that which bedevils us, whether it be this Guild of Thieves, or something else. Or both.

"We will soon have Kerla Cwan, who can lead us back to the Thieves. But the galaxy must yet be searched, by mind and by body. I call on you for your Adepts, all of them, to seek out and find and bring to me he whom I will empty, the key to part of this puzzle.

"A boy named Asher Tye!"

# Chapter 18

He had learned at last to empty his mind of emotion on command. He could drop fear and hatred and anger out of himself with a single gesture of the will, like dropping something sticky into a hole. It was funny, Asher thought. After years of October Guild training, he had not been able to accomplish that particular thing, no matter how hard he had tried. And now, he seemed to have succeeded by a kind of back door, through the effects of hard, fast exercise. And because in his fatigue he had stopped worrying about it, stopped trying, it seemed to have proceeded then to solve itself. He had let it go, and then when his mind tried to pick it up again from habit, he found that he could let it go again.

Tawna presented a different kind of disturbance to his mind, one with which he had no practice. And yet some of the strength gained from his struggle with anger seemed to bring a little wisdom with it. He guessed, from time to time, that no matter what happened with Tawna, he would get through it, could use it to become stronger and better. Even if nothing happened with her, which was the possibility that made his mind quail.

And yet, he was having a very hard time separating the physical demands of his body from the emotional pressures of his loneliness. He imagined her sometimes as the eager and skilled partner in elaborate lovemaking, which he envisioned in such graphic detail that he had to close his mind down for fear of obsession. And at other times, he saw her as the best kind of friend, someone to share with, without the constant fighting one-upsmanship that was the rule in most lives.

Nor did her attitude help, for she seemed torn between Teel and himself. She seemed troubled when she was with Asher, and he could see how she felt when she was with Teel.

There came a time when Asher decided on a last-resort effort toward releasing his Skill. It was no longer a question of leaving. He was beginning to wonder what else he would learn if he stayed a while. But he wanted the Power back. If he could not pin down the source of the drug, could not get away from it by eating some foods and avoiding others, then he would stop eating and drinking altogether. If the water were drugged, then the water supply for the whole underground fortress was, and he doubted that. But it was time to go all the way. He would go for up to a week without food, and as long as he could without water, and see what happened.

The second day of his fast, he was weak and clumsy in martial arts practice. Clemmy frowned at him when he failed to block a routine kick. But otherwise he felt pretty good—a little lightheaded, the pangs of hunger coming and going. If anyone noticed that he was not eating, they did not comment.

The third morning their group of human trainees under Teel was called up to the surface for a drill. They put on tricklers, and for weapons they carried short kendo sticks, sheathed like swords. Their task: to sneak up on a group of warriors in a little forest clearing and overcome them. It would be hard: two of the group were Rollers, with their incredible hearing. Sneaking up on them would be well-nigh impossible.

The six of them—Dov was sick—stepped out of a hatch that looked like a celery tree with a door in its side, and huddled for a moment under the forest spines. Asher felt a raging thirst, but was strangely not hungry at all.

"The enemy is four hundred meters that way," Teel said, gesturing. "Any ideas?"

"Yes," a voice spoke up. It was Rasha. Surprised, they all looked at him. No one could remember him coming up with any ideas before.

He told it to them, and they could think of no other way.

From their survival backpacks they all took their mess kits. One by one, they strung the metal plates loosely together on a piece of cord. Grinning, Teel handed Asher a metal spoon.

"You're the pigeon, creep," he said. Asher didn't like the grin, and he didn't like Teel. But he took the spoon and the plates. He was a Warrior; he would obey.

And so it was that the defenders in their clearing were startled to hear a tremendous racket from the forest. After a moment, Asher Tye came into their view, banging the spoon against a bunch of plates which rattled against one another. And Asher was singing tunelessly at the top of his lungs.

"As I was walking in the park one day . . ."

The six defenders looked at each other. The two humans in the group had their kendo sticks drawn, but Asher's was sheathed. The two Rollers seemed agitated; they swayed this way and that, trying to pierce through the din. The two Ghiuliducs shouted at Asher in their thin voices, telling him to shut up, and of course their voices added to the clamor.

Asher walked into the middle of the clearing, and as he did so the humans there grabbed at the plates and wrenched them from his hand, throwing them on the ground with a final clatter. At that instant, with a banshee shriek, the five attackers leaped from different spots in the surrounding vegetation. The Rollers had not been able to hear them coming over the noise Asher had made.

The fight was short. Sticks flailing, Tawna and Clemmy quickly probed through the guards of the agitated Ghiuliducs and touched them. The Rollers had no reach with their spindly arms, and Ran and Rasha touched them too with their sticks. Asher whipped his stick from his belt and touched one of the humans in the back; the latter would be shamed that he had not guarded himself.

Teel leaped in and engaged the last human, who was quicker than his comrades had been. In a barrage of blows, Teel fell back, and as he brought his blade back for another strike, the weighted stick slammed against the side of Asher's head, and he fell like a stone. Teel's follow-up caught the defender on the bottom of the chin.

Teel's squad stood confused for a moment. Teel, they knew, was in trouble. A leader never "killed" one of his own, by accident or otherwise.

"Back to the underground," Teel ordered. "I'll take care of Tye here. Clemmy, you're in charge. Take the prisoners in."

Clemmy looked worriedly at Asher. "Can't we help you, Teel? We'll build a stretcher . . ."

"He's not hurt that bad," Teel said roughly. "I'll bring him around. See you down below. Now go!"

Obedience was ingrained in them all, so Clemmy went, prodding a reluctant Roller along with her kendo stick. As she disappeared from sight, she glanced back once, and saw Teel bending over Asher. Then the trees blocked her sight.

After all, she thought, Teel is the squad leader, and he is in enough trouble already. He could even lose command of the squad. He wouldn't take any risks now.

But he would.

\* \* \*

"Out cold, are you, Tye?" Teel murmured, sitting back on his heels. "Then I don't have to hit you again. Too bad. I almost got to like you, Tye."

He was talking now, out loud, looking off into space, and there was the glint of unbalance in his pale blue eyes.

"No one will know. I wish they could. They would learn that no one, *no one!*" he shouted, "can do what you did to me. I wish I could squeeze your mind like you squeezed me that day, you . . ." His wormy lips writhed, and he seemed to grope for a word bad enough to encompass all the hatred that had festered in him all these months, but couldn't find one. "Clemmy will wonder, and maybe Ran," Teel began muttering again. "And Tawna's a little sweet on you, I guess, poor baby." He grabbed Asher by the armpits, and began to pull him into the forest. "A little this way, perhaps, and a little that way." There was shrillness in his voice. "So deep into the trees that if you wake up, you won't know where you are or where to go. You will die and never know that I killed you. Too bad. But *I* will know."

A half hour later, he laid Asher on the leaf mold, face to the dirt, and stood up, stretching his own back. Then, with deliberation, he kicked Asher in the side with a booted foot.

Reaching down, he turned the valve of Asher's trickler on high, and the oxygen began rushing from the tank, wasting itself into the air as a relief valve popped open. He undid Asher's backpack, which held the emergency transmitter. "Came off as you crawled along in a daze, I do believe," he muttered. Then he backed off the way he had come, brushing out all signs of passage.

Halfway along he left the backpack. At length he came to the clearing where the battle had been fought.

"Now the hard part," he muttered, looking up at the trees. "But I can take it. I can take anything." Again, that ghastly smile.

A few yards back along the trail, there was a tree

with a few tentacles that reached down almost to head height. He came and stood under them now, looking grimly up.

He looked around and located a partly rotted piece of tree trunk, and dragged it close under the tentacles. The tree, as if aware of what was going to happen, waved the tentacles menacingly, and a few dead spines pattered onto Teel and the forest floor.

Teel stood on the trunk. He muttered: "Got to protect the eyes," and put one forearm over them. Then he stretched to his full height.

The tree lashed at him in a paroxysm of excitement. A dozen needles impaled his arm and forehead, stopping short at the bone of his skull.

Teel screamed and staggered back off the trunk, falling. He did what anyone would have done, lashed by one of the trees. While the tree above him bent and reached and tried to claim its meal, he tore the spines from him, one by one, blood flowing down from his forehead and into his eyes.

Unlike the spines of the tree trunks, the tentacular spines had poison in them—nothing like the poison in the spines of the animal that Asher had once killed, but poison nonetheless. It was a paralyzing sort of poison, one that relaxed the body into a sleepy daze, and then into sleep itself.

Teel did what had to be done; as if trying to reach the underground hatch after so common an accident, he staggered toward it, the poison slowing him gradually and, when he was still a hundred yards away, bringing him to a stop. The pain was gone now, just a pleasant hazy fog around him. He stood there, swaying like one of the trees themselves, smiling his thick, brittle smile, dreamily. And then, like a falling tree, he toppled forward onto the ground.

An hour before Teel's and Asher's oxygen was due to run out, an alarm sounded in Rashid's quarters. The watch commander on duty told him that two warrior trainees had not yet come in.

The second-in-command—Nin Tova was off-planet—threw together a search party, which poured out of the hatch and onto the noonlit sward of the forest. They quickly found Teel.

"A tree got him," the leader of the search party reported back to Rashid.

"The blundering idiot," Rashid had growled. He already knew about the blow that had stunned Asher, reported by the other humans in Teel's squad. That made two goof-ups in one day; Teel would pay for it dearly.

"The other guy must have wandered off," the leader said. "We're fanning out. The Rollers will hear him; he couldn't have gone too far."

But the hour passed, and Asher Tye was not found.

Rashid was pale as death. They had never lost a warrior to the planet before. How could he tell Nin Tova?

It was a long time later that the grim report came in.

"He is dead by now," the search leader's voice said, roughly.

"Find the body," Rashid said.

An hour and forty-five minutes before, Asher had come to. Perhaps it was the extra oxygen that was pouring through his trickler and out the escape valve. In any event, his head felt as if it were full of rocks, banging from side to side.

He sat up, dazed, and looked slowly around. Thirst hit him like a hammer blow. His mind did not register for a moment what he saw. He had no idea what he was doing here; he had not even seen Teel's stick coming. One minute he was poking an enemy with his own kendo stick, and the next he was sitting on his backside in the middle of the forest.

The trickler . . . funny. It was on too high. He valved it back, and looked at the readout. Seventeen minutes left. Plenty of time . . .

Then Asher noticed that his backpack was missing. That was more serious. But he knew the way back to . . .

Wait a minute, this is not the clearing, Asher thought. He looked wildly around. Nothing was familiar; it was a bit of the forest, just like any other bit. Tunnels and trees, tentacles waving lazily overhead. No footprints, no backpack, and no clearing.

Asher moved to each opening, and looked through into sameness. More trees and more tunnels. His head was still not working right. Absently, he fingered a lump on the side of his head. Something had hit him for sure. But where was he?

And then the full enormity of the spot he was in hit him.

Fifteen minutes left . . . no radio . . . no idea where he was.

And yet . . . and yet . . . Where he should have felt blind panic eighteen months before, now he found only calm; he was analyzing his predicament, not running panicked around it in his mind. Good, good, he thought. Now how do I get out of this?

He remembered the fundamental rule of being lost in the woods: Do not panic (he had done that part already), and stay where you are. If you stay where you are, you will not wander farther from the search party that soon will come after you. Unless you are in immediate physical danger from cold or an animal, stay where you are.

An animal . . . Asher remembered the spine-thrower he had defeated in that same forest long ago, and shuddered. Here he had only his kendo stick, a pitiful weapon against such a beast. And as for his Skill, that had defeated the beast then . . .

He reached into his mind and it was there! The Power was there! He could feel its surge, and his answering response. He could touch it again! The drug must have washed out of his system at last.

He played with it, felt its surges and eddies, probed into its chasms and touched its heights.

It felt good, all the Skills back with him—Shadow, Cloak of Unnotice, Levitation, Time Stop, Green Flame, Death Trance, Psychokinesis, all the rest.

It felt so good that Asher sat and enjoyed it, forgetting that he was in critical danger. But at last he did remember, and glanced at the air gauge.

Eight minutes! Eight minutes to find the hatch or a search party. Eight minutes, or his air would run out, and ten minutes after that, the thinness of this planet's oxygen not being enough, his brain would die.

Could he reach someone with telepathy? He doubted they would know what was going on, and they certainly would not be able to respond. And what could he tell them? The shape of that particular tree to his left? Bah!

Eight minutes . . .

He had to be close to the clearing; he could not have crawled very far. Where were the others? Where were Tawna and Ran, Clemmy and Rasha, and Teel? Still he did not suspect the truth; it was too monstrous, and it just did not occur to him.

The sun was directly overhead, and was no help for direction. Even if it had been, he had no idea which way to go. Reaching into himself, he cast his mind out through the trees, but the search party was not yet on the surface, and he touched no one. He could feel the many minds underground, dimly, but that was no help, and he could not figure out the direction.

Six minutes. What could he do? The Green Flame? There would have to be air cars out for smoke to be seen, and he sensed no minds up in the air. What else among all his Skills would save him now? He could think of nothing. He might as well blank out and die . . .

Blank out and die . . .

Wait a minute.

Hurriedly, he scratched a message into the leaf mold with a rigid finger.

Then he settled down, and a little while later, his air ran out.

Three hours later, Tawna burst into the tunnel where Asher lay and found him. "Oh my . . . no!" was all she said at first. Tears streaming down her face, she knelt down and touched his throat, and found no pulse. The trickler was empty. She shook him, and he did not respond. She put her ear against his chest; there was nothing.

Her radio summoned the others. She stayed kneeling there, crying without control, and didn't see the scratched message. A Roller came in then and rolled right over it, flattening its edges. Then the rest of the search party poured in and scuffed the remains of the message away.

They carried Asher all the way back to the hatch, moving like a funeral procession.

"We found Asher Tye," the voice of the search leader echoed in Rashid's ear. "He is dead . . ."

# Part III:

## RECKONING

# Interlude

The lord high commissioner sat behind his desk and watched as the admiral of the galactic police wheeled himself in. The admiral was a Chait—a being from a chlorine-based planet who was almost as smooth as a billiard ball. The living beings there had evolved wheels instead of legs. The admiral was encased in a breathing machine that covered everything except the wheel. Even from across the desk, the commissioner could feel the cold which seemed to radiate from the encapsuled figure, and could catch the eye-watering scent of chlorine in the air.

The lord high commissioner did not believe in preliminaries. He launched right into his subject.

"I want you to go after the October Guild," he said, authority in his voice. "The commissioners agree that they are a threat beyond anything we have ever imagined. How would we even know if they were controlling key individuals? Or everyone, for that matter?"

The galactic police were one of the few glues that held the incomprehensively diverse species of the galactic concourse together. No one else could trace smugglers or deal with pirates. The admiral had as much power as anyone in the Milky Way.

"May I make a suggestion, sir?" the admiral's voice box said.

"Of course, of course," the commissioner said indulgently. "You are the expert here; I'm just a country politician."

There was no reaction from the alien.

But then the commissioner himself started, as if some idea had leaped into his mind. As a matter of fact, that is exactly what had happened.

"The October worlds are not so important," the alien admiral said quietly.

"The October worlds are not so important," the commissioner mused thoughtfully.

"We face a far greater threat in the sinister Guild of Thieves," the admiral suggested.

"Far greater," the commissioner said.

"They disrupt the dealings of honest businesspeople," the alien said.

"Disrupt," said the commissioner.

"They must be tracked down and eliminated," the admiral said.

"Yes," the commissioner nodded.

"That has top priority," the admiral said hypnotically. "We can forget about the October worlds."

"Yes," the commissioner said again, his eyes vacant.

"We will go on double-alert," the admiral continued, "and put all available forces in search of the planetary base of the Guild of Thieves."

"Of course," the commissioner said, entirely convinced. Nothing had ever sounded so logical.

Cor-Reed let himself out. It had not been hard, maintaining the image of the chlorine-breathing alien. Nor had it been hard to penetrate the rather simple mind of the lord high commissioner.

Later that day, he stood in Shadow and watched as the commissioner instructed the real admiral to throw his forces into the search for the Warrior Planet. And, he added, to look for two humans, one Kerla Cwan and one Asher Tye, and a Digger.

# Chapter 19

Teel, bandaged around the arm and forehead, stood before Rashid at the front of the center aisle in a tiny amphitheatre. His squad sat on fixed chairs behind him on either side. On a table on the raised stage lay the body of Asher Tye. A sheet was pulled over his head.

The Digger was there, too, off in one corner, not moving. He might as well have been a piece of furniture.

"That's all of it," Teel said humbly, looking down at the floor. "When I was dragging him over that rotten log, I stretched upward to work out a kink in my back. I just wasn't thinking clearly; I had hit one of my own squad members and I knew I was in trouble. Then the tree got me, and Tye must have awakened in a daze and wandered off while I was lying there."

Rashid's powerful arms were crossed as he leaned his backside against the table on which lay what remained of Asher Tye. The doctors had long since given up hope and left. There was no breathing, no heartbeat, no brain waves at all.

Then Rashid yelled. For once his speech lost that clipped character by which almost everyone knew him.

"You did more than fail," he roared. "*You killed a Warrior*."

Teel seemed to shrink away from the violence of the words.

"He would have been better than you," Rashid roared. "He could have been the best. You *killed* him."

Fear flitted for a brief moment in Teel's eyes.

"It was two terrible accidents," was all he could stammer. The words sounded false. Among the squad, Tawna, Clemmy, and Ran stirred, while Rasha sat stolidly still.

"I'll break you," Rashid said savagely, his voice dropping, hands now in fists. "Run you out of Guild. You hated Tye, and you had not control because of it. We no want such in Guild of Thieves!"

"I'll do better, Rashid, please," Teel murmured. He glanced at the Digger with unease. He knew that the alien had psychic skills beyond the blocking of weaponry, but just what they were neither he, nor any of the Thieves save the Nin and Kerla Cwan, knew in any real detail. But the little alien was just crouching there, seemingly oblivious to everything, and Teel could feel nothing poking around in his mind no matter how hard he tried.

Emboldened, Teel said: "I know I had a problem with Tye, but let me pay for it and learn control, please. I never wanted anything like this to happen to any of my squad, never. Please believe me. Break me down to a new recruit if you have to. Please . . ."

And he meant most of it. Now that Tye was no longer a problem, Teel was facing the likelihood that he would be forced out of the Guild. It was the only home he had anymore, anywhere.

"Please let me stay," he said, voice breaking.

Rashid Kalani seemed to soften for a moment. "That be for Nin," he said more quietly. "Now you go. Not leave room; wait for call from Nin."

Teel turned away. As he did so, elation tore through him, and he struggled to keep it from showing on his face. Tawna, Clemmy, and Ran were watching him closely.

He had just reached the door when the purring voice of the Digger came.

"Stop." And then: "Turn around."

Sudden panic filling him, Teel did so. Soundlessly the Digger moved forward. The aisle stretched between them like a rope ladder.

"Girl, say it," the Digger burbled. In her chair, Clemmy started.

"What . . ." she said.

"Say what is in your mind," the Digger said.

Clemmy frowned. Training in squad loyalty struggled with truth. Truth won.

"I believe he killed Asher somehow," she said at last.

"Clemmy!" Teel snarled. She did not look at him.

"Why?" asked the Digger. The others looked at the young girl. She was not as frighteningly skinny as when Asher had first seen her, now that nearly two years had gone by.

"I saw it in his eyes, out there in the forest," she said simply.

"That means nothing," Teel said harshly.

"Silence!" Rashid roared. "Digger. Continue."

"I believe it, too," another voice interrupted. It was Tawna. Her voice came as if from a great, sad depth. "One time we found him standing over Asher, who was hanging down an air shaft. He said he was pulling Asher out, and Asher never said anything else, but I always wondered. But in the end I believed Teel. I . . . felt for him. And he was my squad leader."

"And now?" the alien burbled.

"I could believe one accident because I wanted to," her reluctant voice came. "But I cannot believe two more, both on the same day." Then she looked at Teel, and in her eyes Teel saw the struggle going on.

"It *was* an accident," he said desperately. "How could I plan hitting him like that? I couldn't know that he would be right there in that spot at that exact moment. How could I?"

"He is a master at kendo," Ran said, speaking quietly. "The chance came, and he took it."

And then, finally, Teel cracked.

"Traitors!" Teel yelled at them, control gone all at once. "You owe me! I trained you to be what you are. I trained you to be like me!"

They just looked at him, saying nothing. Teel was trembling. His tanned skin was as pale as paste.

"Like you, yes," the Digger burbled in his eerie way. "Like you in many ways. But your soul you could not teach. These decent warriors would not learn."

Teel was still trembling, still wracked by a terrible combination of fear and elation and rage.

"What are you all, galactic police?" the blond boy raved. "I want the Nin; she will judge me. I want her to hear facts, not these jealous ravings from stupid and incompetent trainees."

"And so she shall," the Digger said. Teel's shivering lessened. "Every word we utter and will utter in this room, she will hear. It is all being recorded." If it were possible, Teel's skin went even whiter. The trembling began again. He looked around desperately.

"Rashid, this is not fair." Teel appealed to the only recognized authority there. "It is my word against this squad of traitors. I was there and know what happened. They're making wild guesses and that's it. I didn't like Tye, but I didn't hate him. I didn't kill him."

"We shall see," the Digger hissed. Teel shrank back. "What do you mean? Rashid . . ."

"I peel your mind like an onion," the Digger murmured. "I empty out your mind."

Teel opened his mouth in a soundless scream. He seemed rooted to the floor. He wanted to run, and he couldn't move. He felt something all around him, a presence like water in which he was sinking, down and down, and all the feeble blocks that he had raised were gone as if they had never been.

The squad and Rashid Kalani watched in horror, but Rashid made no move to interfere. This was the Digger's job.

The shaking returned and Teel's eyes seemed to bulge outward, as if a gigantic pressure were building up inside him, a dam about to burst, a bubble about to pop. His mouth opened again and drool trickled out, and the jaw was jerking uncontrollably.

And then, finally, the words began. The Digger worked his relentless way in, and layer after layer peeled away from Teel's mind.

And everything came out.

A long time later, two guards took Teel away. His mind was back again, but he had been wrung out like a wet cloth, and in him was utter exhaustion and utter despair. The rest of them were in no better shape. Somehow the mental violence had spilled over onto them, and they wanted nothing more than to hide and sleep and forget what they had seen. They didn't want to think about Teel anymore. Yet they all knew it was not over. There was still the Nin. She would mete out punishment when she returned from off-planet. They wondered what that punishment might be.

Digger was left alone in the little amphitheatre. His feet made clacking sounds on the glass-like stage as he moved to look at the still, shrouded form of Asher Tye.

He hissed. Then words came, so rapidly that a listener could not have made them out through the waving alien cilia.

"Satisfied, Asher Tye? From somewhere did you witness all this? Did you plan it this way? Did you have any idea what would happen here? Why did you not tell Rashid or the Nin of the air shaft incident? They would have investigated. *I* would have investigated. A lesser evil went unpunished because you did not want the betrayal of your squad leader on your conscience. It made room for the greater evil to come. Evil happened to you; evil happened to Teel. You could have stopped it. And I, in the middle of a mission, have to come back for this. Learning you have done, Asher Tye. Yet you did not learn enough."

The steam kettle sound stopped for a moment as the alien cast his mind over the still body on the table. Then the staccato sound came again in one brief explosion.

"And have I taught you nothing about your mind, Asher Tye? You even mishandle something so simple as the Death Trance. You should be able to waken yourself, and you cannot, and you are so far away that you are not even trying. Even I will have a difficult time pulling you back.

"But I will try, Asher Tye. Missions await, but before I leave this space again, I will try."

The alien stood there for two long hours. The air around them crackled from time to time with mental electricity. The lights flickered once as their power was negated by another power in the room. Shadows flitted around the two forms—specters of a sort, mental ghosts taking their brief place in parallel with the Digger's mind—and they faded like steam into droplets of mental substance that reformed into different shapes, again and again.

On her remote planet, the October One stirred. She had felt something in the firmament, some exercise of Power that did not seem familiar to her. She tried to focus on it, and she could not. Faintly disturbed, she called on a few other October Ones to join her in a mental link to track down the tiny ripple. But before they could do so, it faded and disappeared altogether, leaving the October One with a vague and formless unease.

And on the Warrior Planet, the Digger hovered four feet in the air, looking out over the covered body on the table.

"Now," he said, his voice almost understandable. "Arise, Asher Tye!"

# Chapter 20

The Nin strode in. She moved like a panther, gliding across the floor, her superb body in extreme coordination, aware of the movement of every muscle, the passage of every thought. The warriors stood, row after row, and watched her soundlessly. Nothing could be heard. They stood in a glassy cavern of utter silence; it could have been a tomb.

All eyes were on the Nin, but some of them glanced too at Teel. The blond boy was alone in the center of the amphitheatre, watching as the Nin came forward. He was trying to tough it out, but there was a quivering along his jaw, a spasm of the muscle that he could not control.

The Nin had seen the tapes. She had listened to the testimony of the squad and of Rashid. She had listened without comment to Teel, watching his holographic image as her ship spiraled toward the Warrior Planet.

As always before planetfall, still inbound aboard her intersystem shuttle, she had triggered a routine scan of the cubic parsec of space closest to the purple world. In that vast emptiness, nothing moved that the Guild's computers did not already know. There were comets, and planetoids, and the rocky debris of a solar system, thirty-one planet-sized bodies of various compositions, and the Warrior Planet itself swinging slowly around its sun.

The only starships were a full solar system away, fourteen guild cruisers in parking orbits around a mining colony three light years out. The star they orbited was a dull red giant, the rocks they harvested rich in platinum. It was the false front that shielded the Warrior Planet from the rest of the galaxy. Only one ship at a time was ever allowed to fly in transit between the mining colony and the purple world, and that ship a shuttle that could land and be concealed. And even should the shuttle be boarded by a galactic official before it jumped into interspace—highly unlikely—it would be described as on a regular run to the nearest source of oxygen, which happened to be a purple world whose thin air would be compressed into tanks and delivered back to the mining colony. That was true, in fact, as far as it went.

Now, in the cavern, the space between Teel and the Nin lessened, and the tension of the warriors increased. The Nin's face was not the blank that it should have been in such a moment of dispassionate judgment. There was something harsh there that made the assembly fear. She carried a samurai sword in a plain black scabbard at her side, and her left hand was clenched around the haft.

Teel too was armed. It was that that made them all afraid. He too carried a sword, and his right hand was fingering it. But there seemed to be no confidence in him—just bravado, nerve.

Of the Digger, there was no sign.

The Nin stopped three feet away from Teel. He had crouched in a defensive stance, blade pulled half out of its scabbard. Sweat gleamed on his forehead and stained his loose warrior's shirt. The sash of his rank still stretched from his right shoulder to the left side of his waist. Squad leader. Master of the kendo stick, and therefore the sword.

She just stood there, apparently as relaxed as if she

were waiting for a bus. Only her face showed that nothing normal was in her mind.

As the silence lengthened, Teel's body began moving. Imperceptibly at first, little spasms twitched his hands, shuffled his feet, moved his head forward and back. The jerking increased as the seconds passed. His efforts to stop the movements were clearly visible in his face, and if anything, the crowd felt pity. Teel's warrior training was not holding. Emotion was crowding through his mind into his body, fighting the remnants of his control. He was losing. He could stand the waiting, the Nin's piercing eyes, for just so long. And then . . .

"Noooooooo!" his shout suddenly rang out, his sword whipping from its scabbard in a motion so fast that some of them jumped from it. "You will not make me a Toby O'More!" The end of his blade quivered an inch from the Nin's neck. "I killed Tye," Teel screamed. "I killed him, and I cannot take it back!"

Then he lunged. It was more a forward jerk of his arm, the razor-sharp blade driven forward to cut the Nin through to the bones at the back of her neck.

But she had moved. No one had ever seen a blow come so quickly, or ever would again. Her left hand had drawn her blade and whipped it upward in an inside cut that should have been far slower than Teel's lunge, because the blade had so much farther to go. But before his point had touched her skin, her blade had slammed into his, and he reeled sideways from the torque of the blow, off balance for the briefest of moments. And in that instant, in a movement that somehow appeared to be the logical follow-through of her block, she slashed downward and cut the sash across Teel's shoulder from one side to the other, just deep enough that a scarlet thread of blood came.

Cut in two, the sash fluttered down and hung from Teel's waist. He stared downward at it, and then back to her, on one knee, blade now at the ready. But hers had slipped back into its scabbard, the last and still logical follow-through of her incredible movement.

Teel knelt on one knee, and stared into her eyes. In his, there came a kind of wonder, a kind of expectation. It was the same thing that a saint must feel, just before martyrdom.

"Kill me," he said then, his voice hoarse.

Then the Nin spoke. All were surprised. Indeed, this would not be the silence that she had inflicted on Toby O'More.

"Would you take it back," she spoke deliberately, each word a separate sound, "if you could?"

The question hung there. It seemed to take Teel by surprise. The Nin's left hand rested easily on the haft of her sword. It was as if she had never moved.

"I . . ." Teel said, stopping. The question could never have occurred to him before. Then his nature took hold:

"No!" he shouted. "You play with me! He is dead, and it is done, and . . ." And he launched himself into space, his sword cutting the air, the most dangerous hand-to-hand weapon man had ever created, trying to cut Nin Tova's body from shoulder to knee.

She stepped backward; it seemed a casual move, but Teel's blade cut only empty air. He swirled it around in an arc and came in again. This time she stepped forward, a step that moved her like a bullet from a gun. His hand, clutching the haft of the sword, slammed into her side with little force. She brought her fist from the haft of her weapon and drove it into Teel's stomach, in the center just below the ribs.

He lay on the glass floor, mouth open like a fish's, and air would not go in. He panicked for a moment, stunned by her blow. She could have drawn her sword then and cut off his head; instead, she stepped back and watched him.

His lungs suddenly began working again, and the black mist cleared from before his eyes.

"Would you," she said again in that same deliberate fashion, "if you could, do it again?"

"Would I kill Asher Tye?" Teel gasped, trying to bring his thinking into focus.

"Aye," she said quietly, gently, softly.

Teel's head whirled around and around. She was pressing him with something that had stirred in him already, that he had crushed out of himself, or so he had thought. The idiocy of what he had done had come to him during the three days and nights that they had waited for the Nin. He had taken a future and destroyed it. He had thrown away his training, made himself an outcast, if the Guild did not kill him outright. And the reason, revenge, was not even remotely as sweet as he had guessed it would be.

"I would kill him again," he said then, climbing again to one knee, but there was hesitation in his voice. They all heard it. It was clear to everyone, alien and human, in that vast closed-in space, that Teel could not stay in the Guild, for he could never again be fully trusted. And still the Nin was teaching him, trying to salvage something out of the training her Guild had given him.

"I will give you that chance," her clear voice rang out, startling them. "You may kill him again." She took a step backward, and into the cavern walked Asher Tye.

For a long moment Teel looked at him, not believing his eyes, not knowing how this was happening or what to do. Asher seemed whole and strong. He walked confidently forward, and he too wore a sword, though he was no match in swordsmanship to Teel.

The silence hung, and hung. Asher reached the Nin and stopped. Teel stared at him, his whirling mind trying to settle someplace, trying to decide what was right and what was worth doing, now that most of what he had worked for all his life was lost. He had seen Tye's body, and yet here he was. And now, what? A spectacular exit, to attack and die beneath the blade of the Nin? To kill Asher again, if they let him? Or what?

Meanwhile, Asher did not know what to expect, but of one thing he was certain: he trusted the Nin.

Then Teel saw the sash. It ran from Asher's right shoulder to his left side.

Squad leader. Asher Tye.

It should have brought him to a blinding rage. But strangely, it did not. Teel looked sideways, and saw his former squad looking at him. On Ran's face there was pity. On Clemmy's, confusion. On Rasha's, nothing at all.

And on Tawna's face, there was fear.

He looked back at the Nin Tova and Asher Tye. And from his mind, he felt an enormous load rise and scatter away.

"You are not dead," he said to Asher in wonder.

Just then, Rashid Kalani came running into the arena. The faintest ripple went through the group. All knew that Kalani was watch commander that hour of the day. Why had he left his post in Control, where instruments constantly scanned the planet and its near space?

Quickly he whispered something to the Nin. She stiffened, and wheeled away from Teel toward the crowd. "Code five," she said loudly.

There was the briefest hesitation, and then their training took hold. The room erupted into chaos. In seconds, everyone was gone.

The Warrior Planet was under attack.

# Interlude

With the suddenness of the blink of an eye, enemy starships burst into the Guild of Thieves' starspace. One hundred fifty-three ships poured out of interspace, and within an hour, the mining colony was encircled and cut off.

The moment the ships had appeared, the colony tried to burst a tachyonic message to the Warrior Planet, but the invaders had already cast a net of static around the mining world. But the colony sent a backup—a tiny robot probe. It was so small, and so positioned on the far side of the colony planet from the incoming police ships, that its existence was never suspected. It blinked out of normal space and disappeared, emerging sixteen hours later in close proximity to the Warrior Planet.

Then it broadcast its holographic warning, on a radio wave that would have taken three years to travel the distance from the mining colony to the purple planet in real space. And a moment later, it blew itself into pieces the size of dust.

For the police had found Kerla Cwan. And she had betrayed the Thieves.

# Chapter 21

They had traced her from her fistfight on Greystoke to the gambling world of Glitz, where she had apparently kept a pension fund embezzler from losing eighty million credits, then turned him into the police, saving retirees on one planet their food and housing money. Then Cor-Reed had caught the scent of the Digger, elusive as it was, and was able to trace the two of them through the spaceport onto a common shuttle to the nearby world of Clamour, where native animals defended themselves and killed one another with gigantic blasts of sound. The human bubble cities could not entirely dampen the uproar from the swarming life outside, so Cor-Reed had spent a difficult three months trying to trace the two, and after a particularly bad blast from outside, had lost the hearing in one ear for a week. Then he had found that the Digger had disappeared again, but Kerla Cwan had signed up through a travel agent for an outbound yacht headed for Pommel with intermediate stops at lesser pleasure worlds. Hoping that Cwan had some target on the yacht that would keep her on it all the way to Pommel, Cor-Reed had commandeered the fastest private starspeeder in the system and had headed straight for Pommel. He did not guess that she was on her way through Pommel to Caldott to rejoin the Digger. If he had, he would have waited until both were together, and then tried to take them.

He, and a dozen police, had waited for her as her shuttle landed. The police thought that she was an industrial spy from one of Pommel's competing vacation planets—Cor-Reed had arranged for that. Cor-Reed had held her mind closed and prevented her from using her Skill. And so she was taken.

"All I know is that there is this rock colony, see, around a red giant sun, and somewhere nearby is the Warrior Planet, I swear to you," Kerla whimpered at the grim police faces around her. Cor-Reed stood in Shadow as they tortured her body, and listened. For two exhausting days now he had held her mind closed and prevented her from using it against the police. Otherwise, she would have walked right out of the police trap, and left them scratching their heads in bewilderment.

When four hugely muscled human women and one equally muscled man took her into a dank little room full of scalpels and needles and matches and knives, he followed. He watched with disinterest; it was necessary, he thought, for her mind was powerful, despite its lack of full training, and he had not been able to break through even yet.

They tortured her. Through her haze of pain, he went into her mind and started to dump it out in front of them. The barriers were down for the briefest moment.

But she felt him doing it, and screamed. She threw up powerful mental walls, and Cor-Reed realized that she could still stop him cold.

"Get out of my mind, wizard," she yelled, struggling crazily in the chair in which she was lashed, eyes scanning wildly around the room. The five torturers looked at her in amazement.

"Where are you?" she yelled. "Take off the Cloak,

you . . ." Her powerful, undisciplined mind was struggling against his, and he put all his strength into a mental probe that he then threw into her like a spear.

For a moment, it broke through the barriers and she heard him. Instantly, she was quiet.

"Ah, Cor-Reed, is it?" she muttered, eyes less wild now. "The fright-wig One's pet. If I tell them about Tye, this thing will stop, is that it?"

The torturers were standing back from her, trying to figure out what she was talking about.

"And then what?" she continued, her voice rising. "The thieves have treated me right. The October . . . WOULD HAVE ME ERASED!"

And then, as if her pain were not there, she aimed a blow at him. It was like a mental kick, with pointed needle toes. It pierced through his blocks and numbed him, drained him, staggered him. But he had been trained for years longer than she, and his mind instinctively reeled away from the attack, wrapping itself in a tiny ball as hard as a diamond.

Then, suddenly, he thrust that ball outward, and its hardness shattered her needles and drove against her mind.

The torturers moved in.

Later, Cor-Reed knew that he could not have broken her down if her body had not been in such agony. The waves of pain, inflicted by experts, had broken her concentration at last. She had been tough, he thought; the pain had been gigantic. His rodent face rippled briefly as he remembered the blast he had encountered when he had finally entered her mind. He had her then, in the end, and he emptied her.

And then, once he had everything, he knew that he could not risk letting her, Skilled, loose again. So . . .

The mental hammer blow that he delivered could not be seen by the torturers; they believed for the rest of their lives they themselves had killed her.

\* \* \*

He beamed a message to the October One, who instantly ordered the appropriate October to mount a probe to the world of the Diggers. The Other had said that Diggers' Power was inconsequential, and yet here was one who could release an Apprentice from the Psychic Probe. Was this single Digger a mutant of some kind, or was the entire race a danger? Few Diggers traveled among the stars, she knew already, and there were not enough of them to account for the failed missions. But with the missing failed Apprentices . . . Perhaps that was one of the few Skills that this Digger race did have—the ability to intervene in and overturn Erasure. No, she had to find Tye for another reason now; for Tye would lead her to this single, pestilential Digger.

The "miners" were trained members of the Guild of Thieves. They sent out their probe to warn the Warrior Planet, and then, with fierce efficiency, they evacuated their colony into the fourteen Guild cruisers and vanished into interspace. The entire operation took forty-four minutes. They did not go to the Warrior Planet; if it too were under attack, they could accomplish nothing there except capture. Instead, they headed for the first fall-back planet in the Nin's intricate safety plan.

Cor-Reed had gone from Pommel to Caldott, and there he studied the star charts, looking for the lonely mining world that Kerla Cwan had described. There were one hundred fifty-three that superficially matched, but most were in isolated regions of the galaxy outside of the human sector. Fifteen had been possibles, but after seeing starship records of the number of visitors to those worlds, Cor-Reed had picked the one with the fewest. Then he had "persuaded" the lord high commissioner to send out this expeditionary force. The admiral himself had been sent, and with him in his flagship, in Shadow, went Cor-Reed.

The police ships found an empty planetoid, riddled with mine holes that would take days to explore. There were records encoded onto the planet's computer memory, but they seemed to deal mostly with mine inventory. There were no people, no papers, no telltale signs of the nearby Warrior Planet. And there were no minds for Cor-Reed to explore. Yet this was the key, he thought; why else had the miners fled?

He should have, he now realized, reached out and stunned all the minds that he had sensed on the colony, before they had gone into interspace. He had not done so to avoid revealing himself to the police. Now he wondered if he had blown any chance of finding the Warrior Planet.

Yet Kerla had said that the planet was "nearby" the mining colony. "Nearby" could mean one parsec or a hundred in this vast ocean of stars that is called the galaxy, and this region was densely populated with stars.

But somehow, he believed that nearby meant just what it said. There were no likely candidate planets among the moon-sized or smaller debris that encircled this red giant sun of the mining colony. But there were five or six stars within four light years that he had the Skill to probe.

Sitting in the admiral's chair, while the admiral himself wheeled about on the planetoid, he put the Cloak around him and looked at the starcharts that the flagship obligingly called up for him.

Then, gathering his strength, he sent his mind outward.

The probe's message triggered Code Five, yellow alert, on the Warrior Planet. It meant that hostile starships were in the immediate region. It was just short of Code Six, full battle stations, red alert, and Code Seven, invasion.

Asher brought his squad at a full run to the escape ship near the little museum where the disintegrators and other artifacts were kept. Their job was to check the readiness of the escape ship, and then load it with contents of the museum. Throughout the underground burrows of the purple world, squads of warriors were closing off elevators to the surface, checking and reshielding all sources of heat or electromagnetic radiation that might give them away, and loading other escape ships with the vital records of the Guild. The Nin had long foreseen that there was no point in resisting a full police attack, should it ever come. The Guild was not based on advanced weaponry, but on one-on-one encounters, sleight-of-hand, trickery. To resist a police attack, with its gravitational cannon that could shatter a planet, and its endless squads of men and aliens armed with energy blasters that could melt a mountain, made no sense at all. If an attack became imminent, the Guild would climb into its escape ships, blast through the tunnels and, far from the underground warrens, pop to the surface, flash through the thin atmosphere, and disappear into interspace. They would join the mining refugees at the first, second, or third fall-back planet, and then drive to the world they had long since selected as a likely candidate for a new Warrior Planet.

The plan was perfect. But it had not considered the possibility that an October Adept might be working in league with the police.

It took Cor-Reed seven hours to scan the first nearby star. The effort left him exhausted. He no longer sat in the odd-shaped chair that the wheeled admiral had returned to occupy. Now he was in an unused stateroom, lying on the gigantic bed, staring blindly upward, touching worlds, moons, and planetary garbage with his mind.

The first was a system with a giant yellow star, a white dwarf, and a looping neutron star too small to do the gravitational damage it might otherwise have done to the system's planets. Planets . . . eighty-nine of them, a staggering number, and only a few outright impossibilities. Those were the gas giants, on which human beings never ventured. But there were dozens of rocky worlds like the Earth, further dozens of icy worlds, and even one water world. There were hothouse worlds that human technology could overcome, especially if buried underground. And he had to play his mind over every one, probing beneath the ground, casting about for ships, sniffing for heat where there should have been none, or coolness or water where it was not likely.

It was precise, maddening, detailed, tiring work. When Cor-Reed mentally fingered the last cavern in the outermost planet of any consequence in the system, he drew his mind back into himself and entered a dazed trance near to sleep. Yet he had three more systems to check.

At length, wearily, he floated his thoughts up to those of the admiral and looked in.

The Chait, he saw, was frustrated. He had expected a grand campaign against hostile, piratelike forces. Instead, he had found a ball of metallic rock riddled like Swiss cheese, and his soldiers engaged in a long and futile exploration of miles and miles of empty mine tunnels.

But he would wait it out. Perhaps they would find something, some clue to the insidious Guild of Thieves. There was no other way.

Cor-Reed calculated that that gave him another two days. Good. He dropped into an exhausted sleep.

He came awake four hours later, somewhat refreshed. He thought about the October One, waiting in baleful impatience on her world. She had pushed him hard to find Kerla or Asher Tye, in a way that he had not seen before. For the first time, he had felt as if he had been treated as a servant of some kind, and he did not like it. Yet he also knew of the inexplicable disruptions in the October Adepts' missions, and the insults to the Guild's reputation that were even now making their way among the important beings of the galaxy, the beings of business and profession and politics.

It seemed to be making the October One impatient,

even worried. The idea of a Third Force, beyond the October and the thieves, seemed to haunt her.

Perhaps, Cor-Reed thought, we have had a mental monopoly on wizardry too long. It has made us prickly and sensitive and afraid.

Wearily, Cor-Reed cast his mind outward again. Ah . . . the next sun had only a dozen planets, and five of them were gas giants. There were a few large moons to worry about, but the task would be much easier than the first planetary system had been.

One of the worlds had life. It was a methane planet, and on its cold shores hulking shapes moved soddenly among the ochre vegetation. Each mind was about as advanced as a slug's.

Cor-Reed moved on.

Another planet had life, too. It was an oxygen-water world, and it not only had life, it was teeming with it. On every square inch of its surface something was living, crawling, floating, oozing, or just sitting there.

Inside, Cor-Reed groaned. The world was like a mental jammer. There were so many thoughts there that he could not fully probe all of them. A clever Adept could shield a large group of thinking beings, to make them seem as animals. Cor-Reed would have to sample a wide range of minds on this world, before he could be relatively convinced that none of them were Warriors.

Two dominant life forms, each of similar intelligence, apparently battled there. They were somewhat above a Cro-Magnon, perhaps. One was on five legs, and the other flew on leather wings. Cor-Reed saw fearsome battles and felt blasts of pain that shook him, but he scanned grimly.

The effort took nearly five hours before he was satisfied. He had found nothing.

The Chait admiral was showing signs of impatience. Cor-Reed drew back from his mind and decided to visit the third system immediately. He might have to coerce the admiral into staying around this region, but for now, he wanted to stay out of the wheeled being's thoughts as long as possible.

So he sent his mind outward to the next system, a routine setup with white-yellow sun and thirty-two worlds.

He came a whisker from detecting the probe as it flashed into a million pieces. It had been just sixteen hours since the police attack on the mines. On the Warrior Planet, Code Five had just begun.

The Adept's mind touched the planets, one by one, in the quick preliminary scan, rejecting the gas giants and identifying the likeliest worlds. Wearily he began his careful checking, from the outermost planetary bodies inward. It was five hours before he reached the planet of purple trees.

# Chapter 22

For a while, Asher's squad worked feverishly, cleaning out the museum and loading it into the escape ship. It was hard, careful work. Each museum piece was irreplaceable, especially the disintegrators; they saved them for last, so that they could unload them first when the time came. Everything else they lifted with care from the glass cases and placed in boxes filled with plastic down. Once the lid was closed, each box could have been dropped off a three-hundred-story building without even jarring the contents, so shock-absorbing was the packing material.

"Turn one of those babies on," Ran said as they worked, pointing to one of the disintegrators still in the glass cases, "and they'd have to vacuum up our atoms before they could bury us."

"Even worse," Rasha chimed in with a kind of unholy glee. "Without any control, the disintegrator would disintegrate straight down. Gravity would pull it toward the core of the planet. When it broke through the mantle, the molten center of the planet would erupt out through the hole the thing was making. This whole place would become one gigantic volcano."

The others frowned at him. The thought was mind-boggling.

"Let's not turn one of the babies on, then," Asher suggested. They all thought it was a good idea.

It took them six hours. From time to time, Rashid or the Nin herself would pass by and tell them how well they were doing, and they were in constant contact with Control via a holographic transceiver.

Rasha worked now in utter silence. Clemmy did twice the work of anyone. Tawna worked absently, her mind somewhere else. Ran joked and sang and cheered them all on. Asher gave orders, which they all obeyed.

The squad was one short.

"Rashid," Asher asked one time as he was passing through. "What happened to Teel? I lost track of him when that Code Five took us out of the amphitheatre."

He frowned. "Don't know; wish did. Somehow slipped out in uproar; somewhere in tunnels. Roller squad after him."

Asher saw Tawna listening closely, and for the briefest instant he felt jealousy.

"If he come, take him," Rashid said, "or, if must, kill him."

"Just the disintegrators and we're done," Asher said at last. He surveyed the work with satisfaction. The museum was empty, save for its glass cases and the deadly machines. The escape ship was well packed, systems checked, ready for flight.

From time to time, Asher saw Tawna looking up the empty corridor toward the larger part of the underground complex. On her face there was conflict. Asher thought he knew why. She had been watching Teel closely during those last moments in the amphitheatre.

She had seen that there was something still there. She had seen the twisting unravel a little.

"Tawna," Asher said. "I . . ."

At that moment, something touched Asher's mind. It was faint at first, far away, but there was something in the flavor of it that made him forget Tawna and everything else.

It was a mental probe of some kind. It was nearing the Warrior Planet, poking around its neighboring planets and moons, looking for something. It had disturbed the mental background that Asher, like any near-Initiate, had been taught to feel from moment to moment, like a body sensing the temperature of the air.

It was not yet aware of Asher, or of the minds moving under the purple planet, any more than someone splashing in a lake is aware of what his waves are hitting on the other shore, or of the fish beneath. Its own mental background was far away. But the stronger and closer its probing came, the greater the danger they were in.

"Asher, what's wrong?" Tawna asked. The others heard the tone of her voice, and came over nearby. Asher's eyes held the blankness of inner sight.

"I sense . . ." he said to them in his lowest voice, his eyes still unfocused, speaking in a monotone, "I sense some kind of mental presence outside. It is . . . looking . . . for . . .

"Us. . . ."

"What is it?" Tawna asked, grabbing at his sleeve. Ran, better trained, turned to the transceiver and called up the Nin.

"Go ahead," she said, flickering into three-dimensional view. Behind her, dimly seen, was another of the escape ships. Ghiuliducs were moving back and forth from storerooms into the ship.

"Asher Tye senses something . . ." Ran began. Asher threw up his hands and clutched at his head.

"I've got to try!" he said, almost screaming. "But I don't know enough . . ."

He had been shown, once, how to disguise the aura of intelligent thought to look like the thoughts of animals. But the Power needed was enormous, and it took great Skill to shield that draining of Power from the probe of another mind.

For a moment, Asher's eyes cleared, and he saw the Nin's image, standing between the squad members.

"We are being sought by a mind of great Skill," he said shakily. He reached out a hand to her.

"October?" she asked grimly.

"It has to be," Asher said. "We need the Digger!"

"He is off-planet, Asher Tye," the Nin said. "Can you shield us?"

"Ahhh. It moves closer, closer. I must try. But there are things I don't know . . ." Asher sank to his knees, arms held outward, trembling. "I will try," he said, his voice muffled now as he held his head between his forearms, and sank his forehead to the floor.

Pushing all fear aside, he brought his Skill into plan and, delicately, as if he were moving around a cat and trying not to awaken it, he spread a mental net around the underground of the Warrior Planet. Power flowed into him like oil, feeding upward and outward, as if it itself were magma from the core of the planet. As lightly as touching a feather to an eyeball, he deflected all intelligent thought back into itself, so that all that was left were animal radiations of hunger and fatigue and contentment and fear.

The mental probe left the planet's nearest moon, and came downward.

It hovered over the whipping trees, and the waters, and the bare spots of the planet. Asher closed himself off to it, letting not even a faint hint of intelligence escape from the blanket that he had cast over the planet.

But Cor-Reed was an Adept of the October World.

"Why, Asher Tye," his thought thundered suddenly into Asher's brain, "would so many animals be clustered underground?"

Asher clawed his way to his feet, and staggered back.

"Cor-Reed," he screamed. Then his eyes caught those of the Nin. "The October—it's aware of us!"

And then Cor-Reed caught him with an energy bolt of mental Power, and he tried to throw up a Shield. But he had been distracted by the need to alert the Nin. The squad rushed forward to catch him as his body sagged.

"All call," the Nin said. To the squad, it seemed as if nothing had happened, but now her image was in all areas of the underground, and every warrior could see her.

"Code Six," she said.

Cor-Reed threw all caution away. This was his chance to take Asher Tye, but the Warrior Planet was sixteen hours away via the illogical pathways of interspace. If the thieves evacuated before his squadron could get there . . .

He wheeled out of the stateroom in the guise of the admiral himself, knocking over two Chasers as he rushed blindly up to the bridge of the flagship.

"Set coordinates eight-oh-seven-six-nine-six break three-eight-one. Interspace, now. Nova priority—do it!"

The communications officer, a red-haired human, gaped.

"But admiral! I was just talking with your image from the mines. How . . ."

"You donkey!" the "admiral" screamed. He wheeled up to the officer and stimulated certain nerve synapses in the red-haired brain. It was as if someone had thrown a cup of raw bleach into his face. The man staggered back against his console, choking and clawing at his eyes. Tears streamed downward.

"Take this maniac away!" Cor-Reed screamed to the security officer on duty.

The first officer watched the scene, gaping.

"Interspace!" the "admiral" shrilled. "Computer, flag override, voice ID, all ships, interspace now!"

The ship's computer verified the admiral's voice, and linked with the master computers on all the squadron's ships. In perfect synchronization, one hundred fifty-three starships spun out of orbit and headed for the interspatial jump point less than an hour away.

On the mining world, the real admiral, hearing loud shouts, wheeled out of the mine entrance that he had made his headquarters and looked up. The hard dots in the sky that were his ships were leaving formation and dwindling away.

The Chait ranted and raved into his holographic communicator. He sent order after order into the void. But Cor-Reed had put the squadron on communications blackout. The incoming signals were recorded and ignored.

Then Cor-Reed did the one thing that neither Asher nor the Nin had ever suspected could be done.

On the Warrior Planet, the squad was clustered around the still form of Asher Tye. He was breathing strongly and steadily. But nothing could wake him, not shaking or slaps or water to the face. Finally, they tried a drug like caffeine, injected with an air sprayer into his arm. It seemed to do nothing.

Tawna looked up and saw the Nin striding down the corridor toward them.

"We can't awaken him," she told her. The Nin frowned.

"The October knows where we are," the Nin said. "I am going to order full evacuation. We can't . . . ahhhhhh!"

A half-scream erupted from her throat. She saw Tawna go down, and behind her Rasha and Ran. Clemmy reeled as if someone had slapped her hard.

The wave of Cor-Reed's mental blow receded, and the Nin shook herself. Clemmy was on her knees, moving her head from side to side.

The Nin flicked on the holographic unit and, holding herself against one of the glassene walls, spoke into it:

"Code Seven," her voice croaked. "Full . . ."

And then Cor-Reed's mental blow hammered again. It was as if someone had landed a hundred-pound sack of flour on the Nin's brain. Clemmy fell as if struck by an axe. The Nin felt the floor of the corridor come up and hit her knees, then her shoulder as she twisted instinctively.

All over the underground, activity was stopping, the Nin thought desperately. Machines, without direction, were grinding to a halt. Rollers and Ghiuliducs and Therds and humans were out of action. Somewhere in the corridors, Teel too must be down.

The Nin clawed her way to her knees. The immense weight on her brain was lifting slightly. If only . . .

Then Cor-Reed hit again. The Nin never felt the floor as it struck her on the cheek, splitting it open and sending a tiny trickle of blood downward, to congeal in a little pool.

For a moment, the "admiral's" form wavered out of focus, and Cor-Reed desperately brought it back again. No one on the bridge had noticed.

He had never attempted such an attack from so far away. Even now he had no way of knowing how long the warriors would be down. And now, as he mentally fingered the faint collective aura of the dormant warrior minds, he wondered if he had made a mistake. For he could not separate Asher Tye's aura out from the others as long as unconsciousness held. From his training, Tye might be more resistant to mental attack than the others. And the trouble was that the squadron was going into interspace—had to, to reach the Warrior Planet.

In interspace, his Power would be gone. He would not be able to reach outside the ship. For interspace involved the creation of a tiny artificial universe that then skimmed the surface of the larger one. By definition, there could be no linkages between one universe and another, of any kind, mental or not.

He sent another mental blow against the Warrior Planet, and another, as powerful as he could manage and still retain the admiral's shape. But he could not seem to send the minds deeper into blackness. They were too far away.

Cor-Reed had no other Skills he could draw on now. During all the search, he had assumed that he or another Adept would encounter Asher Tye when both were in the same solar system, and take him unaware. But sixteen hours away . . .

He sent out another bolt, and felt it curve back upon itself. Frantically he negated it, and saved the crew from the reflected blast.

The flagship had entered interspace.

# Chapter 23

Asher groaned and rolled over. For a long moment, he stared up at the glasslike ceiling, wondering where he was.

He looked sideways and saw Tawna's face only inches from his. Her eyes were closed, her lips half open. She was breathing slowly and steadily.

Asher stared at her, seeing the beauty even in his daze. But why . . .

He spun his head around and looked the other way. He saw the crumpled body of the Nin, powerful-looking even lying helpless on the floor. The Nin . . .

Asher sat up suddenly, and the tunnel reeled. He waited a moment, willing his brain to steady itself. It did so with amazing rapidity. In fact, the lucidity and speed of his thoughts startled him.

Now he saw all the other members of the squad, scattered around the floor where they had fallen.

Wha . . . ?

And then he realized what must have happened, and with the lightning reflexes that he had learned as a warrior, he threw a mental Shield around himself. Should an attack come now, he would not be unprepared.

Cor-Reed . . . his old teacher. Ferretlike in body, with the mind of a python.

In Tawna's hand, Asher saw something. He reached down and pulled the air sprayer away from her. He read its label, and suddenly knew why he was recovering so quickly. The caffeinelike drug was making his mind speed, as if he had swallowed eight cups of coffee. It would keep him awake for a long time, now that he had shrugged off the effects of the mental assault.

He stepped over to the Nin and shot a dose into her, then leaped backward, guessing what might happen. The Nin stirred, and then Asher found himself facing the naked blade of a samurai sword.

"It's you. Asher Tye," the Nin said then, and dropped the blade. Asher saw it waver as the Nin gained full control of her body, and then the blade disappeared into its scabbard. Asher was suddenly struck by a certain gauntness in her face, around the cheekbones and eyes . . .

"The October attacks have stopped," Asher said to her. "I can sense no psychic presence in the solar system now."

But the Nin was scanning the underground with her holographic transceiver. Everywhere she looked, she saw bodies lying helplessly.

"Yet they know where we are," she muttered grimly. "Why this recovery time?"

Asher knew the answer almost at once.

"Interspace. Cor-Reed must be in interspace!" He looked upward, as if he could see through the ceiling of the passageway. "When he comes out, he'll batter again, and he'll be right on top of us."

Then the Nin asked the question. "Can you shield us, Asher Tye?" She regarded him narrowly. Only a few days before had she taken the Skill-stopping drug out of the water supply. And now, all she had worked for—her entire Guild, the war against October and the real thieves of the galaxy—rested on the shoulders of this young man. There was, she knew from the miner's automated probe, a full police squadron with the October Adept.

"I don't know," Asher said slowly. "He caught me by surprise last time. The Digger taught me . . . I don't know. It all depends on how long it lasts."

"Yet if we can be in interspace before the wizard comes out . . ." The Nin grabbed at Asher's hand. There was a large supply still left in the air sprayer.

"Give them all a dose," the Nin ordered. "Everyone you can. Do it squad by squad. When yours awakens, send them out to awaken another squad, and have both squads waken others. It won't take us long to wake up the whole underground. And when everyone is awake, immediate evacuation. How long do we have?"

"He was on the miner's world? That's sixteen hours away . . . add one to get to the jump point . . ." Asher consulted his wrist computer. "How long ago did I go down?" he asked it.

As if someone had thrown a bucket of paste over him, his face drained of color. He looked up at the Nin, and in his eyes there was . . . fear? No, he felt no fear, not anymore. Nor anger.

Grimness. Desperation.

"I went down sixteen hours and eighteen minutes ago," he said quietly. The Nin turned and ran up the corridor, pulling an air sprayer out of the medical kit on her belt.

Asher bent down and, one by one, woke up his squad. Quickly, he gave them the orders, and with the precision of trained soldiers, they obeyed. They were gone down the corridor in moments, Clemmy leading them.

But Asher stayed behind. He had to prepare himself for the attack.

It came twelve minutes later. The squadron burst out of interspace, and as it did, Cor-Reed sent a powerful blast against the Warrior Planet. It rammed up against it, and then bounced away.

The planet was Shielded.

As the Chait admiral, Cor-Reed ordered a full power dive through the planetary system toward the purple world that they now saw on their view screens. Dimly he sensed the minds on it, and knew that it was not evacuated. But even as that thought crossed his mind, the flagship told him:

"Escape ship leaving planet's surface."

It was much too far away for the guns of the squadron. Cor-Reed reached out his mind to blank out the minds aboard the other ship. But even as he did so, something interfered with his concentration, and as he regained it, the escape ship shot out of the atmosphere and immediately entered interspace.

Had it been a larger ship, it would have blown apart trying such a maneuver so close to a planetary mass. But since it was so small, it probably had made it.

"Another escape ship . . ." Cor-Reed had seen it on the screen. He made another half-hearted attempt, but his thought was again deflected and that ship too entered interspace.

"Asher Tye, I taught you!" Cor-Reed thundered mentally. "I know everything you can do, and everything you can't do. And one thing you cannot do is resist me!"

The Shield tightened, if anything. Cor-Reed gathered all his strength, reached deeply into Power, and shot a razor-sharp bolt of mental force against Asher's Shield.

Lying on his back within the museum escape ship, still within the bowels of the planet, Asher felt his mind go numb. He fought desperately to maintain the vast Shield that he held around the planet. His vision blurred, but he closed his eyes and held on. Cor-Reed gathered himself for another blow.

"You cannot win, Asher Tye!" Cor-Reed thundered at him. The mental words were getting through to Asher; the Adept could sense it. But instead of the overwrought, emotional Asher Tye that he once had known, he felt a gigantic calmness. Asher wasted no energy in forming a reply. He put all his Skill, all his knowledge of the Power, into the Shield.

The planet was emptying rapidly now as squad after squad boarded their ships and shot down the escape tunnels. But Asher's squad was still out. It had awakened the last warrior way on the other side of the underground, and was now racing back through the tunnels toward the museum and escape.

Cor-Reed urged his squadron faster, and sent another blow against Asher Tye. He felt the Shield wobble, then reform, and felt an instant of triumph. Asher Tye was strong in his icy calmness, yet he was not even an Initiate. Cor-Reed struck again.

The Nin entered the museum ship and saw Asher's body tremble from the blow. She herself felt the faintest edge of it, and the power behind it staggered her. She bent down and whispered into Asher's ear, as if sound would break his concentration.

"In two minutes, this will be the only ship left on the planet," she whispered. "Just a little more . . ."

Eighty light-years away, the Digger became aware of Power ebbing and flowing. He cast his mind outward, and felt the rage of Cor-Reed, the stoic resistance of Asher Tye.

The October One sensed it, too. She tried to send mental help, added Power, to Cor-Reed, but he was too far away, and never trained in long-distance linkages. She called upon the ten thousand Octobers, their thoughts linking across the vastness, light-years of emptiness and dust and scattered photons of energy. She had always kept the knowledge of linkage across interstellar space away from her trainees, for then they could never rise against the October Ones. Yet now, she wished she had taught at least one. If Cor-Reed could feel the attempt, could take some of the Power that they offered and use it . . .

But he was concentrating on the attack on Asher
Tye.

Asher was almost dizzy from the drug. He had diffi-
culty in concentrating his Skill, in focusing the Shield
around the minds in the escape ships until they were
freed by the veil of interspace. The police ships were
almost upon them now; soon he would have to shield
against weapon attacks as well as mental ones.

Another ship escaped, and for a moment he felt a
kind of void. Then he did a quick scan of the planet,
and felt a burst of relief. There seemed to be no other
minds left in the underground, except for the flickers of
his own squad and a sleeping numbness that must be
Teel, whom the Rollers had not found. The hard part
was over. With so many fewer minds to cover, he could
draw his Shield inward and concentrate it. He began
doing it.

"Just one more ship," the Nin whispered. "And then
us."

Asher's eyes flew open. "One more?" he said, his
Shield wavering. "Where? Where? I sense no minds . . ."

An escape ship was thundering down its tunnel. Inside, two warrior Therds crouched over the controls.
The Police ships were very close.

"I can't sense them!" Asher said frantically. He grasped
the Nin by the shoulder, sitting partly up, his overstim-
ulated brain casting wildly over the planet.

The Nin, puzzled, said: "There are two warriors
aboard, both Therds. Why . . ."

"Therds!" Asher screamed. "I can't sense Therds."

His mind, spinning from the drug, tried to throw up
a planetwide Shield again. But it was still tentative and
incomplete as the Therd ship broke cover and blasted
through the atmosphere toward the escape point.

Far above, the lead police ship detected it. Automati-
cally, the gravity cannon locked onto it and, with the
incredible rapidity of computer thought, burst a warp-
ing bolt of gravitational force toward the escaping ship.

"Escape point, six seconds," the Nin breathed, watching the holography. Asher tried to find the ship, tried to place a Shield around it that would deflect gravity. But he was frantic, and Cor-Reed chose that moment to attack again. Asher instinctively threw up a desperate defense around the minds he could feel. "Five. Four. Three . . ." the Nin's voice said.

And the gravity bolt hit. The Therds felt space twist around them, and saw, for the briefest moment before blackout, the ship rip apart as if it were a wet paper bag. They would have screamed in their way, but air was gone and there was nothing left to carry the sound.

And then they died. Tumbling crazily, they and the fragments of their ship shot past the escape point and disappeared into the darkness and debris of the planet's near-space.

The Nin sat back on her haunches, her mouth open a little, eyes blank. Asher staggered to his feet, as if he could do something, anything, to reverse the last sixty seconds. Outside, some of the squad members had returned, and they could hear them moving.

The Nin turned her eyes toward Asher Tye, and in them was such pain that Asher could not hold her gaze, was forced to look down at the floor.

"Asher Tye," she said numbly. Then, seeming to gather herself, she stood up, fluidly, and seemed to flex her body in parts, one by one, as if to make certain it was still there. Then she stepped over and, incredibly, took Asher by the hand and forced him to look into her eyes.

"Without you, Asher Tye," she said carefully, every word a tool, "I would have lost the entire Guild to the police. Now I have lost two warriors, and we will mourn them. But the Guild lives."

"They could have been effective weapons against October," Asher said dully. "For the October Skills could not sense them."

"Indeed?" the Nin said, calculation in her eyes. Learning, always learning . . .

Asher could find nothing more to say. Nor did he dare cease his mental war with Cor-Reed. There had come a blast of gloating triumph a moment before, and that moment had been enough to consolidate his Shield again, back around the few minds left on the planet.

They stepped out of the ship into the museum corridor. The squad was there, except for one. Tawna . . .

"Where is she?" the Nin demanded. Asher stood silent, still shaken by the death of the Therds. Above them, police ships ringed the planet, and twenty-four of them shrieked down through the atmosphere toward the clearings above the underground.

"I believe," Ran said, "that she seeks Teel."

# Chapter 24

While Asher stayed at the entrance of the museum and fought Cor-Reed, the others ran toward the spot where he directed them as he sensed Tawna's flickering mind. They found her deep in one of the least-used tunnels of the underground. She was cradling the head of Teel, who lay as if dead on the dusty glassene floor.

She looked up as they came. "My air sprayer is empty," she said in a matter-of-fact voice. "Please give me one of yours."

Rasha moved forward, but Nin Tova held out her arm. "No," she said. "Leave him be. We cannot have a rebel wide awake among us now."

Tawna's control trembled.

"No. You can't leave him here like this," she said shakily. "Please . . ."

"I can, but I will not." She motioned to the squad. "Carry him. Double-time, back to the museum. We will be lucky if we get there before the police."

There were sounds up above now—basso sounds of machinery and earth blasters. The walls of the underground trembled, and at one point, they felt the air move suddenly, then quiet again.

"They have breached the underground, but stopped

the air from leaving," Nin Tova said. "They would take us alive."

Their primitive weapons would be useless against the police, they all well knew, Their training was not for fighting modern firepower, but for honing the self for control, clearheadedness. One on one, they were each among the deadliest humans in the galaxy. Grouped against the police, they had no chance at all.

They heard movements up the corridors. They ran, carrying Teel by his shoulders, stumbling. Then the Nin picked him up and slung him over her back like a sack of potatoes. They all ran, and could scarcely keep up with the Nin and her burden.

They reached the museum corridor. Asher crouched on the floor, his eyes glazed.

"He comes. He comes!" Asher mumbled brokenly. Sweat beaded and plowed furrows on his brow.

"Put Teel in the ship," the Nin commanded. "Whatever is left in the museum stays. Pick up Asher and bring him along. It is time for us."

For a moment, Asher's vibrating mind shot to what was left in the museum. Tawna and Ran took Teel from the Nin and carried him into the ship. Rasha and Clemmy moved toward Asher. The Nin took a step up the corridor. Sound was there, close, close . . .

And then Cor-Reed was there. The Nin looked toward him, and froze. She knew him, this man. Indeed, images of him had haunted her sleep for three decades.

But he, she saw, did not recognize her. Perhaps there was some advantage in that. She dropped her hand, caressing her sword hilt. A boiling rage swept through her and out, leaving her mind as cold and centered as a pick in ice.

The Adept was at the front of a platoon of police, armored and blasters drawn. Behind the Nin, Rasha and Clemmy were holding Asher up.

The Green Flame. The mental bolts. The squeezing of the mind. All useless, Asher sensed, gazing at the wizened face of his teacher. *If I can shield these few humans for a few moments more, we might yet win.*

"Into the ship," Asher croaked, shaking off Rasha and Clemmy. The Nin glanced at him, and then forward again. Cor-Reed scowled and, raising his arms toward the sky, said: "You willll. . . . obeeeeeeyyyyyyyyy. . . . mmmmmmeeeeeeeeeeeeeeeeee!" It was the Voice, the pied-piper trick that resonated in the minds of humans, leading them to obey, forcing them to obey . . .

But the four humans heard nothing. Asher had blocked their hearing.

He gestured, and Clemmy and Rasha stepped toward the ship. Cor-Reed raised his arms again, and Asher became aware that he was appearing as something else to the soldiers behind him. *That alone was taking some of his Power away. Yet he was a full Adept, and Asher not even Initiated.*

"I sought you these months," Cor-Reed said thunderously. "I find you at last, and you must be mine. By the Power of the October, you must be mine!"

Asher heard him, not with his ears, but with his mind. Like a nutcracker with an almond, Cor-Reed squeezed at Asher's Shield. The air began to shake, and the soldiers behind Cor-Reed quailed. Asher's Shield began to become visible as a shimmering barrier of force; tendrils of white power shot from Cor-Reed's eyes and deflected off it. Clemmy turned and pushed Rasha. They stumbled into the airlock of the ship.

With a cry that held all the fury of a lifetime of hidden hate, the Nin whipped out her sword and leaped at the Adept. Startled, he drew back, his attack against Asher vanishing all at once, and nearly caught the blade in his throat. It was only at the last possible instant that he managed a barrier between his body and the weapon.

Enraged, he beckoned at the police, and to his surprise felt her press forward. She was rigid, every muscle in her whipsaw body straining, focusing in warrior fashion on a single point before her, three inches inside the wizard's throat. The point cut into the barrier as if it

were slowly entering hardened rubber. Asher cast a
cloud of darkness over the police, so that they could not
see to aim their weapons. He sensed a babbling confusion among them. Cor-Reed took another step backward, the blade following him. He put more Power into
the barrier, and felt his rearward image as the Chait
admiral slip away. But the soldiers, in darkness, could
not see it go. He tried to jab at her mind, but to his
amazed horror found that her concentration was total
and as impenetrable as a neutron star.

And then Cor-Reed twisted the barrier with a sharp
wrenching jolt. As if it had been made of ice, the sword
snapped off at the hilt and the blade clattered to the
ground.

The Nin stepped back, reaching for the dagger she
carried in her belt.

*Nin!* Asher said quietly, directly into her mind. *You
must go to the ship. If we have any hope of escape, you
must be in the ship.*

She hesitated. Cor-Reed, who had never faced raw
physical power such as the Nin had just displayed,
seemed berserk at the idea that it might have succeeded against him. Placing his palms outward, at right
angles to his body, he abandoned all simulation at the
Chait and put his effort into calling up the Green Flame.

It roared from his palms and spattered against Asher's
Shield, which had not wavered for a moment. Like
clicking a switch, Asher cracked off the cloud of darkness, and at the same time threw the Chait simulation
that he had reconstructed from Cor-Reed's mental ema-
nations to the doorway of the museum.

"In here!" the Chait admiral screamed, wheeling frantically inside. The confused police beheld an unknown
man right in front of them, blasting green fire at something that they could not see, for the fire itself obscured
it. But they had seen the admiral, and they were trained
to follow orders. In a pell-mell rush, they thundered
past Cor-Reed and poured into the museum.

"Clever!" shouted Cor-Reed. The Nin had reached

the hatchway and paused. Asher was taking one step at a time backward, his body shaking with the battle against Cor-Reed. "But your true love, Tawna the Warrior, loves someone else!"

It was the last thing Asher expected to hear, and it shattered his control for the briefest instant, because the Adept had called up the deepest part of him that felt pain. It was the fact that his mind had avoided thinking, but knew all the same. Tawna was the first one he had loved, had believed he had loved, and her loyalty to someone else had not been destroyed by anything that had happened. Cor-Reed, the master wizard, had sensed it all through the ragings of the past few hours, and now attacked him with it, and he was lost.

With the swiftness of one of the Nin's sword blows, Cor-Reed knifed through his Shield and cut the other humans off from him. Asher threw his mind against this new barrier, and could not penetrate it. He had held a planetary Shield against a full Adept, and now he knew in his desperation that it was far, far easier to maintain a Shield than to break through it. And Cor-Reed could now move in on the Nin and the squad, reach into their untrained minds, order them to do anything . . .

A glow of triumph began to fill Cor-Reed's face, to spill over from his thoughts like candy melting over a boiling pot. Asher, wrapped at last in a Shield that covered himself alone, cast frantically around for some weapon, any weapon, that he could use. But all his mental Skills were known by Cor-Reed, surpassed by him in many cases, and nothing the Digger had taught him was really new, just strengthenings of what he knew already.

The soldiers were milling around in the museum room, and in a moment they would be pouring out into the corridor again, and . . .

The museum room.

And then Asher knew what he had to do. A little time ago, he had briefly blamed himself for the death of the Therds. But that had been the sheerest accident compared to what he now must do. And yet, if he gave Cor-Reed another moment of time, the wizard could kill Nin Tova and the squad with a single bolt of mental power.

So Asher reached with his mind. He entered one of the glass cases, sought for and found one of the flare-nosed machines resting there. Then he turned it on . . .

A sound such as no one had ever heard filled the underground. Sudden screams erupted from the museum and were cut abruptly off. The disintegrator field ballooned slowly outward as it powered itself up. It sucked the cases into atoms. Anyone looking toward it could see a black blankness as Asher's mind grasped it and held the iridium up. Air rushed explosively into it, for it was as if a complete vacuum had been created there, a vacuum that ate the air, sucked everything in. The soldiers tried to get away. Some huddled on the far side of the room, where there was no way to escape. Others rushed toward the doorway, trampling each other, but they could not get out, because the air was rushing through it like a hurricane. A body was picked up by the air stream and, with a final wail, blown backward into the void. And then another one. And another. One soldier triggered a blaster at the oval and lightning-flashed blackness, and saw the flame sucked away. Then he, screaming, was engulfed by it, and the disintegrating darkness grew larger.

The sound was so loud that they heard it directly in the brain. It needed no eardrums or nerves in between, for it shook the brain itself. Cor-Reed stumbled back against the corridor wall, trying to escape the force of the slipstream of air thundering down the corridor. His barrier went down; his mental attacks ceased abruptly. Asher lost sight of him as his own Shield went down, as the incredible sound ended all hope of coherent, directed thought.

The Nin had realized at once what was happening, however. Freed of Cor-Reed's power, she stepped forward, grabbed Asher under the armpits, and dragged him backward to the ship. She glanced up the corridor one last time, and through the howling wind around her, the whipping of her clothing as if physical bodies were rushing past her, she could see nothing of the wizard, nothing of the soldiers. Through the doorway of the museum room, she saw an awful expanding blackness into which the substance of the underground was being consumed. Even as she watched, it reached the doorway and devoured it, and her ears suddenly popped as more air was sucked away.

She threw herself then through the airlock and hit the button that sealed it. She knew that her warriors by now were at the controls of the escape ship waiting for the moment she and Asher entered, and she shouted: "Ignition!" The ship trembled; and then it tore away down the tunnel toward the faraway surface.

Asher released the disintegrator with his mind and fell back, gasping. The device, with nothing holding it up, fell suddenly downward, cutting through the planet's skin like butter. All over the underground, police were frantically running toward their entry points, not knowing what horror was raging down below, wanting only to get away from it. They were leaderless now, without immediate direction, for their admiral had disappeared in the chaos below.

In sixty seconds, the disintegrator had fallen 6,400 feet—over a mile—heading down toward the molten core of the planet.

Asher tried to find the Adept, but there was nothing there—a blankness, like the void in the disintegration field. Cor-Reed, dead? It could scarcely be believed.

At length Ran said: "Surface in four minutes."

They climbed into couches that opened out from the walls and strapped themselves in. Most ships did not need such protection, but they would be jumping into interspace close to a planetary mass. Asher devoted his attention to the next problem. He prepared a Shield against the weaponry of the police starships.

The escape ship burst from the ground and screamed into the atmosphere. It was detected immediately by the police. Violating custom, they fired grav cannon at it while it was still in the atmosphere. They used lasers and particle beam weapons. They threw every type of energy weapon they had at the tiny ship.

It all cascaded off and around it. Some bolts reached the planet's surface and caused devastation among the whipping trees. The rest flew harmlessly off into space.

And then Asher, exhausted, felt the Shield implode inward as if the October One herself were nearby and attacking. But he knew that such was not the case, this time. Instead, the little ship had wrapped a new universe around itself, a universe that was very small.

The ship had entered interspace.

# Chapter 25

"You passed out," Clemmy said. Asher looked up at her, as if through a fog. He seemed to be lying on his back. "When we went into interspace, you sort of looked around as if to make sure everything was okay, and then you were out as if someone had hit you with a hammer." The thin-faced girl touched him lightly on the jaw. "Without you, we would have been gone; those soldiers in the underground, the ships in the sky would have killed us." Clemmy was smiling, a soft kind of smile that Asher did not recall having seen before.

Asher shot upright suddenly. A vision had entered his mind. It was the vision of a purple planet shuddering, splitting, gouts of molten magma pouring through the splits—fire, desolation, cinders, and under it all, something sucking and sucking until nothing was left but a blackness eating itself.

He wiped his forehead with his hand, and both came away as wet as they had begun. Clemmy was looking at him with concern, a certain tenderness now on her narrow face.

"What's wrong, Asher?" she asked softly. Again she put her fingers on his cheek.

Asher looked around. He was in the cabin of the

escape ship, its only room save the head and storage. The other couches were gone, folded into the walls, and in their places were chairs. On the screen was the star-lined display of interspace.

The Nin was sitting in catlike relaxation in the pilot's chair, listening to the readouts. The rest of the squad was draped on chairs or pacing around the room. There was one other couch, and on it Teel slept, Tawna sitting by his side.

Asher looked at them, and felt something stab him inside, even as he felt Clemmy's touch on his face. And yet, it was done. Even if Teel were to die now, Tawna would never be mine, Asher thought. He would have to let the pain come, and then let it go. It would fade, and eventually the hurt would be only barely there.

He looked back at Clemmy, his eyes only inches from hers, and saw that she had been watching him closely, and that now there was relief of some kind in her eyes.

"How long . . ." Asher began, eyes not wavering from hers. She frowned.

"You were out seven hours," she said, and pulled away.

Ran hurried over to him and grasped his hand. "You saved our guts down there, Ash, old pal," he said, his eternal smile holding something new now. Asher realized with a start what he saw there.

It was respect.

"You can call me 'Your Squad Leadership,' " Asher said, smiling sourly. The image of the dying planet stayed in his mind.

"Oh, aye-aye, sir!" Ran laughed, coming stiffly to attention, shoulders thrown so far back that he seemed to be falling over backwards.

"Straighten up, you maggot," Asher barked, and Ran stiffened his head even further.

"Don't get cocky," the Nin said wryly without turning her head.

And then Ran did fall over backwards, and there was

a howl of laughter from everyone, even Tawna, and even Rasha, who had been sitting scowling in the farthest chair. All except Asher; he was seeing something else in his mind's eye.

"Enough!" the Nin said, still not looking at them. They all fell silent, knowing that it was not quite a reprimand, but that it had turned them back into warriors. The relief still stood in their minds like a giant puff, full of peace.

There was work ahead, as they set out to find the rest of the warriors and begin building again, on some new planet in another region of the galaxy.

As he sat up, it struck Asher that the Nin had, in a sense, lost everything when the police had found the Warrior Planet. Years of work had been destroyed in a single day. And yet she did not seem swayed by it. She sat as confidently as ever.

Still, it must bother her just a little, Asher thought.

And then he thought: maybe it doesn't! Maybe she had conquered her own flaw in her own way. Maybe she had learned to live in the present, looking into the future, with the past a lesson learned, but nothing to brood about.

It would be a very peaceful way to live, Asher thought; but in his mind, he saw the glare of the insides of a planet pouring out. Regrets would turn into lessons and no more. Worries would be short and then go away.

Asher's eyes caught Tawna's, and she looked at him, no expression in her face. Gone, he repeated to himself. A lesson learned . . .

He felt closed-in in this tiny universe. The mental feel was strange—just the minds he saw around him, and a deadness otherwise. He had felt interspace before, but never in such a small place. Maybe that accounted for the strangeness.

Then the Nin's voice came quietly, and Asher knew that the words were for him.

"It will eat a hole in the planet's middle," she said softly. "It will cause volcanoes here and there as the crust adjusts. If it were made of some infinitely durable substance, it would eventually swallow the planet up. But it is not. It is iridium, and it will not last beyond a day; it will eat itself up. The planet will survive."

The planet will survive . . . A weight seemed to rise.

He opened his mouth to speak, but the Nin's voice cut him off.

"Thirty seconds to exit," she said.

For a moment, the squad gaped. Then Ran, Tawna, and Clemmy hastily took their chairs. They had had no idea that the meeting place of the warriors would be reached so soon. But then interspace was bizarrely illogical. It could be days to the next-door neighbor planet, but hours to cross the galaxy.

This time they would be near no planetary mass, so the couches were not needed. They just sat and waited for the transition. Asher waited for the closed-in feeling to go away as they entered the wider universe.

The seconds ticked away, and then the Nin stiffened.

"There's something wrong," she said. "We've passed the exit point, and we're still in interspace!" The squad looked at each other. They had no experience with this.

The Nin spoke rapidly to the ship, and it answered just as rapidly.

"Something has translated all the numbers," the Nin said, wonder in her voice. "Something has caused some kind of underlay; the readouts say one thing, and mean something else. How can this be?"

A sense of dread was growing in Asher Tye. He looked around at the blank walls of the escape ship, and shot his mind here and there.

"We're locked into some alternate course," the Nin said. "I cannot free it. The computer will not obey me."

"No," said a voice, and they all looked wildly about. "It will obey only me." And as if stepping right out of the wall, Cor-Reed stepped out of Shadow.

Cor-Reed . . . here? With instant precision, Asher attacked him with Power, but it was no use. The Nin's hand was on her sword hilt, but she could not draw it.

Weapons lay useless under the hands of all the squad members as they strained for them, and could not move.

Cor-Reed had had seven hours of mind manipulation time. He had used it to disable them all. He was in absolute control, and knew it. Asher couldn't even raise a Shield.

Cor-Reed's evil gaze roamed the cabin. "Couldn't detect me at all, could you, Tye?" His pointed features twisted. "And you, warrior lady," he said to the Nin, coming up to her and planting his nose against hers, so that she drew back. "I ran right past you in Shadow as you stood in that airlock, and you stared stupidly at the disintegration and thought it was the wind."

Then they saw that Cor-Reed was holding a needler, and pointing it directly at the Nin. He was taking no chances that his mind would not be enough.

"Ah, yes, Tye," he said, turning his face away from the white-faced Nin. They were all as paralyzed as if encased in cement. "Ah, yes, Tye," the Adept said again. "It was a great trick, that disintegrator; I was not prepared for anything like it. I taught you well, Asher Tye. But in the end, I mastered you."

They all said nothing, just stared at him. In each mind was rapid activity. If Cor-Reed left any openings at all, someone would be there.

"And now," the Adept went on, his ratlike face settling into something approaching hatred, "you each have a date with my Master—especially you," he said, turning back to Nin Tova again. "You who have caused our Guild such trouble, you will die this day, I promise you. And you, Asher Tye," he snarled, coming back to him, "you who would have betrayed our secrets to this thieving Guild if you could, I promise you an Erasure that will leave you like a babbling idiot at best, if you live at all."

Asher strained at the mental bonds that enwrapped him, and there was not the slightest yielding in them. The Nin gathered her magnificent muscles and strained at the cords of mental power, and nothing happened there either. The Adept's smile was nasty. There was fear now in the eyes of the rest of the squad.

"The rest of you I will turn into Initiates," he hissed at them. "But first we will empty your mind of the memory of the Warrior Planet. Its skills you will retain, but how you got them, you will never know. You will be the warrior arm of the Subtle Guild to which I belong, and you will forget the Guild of Thieves, because it will be no more. Already I know from your minds the meeting place. With your leader dead and you Erased, I will send out a squad of my own, and they will be defenseless against the Power that we wield. There will be no Asher Tye to help them. They will join us, too, like muscle-bound carrots, the memory of the Guild of Thieves wiped from the face of the galaxy!"

They said nothing; they could say nothing. All their muscles, save those for breathing, were paralyzed. The computer beeped, and Cor-Reed raised one arm to the ceiling.

"And now," he said, like a magician pulling a rabbit out of a hat, "you have a date with Coldness, a date with Power. It is time for you to meet She who will one day be master of the galaxy. It is time to meet . . . October!" And like a veil parting, the escape ship blew itself out of interspace, and into the solar system of the October World.

Cor-Reed's theatrics had warned Asher just in time. Perhaps the Adept was slowing down. He should have knocked Asher out. As it was . . .

For the split second the ship made the transition out of interspace, Cor-Reed's Skill could not function, and in that instant Asher threw a Shield around himself. He could not protect the others, though he saw that the Nin's sword was half drawn before Cor-Reed's Power came down on her again. He had had time only to protect himself.

Cor-Reed turned on him, snarling, made as if to throw a mental bolt at him, and then paused.

"No," he said softly, "I will throw it at her." Tawna stood wide-eyed, still over Teel. "The One wants the Nin, but of this girl she cares nothing," Cor-Reed mused aloud. Asher felt him gather himself for the strike.

"No!" Asher cried. He hesitated for the barest instant, with emotions he only vaguely understood rising up in him.

And then he let his Shield down. He would have done the same for any of the squad, he thought. He was sure he would.

Cor-Reed's Power wrapped itself around Asher Tye, and once again he was immobile. And the ship spiraled in toward the desert planet.

Toward the October One.

She brooded in her fortress, feeling the little ship as it came in. Tye was there, she had known at once. The quest was over. She would reward Cor-Reed well, and then get him out of her sight. She was tired of the rodent-faced man; perhaps she would send him to one of the other Ones and let him deal with aliens for a while.

And now she had the Nin herself! Such a prize she had not anticipated so soon, before emptying Tye. It was satisfying, and yet . . .

Hours before, another shuttle-sized ship had entered October space. She had scanned it and probed it; it had been empty of mind. Its computer was dead save for the command to exit interspace at random, and somehow it had come here, to the October World. She had sent ships to intercept it, but it had come out too close to the planet, entering the atmosphere like a large meteor and screaming through the air at an oblique angle, radiating fire as it burned through the atmosphere, a giant shooting star. It had lit up the night side of the planet for a whole minute before it had hit the side of a mountain, exploding into it as its space-hardened hull finally disintegrated into vapor and molten nodules. Though her search teams were even now excavating it, she knew there would be nothing to identify, and she was disturbed.

She did not believe in random events. This ship had come from nowhere, with no one inside, and had crashed into oblivion. Why? Again and again she probed with her vast and powerful mind—its exit point, the track it had taken through real space to her planet, its fiery descent and destruction—looking for some hint of mind, some hint of purpose, and finding nothing. And in the rippling Power of the galaxy, that tiny point of vacuum that she had guessed at and probed for and never found, that tiny hint of another Presence, was nowhere to be found, and she wondered if it and the coming of this unknown ship were somehow related.

Was it a coincidence that Tye was here, so close behind? Did he have some monumental Power that he had been born with? None of it made sense, and the October One brooded as she prepared to destroy the only threats to her Guild she had ever uncovered: Asher Tye, who was the last remaining Rogue Adept insofar as she knew, and the Guild of Thieves.

Like automatons, the seven warriors marched forward under the direction of Cor-Reed's grim mind. Teel was awake now, his eyes dazed, seeing little around him. The rest of them, including Tawna, still looked for that tiny opening, and did not find it.

They entered the mile-high ramparts of the October One, and in a twinkling they seemed to be entering a vast open space, an amphitheatre cut into tan-colored stone and open to the sky. Walls rose around them at steep angles, cut by galleries and balconies. In them were people leaning over the railings, all humans, and more humans stood stiffly around the floor of the amphitheatre. They walked through them, sometimes coming within a few feet of one or the other, and none of them looked their way. All were dressed in the black shimmery jumpsuits of the October Guild.

"It is an Assembly," Asher whispered to the others. "I never saw one all the time I was here. What you are looking at are all of the members of the October Guild now on-planet—Adepts, Initiates, Apprentices alike."

"There are so few," commented the Nin softly, her face straining with the effort of breaking through Cor-Reed's control. But the only thing the Adept allowed were these whispered words.

"Yes, few," Asher said. "I don't think that many people, in all the trillions, have the ability to learn Skill. Many have pieces of it, glimpses of telepathy once in a while, or the ability to dream a piece of the future. But to control it . . . very few are found with that potential."

"No more than 1,200 or so," the Nin muttered, looking around. "In a fight, we could take them, just the seven of us."

"Only if they didn't use Skill," Asher said.

"We would fry your brains," Cor-Reed whispered in front of them, then threw back his head and laughed. "And now, as we enter the presence of the One . . ." And he closed their lips to speech with a tiny additional effort of his mind.

They had entered the fortress, and yet now they were outside . . . Asher wondered if the scene were holography—the three-dimensional picture of a real Assembly, somewhere on the planet—and that they themselves were in or approaching the chambers of the October One. They seemed to be walking toward a dais, a raised platform at the center end of the amphitheatre. The platform was empty, but . . .

Not empty. A wavering of the background stone was suddenly seen, and there, floating a few inches above the platform, withered legs invisible in ochre robes, was the October One.

The crowd made no sound, and yet it was as if a collective sigh had risen toward the heavens.

The October One was turned sideways. One baleful yellow eye was scanning the crowd, its iris dilating and constricting again in a slow, awful rhythm. They could see nothing of her near-vertical mouth, but as they drew nearer, the crackling in her hair came to them, and they could see the tiny flickers of static electricity as it writhed in a black cloud on her head.

When they were apparently twenty feet away, Cor-Reed stopped them. Directly in front of them was a yellow line etched into the tan rock of the floor. Beyond such a line, Asher knew, no one ever approached the October One and lived.

"You," came the gravel voice of the One. It seemed as if the voice were next to each person in the amphitheater, only inches from every ear. She cast herself on all of them, and they heard every silent word that she said.

"You have troubled my Guild . . ." She was evidently speaking to the Nin Tova. "You and your blank-minded warriors, not fit to drool at the feet of the newest October Apprentice, dared to crawl in where you were not wanted."

The Nin seemed to be choking—Cor-Reed was frowning. Then the October One gave a tiny gesture, and Cor-Reed freed their throats, drawing back as if his mind had been burned.

Asher gasped: "The line! Stay behind the yellow line!"

But the Nin did not seem to hear. All of her attention seemed concentrated on the awful figure of the alien woman before her.

"You and your Guild pollute the galaxy," the Nin said then, her voice harsh from the strain of fighting Cor-Reed. "You misuse your Skill to serve the corrupt and power-mad. You . . ."

The October One gestured again, and the Nin's voice strangled in her throat.

"Enough," the October woman said, almost wearily. "Our purposes are beyond your mental ability to know." The October One's head turned then, and her slit of a mouth came into view. Her skin's yellowish tinge was accented by the tan color around them. She was in three-quarters profile now. Her cat's eyes seemed to bore into the Nin like a drill into steel.

Then something happened. Like a snake crawling slowly out of its hole, Teel's sword began to draw out of its scabbard. The squad watched in horror; they strained, and could not move at all. Cor-Reed was standing to one side, smiling an icy grimace. Asher guessed what was about to happen, and reached deeply toward the Power that he still felt stirring within him. He could not reach it.

The sword emerged from its scabbard and swung upward, its razorlike blade casting images of the sun overhead into the eyes of the watchers as it moved. It came and poised itself above the Nin, and to everyone there it was plain what was coming. The Nin watched it silently now, no expression at all on her face.

"Thus," said the October One, softly, "do you die by your own weapon. And all who see, remember. Remember the end of the Guild of Thieves."

The sword would cut the Nin from shoulder blade to hip, cut her in half from top to bottom, cut . . .

And then the heavens ripped open. They heard the sound of a gigantic thunderclap, and the October One's eyes leaped upward. They were all released from the grip of Cor-Reed as he staggered back, eyes unbelieving, looking at the sky.

But the October One, even looking upward, sent the sword crashing down at the Nin.

Asher threw out a Shield, but it was too late by far. The sword reached the Nin and . . .

She was not there. Like a panther, she stepped inside the cut, shot one hand upward, and grasped the hilt. Wrenching it from whatever mental grasp the One still held, she glanced down at the yellow line; and conscious that the mental grip might seize her again at any moment, she whipped the sword in a blur that no one saw and hurled it straight at the breast of the Master of the October Guild.

It almost made it, but as if she were swatting a fly,

the One batted it aside with a part of her mind, and it hit one of the walls behind her, point-first. So powerful had been the throw that the sword penetrated a few inches into living stone, and quivered there.

But the October One's mind was concentrated upward, and they all looked up then, even the silent minions of the October World.

The sky was torn open as if someone had gripped it with both hands and ripped it apart, as if it were made of blue cellophane that could be wrenched into two. Inside the tear they saw blackness, but it was not entirely black, for as the rip widened, something was growing there—a symbol, a diagram, something in blue sapphire fire . . .

Then, through that rip the atmosphere was rushing, freed apparently of gravity by the same force that was making the hole. Another gigantic thunderclap hit them and, all around them, Adepts and Initiates were blown off their feet by a hurricane blast of wind. The warriors felt it and, with their instinctive trained reactions, dropped flat on the ground, the wind howling over them, hardly touching them now, while October Guild members rose and fell around them, trying to stand, rolling like tenpins as the wind threw them again.

Cor-Reed was hurled off balance by the first blast and, unlike the warriors, had no physical training to fall back on. The wind threw him forward, and even as he reached into himself for a Shield, he looked downward and screamed. He was over the yellow line . . .

And died.

The October One's brain had acted with an automatic response. Most of her attention was directed upward, for she knew what the rip in the sky meant. And when someone had crossed the line toward her, the line beyond which no one had come since her accession on the October World, what was left of her attention had, almost absently, whisked at the invading brain and scrambled it like an egg. Cor-Reed's body had fallen forward in a bloody sliding scrape on the stone floor, never aware that he was going to die.

All around then, Adepts and Initiates and Apprentices were crawling and rolling, fleeing from the sound coming from above, a sound low and high at the same time, a sound so loud that Asher remembered the disintegrators. But this sound was far vaster. Not louder perhaps, but speaking somehow of a power that could rip the sky apart.

Sound, light, chaos—and a symbol formed in the black hole above them.

"You swore you would not!" the October One screamed. "You closed yourself in and swore you would not interfere with us!" Her body was turning now, slowly, so that it took minutes to make a full rotation. They could see her face and the back of her head in turn, every aspect filled with a terrible rage. And where there had been flickerings in her writhing hair, there were now such continuous flashes that her head seemed bathed in fire.

Asher rose to his feet, a Shield around him against the hurricane, and against the October One, and attacked. He cast a lance of mental energy at the October One, and that fragment of her mind that had killed Cor-Reed would have killed him, too, but he was ready and his Shield was up. While she could have obliterated him if she had turned her attention to him, she did not bother, but screamed upward into the heavens.

Far across the galaxy, October Ones stirred and felt what was happening on the October World. They tried to lend the October One their Power, but they could not. When they tried to close the images that they were seeing from themselves, they could not do that, either. And in the shriveled hearts of the ten thousand, a massive fear began.

Asher attacked again, and again he was rebuffed. The Nin seemed to sense what he was doing, and screamed at her warriors: "Attack! Attack! Do not cross the line. Throw your weapons at her!"

Ran and Clemmy reacted almost simultaneously. They hurled their swords in the same motion that the Nin had used, on their knees now, fighting the wind. Close behind came Tawna's weapon. Teel seemed to be coming out of his daze.

And Rasha hesitated. His eyes moved from the Nin to the October One and back again. He seemed to be calculating . . .

And all at once Asher knew that Rasha was playing the odds. For the first time he had a truly clear vision of someone else's long-buried flaw, a flaw that had not been conquered but only suppressed, that now emerged like a frog digging out of the spring mud. For Rasha did not yet know who was going to win here. And despite the chaos around them, the October One seemed to hold the most power.

Then Teel seemed to come alive; he leaped forward and crashed his fist against Rasha's temple. Even as the younger boy fell, he wrenched Rasha's sword away and, in a lightning movement, sent it after the others, straight at the October One.

But it was for nothing. None of the weapons reached the One. She batted them aside in a mental reflex, and they clattered to the stone. But it seemed to make her notice them . . .

Her turning body stopped. One baleful eye was upon them now, and she seemed to gather herself inward like water piling up behind a dam, ready to burst outward.

Then she spoke:

"While I can, I will at least see the end of you . . . thieves who threatened me, and the betrayer Asher Tye." For she now knew who the Digger was; Asher Tye was no longer relevant.

And from her gleaming yellow eye shot a light and . . .

Everything went negative. The light from the eye turned dark, the rip in the sky white, the blue around it black, the tan rock grey, the yellow October face deep grey, the blazing hair black. The squad, the October

Initiates and Apprentices and Adepts around them, all fell like stones, hitting the earth as if life were gone. Asher, whose Shield bent and swayed as it tried to protect him, knew that they might be all dead now, brains scrambled or lifeforce simply driven out of them. Clemmy and Tawna and Ran and Teel, and the fallen Rasha too. And the Nin, whose strength of body came to nothing in the end, against the raw mental power of the evil one before them. And even the One's own minions all around them.

Asher felt his Shield ripped away. He prepared to die.

And then . . .

Everything went positive again. The October One's eyes were on the bodies on the stone. She seemed to shake herself, an almost invisible movement in her robes, and gather herself again.

Her eye blazed, and it all went negative. Asher's new Shield went down, and from deep in his mind there came . . .

The Word. The one that stopped Apprentices in their tracks. The one with the power of the Glance of Command. The one that would stop an October Guild member as if flash-frozen, as if hit by a Time Stop.

The October One laughed.

"Did you keep me from killing them, Asher Tye?" the awful voice came then. "You are truly a Rogue Adept. I had not guessed the Power that I would have to devote to you. And now you try my own Word on me?"

Again that ghastly laugh, and then it stopped as if cut off by a knife.

"And now, die, Asher Tye," the October One said. And she released the Power.

But even as she did so, in the exact split second of release, something welled up in Asher Tye. Even as he had fought her, he had been amazed at the calmness that seemed to flow through him. It was not that he did not care; it was not that he had gone emotionally dead.

It was that he would no more let anger or fear or worry or hate block off effective action. He was utterly warrior-trained now, acting without thought, ready with the right move at the right time, with split-second precision . . .

He said the Word. Not the Word of the October Guild, but another Word, a Word that had been taught to him long ago, a Word that he had dreamed and then forgotten.

And the October One's blow stopped and bounced off. Her mouth went open and her eye went blank. Her hair, which had grown to blinding incandescence a moment before, went black now, all light gone out of it.

For Asher had said the Word of their Teacher. A Word never before heard in the Galaxy. The Sculptor's Word . . .

And from behind Asher there came the Digger.

# Chapter 26

The symbol in the sky was clear now. It had twelve corners, and each corner was like a sun. There was a single point of light inside it, and that point was so eye-dazzlingly bright that it could not be looked at directly.

The Digger clattered up to Asher. Asher could see nothing different about him. He reached out and felt the alien with his mind, and encountered the same alien blankness that he had felt many times before in training, before the Warrior Planet. But Asher knew that the Digger was somehow responsible for all this: the tear in the sky, the chaos around them, and the life still in the warriors, lying on the stone. For something had dampened the blow from the October One at the last second, and that something had not been Asher Tye.

"You are not a Digger," Asher said. Around him, the warriors were stirring, all except for Rasha.

"No," the giant nose burbled. "I sought for Skill when I reached the central Galaxy, and found a little in the Diggers. But they were a form to take, one not easy to see through."

The Nin was climbing to her feet, shaking her head.

267

She looked up at the October One, who had not moved. The wind was fading now, and above them the tear was closing slowly, as if reluctant to go away.

Teel was on his feet now, pulling Tawna up. Ran was up and grinning already. Clemmy was sitting up, listening.

"Why didn't you stop her yourself?" Asher asked the alien in the Digger's form.

The Digger spoke then, and the ciliatic burble was all at once gone from his voice. It came to each of them clear and deep. Yet it did not really seem directed at them at all; it was as if the Digger were engaged in a monologue, talking to himself. And yet when he was finished, they realized that he had reduced it all to simplicity so that they could understand.

"It seems as if the wiser you become, the less you want to interfere with anyone," the Digger said. "You begin to see all sides of everything, and nothing is clear-cut anymore. There is little good that is absolutely good, and little bad that is totally bad.

"When the October revolted and left the Sculptor, I made a promise to myself and to them that I would never confront them in a Test of Power. I would take that threat away, and see what they made of themselves from the training I had given them.

"And they botched it. They sold their Skill, and did not use it for the benefit of anyone but themselves. They sold their services to the highest bidder, and cared not what that bidder had them do. Worse, in their paranoia, they strove to master and control the civilizations themselves, so innately fearful were they that someone, somewhere, would rise up and end their near-immortal lives. But if they controlled the Concourse of Planets, and then the planets themselves, they would be a force for the status quo, for they would see change as threat. The galaxy would stagnate, and that I could not allow."

The alien's clear voice sighed. "The fault, in the end, though, is mine. I taught, thinking that what I had mastered could only be used for the benefit of everyone. But the October, when they taught, left out some things, maybe because I did not stress them enough, maybe because my timing was wrong, and certainly because I read them wrong as students in the first place. The result was the twisting of Adepts until they became like that one." He pointed at the fallen body of Cor-Reed. "They had not trained far enough. When I train again, I will begin with the practice of right and wrong, in little things, and wait until that is completed before I teach Power. For I, too, can learn; it is one reason I sought out the Guild of Thieves. For while its moral vision was flawed, it had clarity, and was logical and clear within itself. There were techniques of learning that I had never before seen, and I have learned now how better to teach when I teach again."

He fell silent then, and above them the rip in the sky closed. The October One hovered frozen.

"She hears," Asher said softly.

"Aye," said the Digger. "She hears deep inside, and for every argument she brings up, I answer it and end it."

Indeed, Asher could sense the flow between them, an exchange of fact and fiction, of good and evil, of best and worst. And he could sense that the October One didn't have a chance. Nothing she could come up with would do her any good. Before this clarity of thought, she could not prevail. Her mythology was toppling. In a way, she was being destroyed.

"Your fundamental mistake," said the Digger, addressing her directly now, "was in forgetting that someday you will die." She seemed to start, even under the spell of that awful Word. "I did not teach you to think of that far-away day, to think of it all the time. To think of yourself about to die, lying sick and in pain. And to think of yourself looking back on what you have done in your life. Would you be mostly proud, or mostly bitter? Did you give other people happiness—any other people? Did you make anyone's life better? As many lives as you could?"

The October One seemed to quail, but the arrogance was still in her, too, fighting for control.

It could not win.

"I had to stop you, and yet I could not attack you directly. I had to hide from you, for what I had taught you, I had taught well. I had closed myself off from facing you, for what I say once is said forever, and therefore, I had to find someone else to face you.

"For years I searched the galaxy. I found the Diggers, but they could not reach enough of the Power. I found my first failed Apprentice of the October Guild, and released him from Erasure; and from that point on, I had a way of harassing and hounding the October Guild through its own skills. In all the time I searched, I found only a few dozen such outcasts from October, but they were enough to cause havoc in the October plans. I taught these recruits how to render their auras invisible to October skills, and then set them loose on the Guild, and so went awry many careful plans of October, without any clue as to why. Kerla Cwan was one of the earliest such. I could not teach her well, but she was good at spotting Erasures; I wish now that I had taught someone else, and left her where I found her, sad and lonely as she was.

"And then, together, we found the Guild of Thieves, and for a while I thought that the warriors could be taught—they seemed to have a crude sense of good and evil, and they were training in instantaneous response—but of psionic ability they had none.

"And I found you, Asher Tye. Do you remember how you felt when you killed that animal during the Test; when you almost knocked the old man over while you fled the Adept on the *Pride*; while you chased the pinkish alien through the jungle?"

Asher remembered, with a clarity that was almost painful.

"You made mistakes, of course—as when you killed

that first animal, and when you did not tell the Nin of Teel's first try at killing you—but the basic core was there. And you were a natural student of the Power. Yet there was that flaw . . . So I sent you to the warriors. I knew that if anyone could cure you of it, they could."

"And we did," the Nin said, with satisfaction.

"Mostly, mostly," the Digger said. "He is still young; there are still aspects to confront."

"What?" Asher asked.

"You will find out," the Nin broke in. Her eyes seemed almost sad as she looked at him. Asher was puzzled. He was about to speak, when the Digger's new voice came again.

"All I really needed to do was to get the ear of the October One, to break through just once, but she had permanent shields raised against me. She did not want further teaching; she thought that she had finished learning. Never think that, any of you. If you do, you might as well die."

The Nin and the Digger were the same, Asher thought. Always teaching. Always learning.

"I had to find someone to break through," the Digger said. "Not necessarily you, Asher Tye. I implanted the Word in you as just another tactic, another possibility for which there might never be an opportunity. What happened was part luck and part foresight; if you plant a thousand seeds, some of them will grow.

"Look at Clemmy, Asher Tye," the alien said. Asher, startled, looked. He caught her gaze for a fraction before it fell, her face reddening. But in that instant, he knew what he saw there.

"Until you die, there is always the next day, Asher Tye," said the Digger. Asher looked at Tawna for the briefest instant; then he looked away.

"No, Tova, I cannot teach you," the alien then said, in response to a question that none of them had heard. "I cannot teach most beings. Perhaps it is a genetic mutation, something inherited that only a few have.

When I find it I can teach. I also find millions who might be more intelligent and kinder and quicker, but if they lack that one thing, the teaching doesn't take.

"Of all of you here, only Asher and Clemmy have it."

Clemmy looked up, surprised.

"Oh, yes, young lady," the alien said. "Do you remember when you kicked the mind out of Asher Tye that day on the Warrior Planet?" Clemmy flushed again and looked guiltily at Asher. He looked at her, and now his eyes were seeing more than he used to. She flushed even deeper, and looked down. "He should have seen that thought when it came into your mind, even in his hyper-oxygenated state. But somehow, you hid it from him. And I see from the Nin Tova's mind that you resisted Cor-Reed's attacks on the Warrior Planet longer than anyone save the Nin herself, and she did so with centering alone and no psychic abilities, which is a remarkable feat on its own."

Again Clemmy looked at Asher. He looked back at her. He wanted now to go into her mind, but he found that he would not; not unless she invited him.

"If you knew that, why did you send him . . ." she gestured at Asher ". . . to us? He could not have taught us even if we had let him try."

The amazing clear voice came: "I sent him . . . for him! He is now more than what he was. And . . . he did come in handy, did he not?"

The Nin smiled her rare, heart-stopping smile. If she had been disappointed by the Digger's inability to teach her, she had already shaken if off with her characteristic adaptability.

"Then I will go and rejoin my Guild and build again," she said, ready for activity again. "There must be a ship or two on this dried-up planet; who is coming with me?"

Ran was, of course. But a cloud passed over Tawna's face. She looked at Teel, and then back at the Nin.

"Digger?" said the Nin, gesturing toward Teel.

The Digger considered. Teel barely felt his mental touch this time.

Finally the Digger spoke: "He has learned the hard way, but he has learned. He will now make a fine warrior. Take him with you, Nin Tova, and Tawna with him."

And then the Nin bent over Rasha. "He lives," she said. She straightened up. "But I will not take him. He can stay here and the Adepts can have him."

The words raised another question:

"Digger," said Asher. "Ten thousand October Ones, and each with several thousand Adepts—how can you purge the galaxy of all of them? Even you do not have such power."

"No, I do not, Asher Tye," said the Digger. "But through this One, I have reached the other Ones; the same stream that flows between myself and her flows between myself and those ten thousand others whom I have known in the past, and who I can recognize among the mental chaos of the galaxy. What you see happen to her will happen at the same time to all of the Ones.

"But of the Adepts and others of the October Guild, you are right. They cower right now, unable to understand that something might attack October and prevail against it. When they come out again, they will naturally cast their minds outward, seeking their One, but their One will no longer be here. Yet they will find something—a mental message, an order.

" 'Seek me,' it will say. 'Join me where I now reside, among the million stars of a particular satellite galaxy, the one known as the Sculptor.' And trained to Guild obedience, they will find ships and come to me, and there, far from the galactic wheel, I will correct what October has done and make them whole again—in body, mind, and spirit—even as I teach their masters with them."

Their masters with them . . .

"And what of you, Asher Tye?" the Digger asked.

It seemed to everyone that the answer was obvious.

Asher would go with this Teacher to the Sculptor, and learn. He was only a beginner in Skill, after all.

But Asher surprised them, and even surprised himself.

"I will do the right thing," he said, and smiled at the word "right." "First I will visit my family. And then I will come to the Sculptor."

"Yes," said the Digger. "Yes. But first you must rejoin the thieves." Asher was frowning. "For you still have much to learn from them."

"Thievery?" Asher winced. "Their physical skills, yes. But I don't want to learn any more thievery."

"Perhaps while they are teaching you, you can teach them," the Digger went on as if Asher had not spoken. The Nin shot him a suspicious glance.

"Psionics?" she said.

"No," the Digger said. "Instinct. For right and wrong."

"You can't teach instinct," the Nin grumbled. But Asher was arguing: "Emotion cannot rule me any more!" he said adamantly. "I can let it flow away in an instant, whenever I choose, or use it as a tool in any way I wish. It is *mastered*, I tell you!"

"Not all of it," the Nin said, sadly again. "Only those emotions you've experienced in detail. There will be more, I'm afraid, Asher Tye."

And then, unbelievably, as he had heard it once before, Asher heard the Digger say: "Good-bye, Asher Tye."

Asher's mouth dropped open. Crashing thunder rolled over them. The sky was opening again.

And then the nose shape that was the Digger seemed to elongate. It was as if the Digger-shape flowed upward into a gleaming steel cylinder, as thick as a pencil and perfectly reflecting, like the shiniest mirror. For a moment Asher wondered if it was the Teacher's real shape that he was now seeing. And he wondered if he would ever know.

Then he saw the October One. She too was stretching upward, still frozen in that open-mouthed stare, growing thinner and thinner as she stretched, until she was just a thin yellow thread reaching upward toward the sky, side by side with the metallic thread of the Digger. He knew that all over the galaxy each October One was elongating into a similar thread, pointing to the star in the Sculptor's eye.

And then the rip in the sky was fully open, and the two threads hurled upward like arrows shot into the sky, straight toward that gleaming center point of light.

And then they were gone, and the sky was whole. And Asher felt a great loss, even as he knew that he would see the Teacher again.

He looked down then, and realized all at once what the Digger and the Nin had been talking about.

For Tawna and Teel were hugging each other.

Instantly, Asher felt the sharp pang of jealousy. Then he looked guiltily at Clemmy. And then, he remembered the Teacher's words, and the Nin's.

Jealousy and guilt . . . Now how would he handle that?

*Here is an excerpt from IRON MASTER by Patrick Tilley, to be published in July 1987 by Baen Books. It is the third book in the "Amtrak Series," which also includes CLOUD WARRIOR and THE FIRST FAMILY.*

# PATRICK TILLEY
# IRON MASTER

The five sleek craft, under the control of their newly-trained samurai pilots, lifted off the grass and thundered skywards, trailing thin blue ribbons of smoke from their solid-fuel rocket tubes. Levelling off at a thousand feet, they circled the field in a tight arrowhead formation, then dived and pulled up into a loop, rolling upright as they came down off the top to go into a second—the maneuver once known as the Immelmann turn.

There was a gasp from the crowd as the lines of blue smoke were suddenly severed from the diving aircraft. A tense, eerie silence descended. The first rocket boosters had reached the end of their brief lives. Time for the second burn. The machines continued their downward plunge—then, with a reassuring explosion of sound, a stabbing white-hot finger of flame appeared beneath the cockpit pod of the lead aircraft. Two, three, four—five!

The watching crowd of Iron Masters responded with a deep-throated roar of approval. Cadillac, who was positioned in front of the stand immediately below his patrons, Yama-Shita and Min-Ota, swelled with pride. These were the kind of people he could identify with. Harsh, forbidding, and cruel, with unbelieveably rigid social mores, they nevertheless appreciated and placed great value on beautiful objects, whether they be works of nature or some article fashioned by their craft-masters. Cadillac knew his flying machines appealed to the Iron Masters' aesthetic sensibilities. Like the proud horses of the domain lords, they were lithe and graceful, and the echoing thunder that marked their passage through the sky conveyed the same feeling of irresistible power as the hoofbeats of their galloping steeds. Here, in the Land of the Rising Sun, he had been taken seriously, had been given the opportunity to demonstrate his true capabilities, and had been accorded the praise and esteem Mr. Snow had always denied him. And his work here was only just beginning!

As the five aircraft nosed over the top of the second loop, leaving a blue curve of smoke behind them, their booster rockets exploded in rapid succession. Boooomm! Ba-ba-boom-boomm. Booom!

Cadillac, along with everyone else in the stand behind him, watched in speechless horror as each one was engulfed by a ball of flame. The slender silk-covered spruce wings were ripped to pieces and consumed. On the ground below, confusion reigned as the shower of burning debris spiralled down towards the packed review stand, preceded by the rag-doll bodies of the pilots.

Steve Brickman, gliding high above the lake some three miles to the south of the Heron Pool, saw the fireballs blossom and fall. It had worked. The rocket burn had ignited the explosive charge he, Jodi, and Kelso had packed with loving care into the second of the three canisters each aircraft carried beneath its belly. Now there could be no turning back. Steve caught himself invoking the name of Mo-Town—praying that everything would go according to plan.

General To-Shiba, seated on his left, was quite unaware of the disaster. Fascinated by the bird's-eye view of his large estate, the military governor's eyes were fixed on the small island in the middle of the lake two thousand feet below. It was here, in the summer house surrounded by trees and a beautiful rock garden, that Clearwater was held prisoner. The beautiful creature who was now his body-slave and who possessed that rarest of gifts—lustrous, sweet-smelling body hair. The thought of his next visit filled him with pleasurable anticipation. As a samurai, To-Shiba had no fear of death but, at that moment, he had no inkling his demise was now only minutes away. . . .

July 1987 • 416 pp. • 65338-5 • $3.95

*To order any Baen Book, send the cover price plus 75¢ for first-class postage and handling to: Baen Books, Dept. BB, 260 Fifth Avenue, New York, N.Y. 10001.*

# TRAVIS SHELTON LIKES BAEN BOOKS BECAUSE THEY TASTE GOOD

Recently we received this letter from Travis Shelton of Dayton, Texas:

> *I have come to associate Baen Books with Del Monte. Now what is that supposed to mean? Well, if you're in a strange store with a lot of different labels, you pick Del Monte because the product will be consistent and will not disappoint.*
>
> *Something I have noticed about Baen Books is that the stories are always fast-paced, exciting, action-filled and seem to be published because of content instead of who wrote the book. I now find myself glancing to see who published the book instead of reading the back or intro. If it's a Baen Book it's going to be good and exciting and will capture your spare reading moments.*
>
> *Another discovery I have recently made is that I don't have any Baen Books in my unread stacks—and I read four to seven books a week, so that in itself is a meaningful statistic.*

**Why do *you* like Baen Books? Drop us a letter like Travis did. The person who best tells us what we're doing right—and where we could do better—will receive a Baen Books gift certificate worth $100. Entries must be received by December 31, 1987. Send to Baen Books, 260 Fifth Avenue, New York, N.Y. 10001. And ask for our free catalog!**

HE'S OPINIONATED

HE'S DYNAMIC

HE'S LARGER THAN LIFE

# MARTIN CAIDIN

Martin Caidin is a bestselling novelist, pilot *extraordinaire,* and expert on America's space program. *He's also a prophet of technological change.* His ability to predict future trends verges on the psychic, as when he wrote *Cyborg* (the novel which became "The Six Million Dollar Man") and *Marooned* (which precipitated the American-Soviet Apollo-Soyuz linkup mission). His tense, action-filled stories are based on personal experience in fields such as astronautics, aviation, oceanography and the military.

Caidin's characters also know their stuff. And they take on real life, because they're based on real people. Martin Caidin spent a stint as a merchant seaman in Europe and Africa, worked for Air Force Intelligence in the U.S. and Asia, and has flown his own planes to many parts of the world. His adventures can be yours in these novels from Baen Books.

— — — — — — — — — — — — — — — —

EXIT EARTH—Just as the US and the USSR have finally settled their differences, American scientists discover that the solar system is about to pass through a cloud of cosmic dust that will incite the Sun to a paroxysm of fury. All will die. There can be no escape—except, possibly, for a very few. *This is their story.* 656 pp. • 65630-9 • $4.50 ————

KILLER STATION—Earth's first space station *Pleiades* is a scientific boon—until one brief moment of sabotage changes it into a terrible Sword of Damocles. 55996-6 • 384 pp. • $3.50 ————

THE MESSIAH STONE—"An unusual thriller . . . not only in subject matter, but in the fact that the author claims that the basic idea behind the book is real! [THE MESSIAH STONE] concerns the possession of a stone; the person who controls the stone rules the world. The last such person is rumored to be Adolf Hitler. . . . Harrowing adventure and nonstop action."—*Science Fiction Review.* 65562-0 • 416 pp. • $3.95 ————

ZOBOA—It started with the hijacking of four atomic bombs, and ended with the Space Shuttle atop a pillar of fire. . . . "From the marvelous, cinematic opening pages, Caidin sweeps the reader along in a raucous, exciting thriller."—*Publishers Weekly* 65588-4 • 448 pp. • $3.50 ————

*To order these Baen Books, check each title selected and return with a check or money order for the combined cover price. Send to Baen Books, 260 Fifth Avenue, New York, N.Y. 10001.*

**Distributed by Simon & Schuster**
**1230 Avenue of the Americas • New York, N.Y. 10020**

# C'MON DOWN!!

Is the real world getting to be too much? Feel like you're on somebody's cosmic hit list? Well, how about a vacation in the hottest spot you'll ever visit ... HELL!

We call our "Heroes in Hell" shared-universe series the Damned Saga. In it the greatest names in history—Julius Caesar, Napoleon, Machiavelli, Gilgamesh and many more—meet the greatest names in science fiction: Gregory Benford, Martin Caidin, C.J. Cherryh, David Drake, Janet Morris, Robert Silverberg. They all turn up the heat—in the most original milieu since a Connecticut Yankee was tossed into King Arthur's Court. We've saved you a seat by the fire ...

HEROES IN HELL, 65555-8, $3.50 _____

REBELS IN HELL, 65577-9, $3.50 _____

THE GATES OF HELL, 65592-2, $3.50 _____

KINGS IN HELL, 65614-7, $3.50 _____

CRUSADERS IN HELL, 65639-2, $3.50 _____

*Please send me the books checked above. I enclose a check for the cover price plus 75 cents for first-class postage and handling, made out to: Baen Books, 260 Fifth Avenue, New York, N.Y. 10001.*